*T*HE GOAT WOMAN OF LARGO BAY BEGINS the detective series featuring Shad, a bartender in a fishing village in Jamaica who is the community problem solver and right hand of Eric, an American who owns the bar and a hotel left in ruins by a hurricane.

When Shad sees movement on the island offshore, he thinks it's just a goat. But it turns out to be Simone, an American who has run away from her professional and personal life in the United States, an intriguing woman who captures Eric's heart. Always keeping his ear to the ground, Shad discovers that a gunshot heard near Simone's place late one night isn't exactly friendly fire, but is tied to a plot to harm Simone and ultimately manipulate local elections. But why does someone want to harm Simone? And what does she have to do with the elections? Only Shad can find out.

An irresistible character is introduced in *The Goat Woman of Largo Bay,* and Royes wonderfully blends suspense and the soul of the islands in this smart debut.

THE
GOAT WOMAN
of
LARGO BAY

A Novel

GILLIAN ROYES, *1947*

ATRIA PAPERBACK

NEW YORK   LONDON   TORONTO   SYDNEY   NEW DELHI

ATRIA PAPERBACK

A Division of Simon & Schuster, Inc.
1230 Avenue of the Americas
New York, NY 10020

First Atria Paperback edition October 2011

ATRIA PAPERBACK and colophon are trademarks of Simon & Schuster, Inc.

For information about special discounts for bulk purchases, please contact Simon & Schuster Special Sales at 1-866-506-1949 or business@simonandschuster.com.

The Simon & Schuster Speakers Bureau can bring authors to your live event. For more information or to book an event, contact the Simon & Schuster Speakers Bureau at 1-866-248-3049 or visit our website at www.simonspeakers.com.

Designed by Kyoko Watanabe

Manufactured in the United States of America

10 9 8 7 6 5 4 3 2 1

Library of Congress Cataloging-in-Publication Data
Royes, Gillian.
    The goat woman of Largo Bay / Gillian Royes.—1st Atria Paperback ed.
       p.   cm.
    1. Bartenders—Jamaica—Fiction.   2. Women hermits—Fiction.
3. Jamaica—Fiction.   I. Title.
    PS3618.O92G63 2011
    813'.6—dc22   2011001220

    ISBN 978-1-4516-2741-1
    ISBN 978-1-4516-2742-8 (ebook)

To the memory of Farah Ebrahimi,
best friend, editor, reader, and loving soul

The winds of God's grace are always blowing.
It is for us to raise our sails.

—KRISHNAMURTI, INDIAN GURU

THE
GOAT WOMAN
of
LARGO BAY

At first he thought she was a goat. Staring at the distant spot, Shad decided there was something about goats that had always irritated him. Nobody liked them, even if they were as common to Largo as fishing boats. But they were rude animals—*facety,* his grandmother used to call them—invading your yard to eat your young tomatoes and glaring when you tried to shoo them away.

The thought came only a minute after Eric had shouted his name and Shad had placed the glass he'd been wiping on a shelf and hurried around the counter of the bar.

"What happening, boss?" he'd said.

"There's something on the island!" Eric, his T-shirt and shorts flattened by the sea breeze, was pointing toward the tiny offshore island.

"I don't see nothing." Shad had squinted at the lump of rocks and its lone tree. "Probably just a bird, or a shadow."

"I'm telling you, there's something out there."

A tall man with the red-brown skin of a northerner who'd been in the tropics too long, Eric was standing

1

statue-still, knees bent, a few feet from the edge of the cliff. Every part of him, the outstretched arm holding a pipe, the swirling white hair, the small paunch even, strained toward the island.

Atop the five steps leading down to the grass, Shad had shielded his eyes against the setting sun. Golden-orange, the island looked like a prodigal son sitting a quarter mile offshore. The water that separated it from the cliff was striped turquoise and aqua, long waves rolling toward the shore, forever restless without a protective reef.

"I see it," Shad said.

"I told you so," Eric said, and straightened. "What do you think it is?"

"Look like a goat, boss."

Eric agreed, because Shadrack Myers was known in Largo Bay as a *smart-man*, in the best sense of the term. He might be small and wiry, they said, but he was as bright as any Kingston professor and as wily as Anansi, the spider of the folk tales. The reason for this, according to the old ladies, was that he was born with a high forehead and the blackest skin a man could have.

"Who'd put a damn goat out there?" Eric asked.

"It only take one renegade to cause confusion," Shad said. And the renegade knew that Eric wouldn't do anything, because a foreign man couldn't afford to make a fuss in a small Jamaican village.

"Why would they want to do that?" Eric said, and put his hands on his hips.

"Probably to separate it from the herd. Must be sick."

"Sick? They can't just take a sick goat out and leave it. Don't they know the place is mine?" Eric said, and raised his arms to heaven just as Shad turned away.

Few people other than Eric noticed the little island anymore, and Shad tried to see it the way his neighbors did, as nothing more than background wallpaper, like the tall mountains behind the village. Looking at the roofless, paint-stripped walls on the island only left a sweet-and-sour feeling in his stomach.

Behind the counter, Shad cut limes into thin slices and prodded the last of the cherries out of the bottle, wondering how to find the owner of the goat. If he started talking about the animal, someone might row out and steal the goat. But if he and Eric didn't do something, the owner might take other goats over, and there'd be even more trouble.

Setting a bottle of wine on the counter, he called to Eric.

"Boss, remember to order more red wine. We running low."

If any customers had been seated in the bar, they would never have known that the slim, midthirties man bustling behind the counter—the shirt neatly tucked into the belted pants—was thinking of anything other than the job at hand. Instead, and as foreigners sipping a beer often did, they would have thought that Shad was the happiest man in Jamaica—and missed the haunted look behind his eyes. They could have been forgiven, because it was easy to assume from his trademark grin, with its gap between the front teeth, that Shad was a man with few problems and a good ear; in other words, the perfect bartender.

While the bar was prepared for evening business, Eric sat on the top step, his back to Shad. The only response the younger man heard was a grunt, accompanied by a cloud of pipe tobacco, as always Canadian maple, which blew in with the sea breeze, filling the empty restaurant.

When it was finally too dark to see, Eric stood and tapped the dead ashes from his pipe bowl against the step. As he plodded past the bar, it was clear to Shad that the goat's invasion was hanging over them both. It had brought back regrets that would linger until they took action.

The next morning dawned drizzly and gray, unusual for Largo in midsummer. Visibility was poor and Shad spent most of the morning placing and emptying buckets under the bar's leaky thatch roof. Near him, Eric, his forehead lined with debt, sat at a wooden table in the bar calculating the cost of a new roof, looking up from his paperwork a few times to ask the name of a workman or a hardware store, glancing at the island while he did it.

"Boss," Shad finally asked, his voice offhanded, "you going out to the island?"

"Nah, I don't think so," Eric said. He looked up and rubbed his knees, the way he did when it rained. "Did you find out who took a goat out? Anyone with a sick goat?"

"Half the goats around here are sick, man," Shad said, rubbing a hand over his shaved head. Speculation in front of Eric was never a good idea, because next thing, he'd be driving all over town asking questions and making accusations.

Two days later, pushing in and straightening chairs after lunch, a broom in one hand, Shad glanced up and saw someone rowing toward the island. The bright purple and red canoe was carved from a single log, like most of the older fishing boats. It beached on the eastern side of the island. The rower offloaded a few bags and disappeared. Staring without blinking, feeling behind him to make sure he didn't miss the chair, Shad sat and watched the person return, again with bags, and row back east around the point.

A goat, a man rowing bags of things to and from the island—they didn't add up to Shad, and he knew everything that went on in Largo. In a community of five hundred in an isolated corner of Jamaica, a village without a police station or a hospital, someone had to make it their job to sniff out—and snuff out—problems even before they emerged, and Shad was that man.

The bartender's vocation as sniffer and snuffer had started in early childhood because he was a fierce runner, and since he was also a nice child, his ability to run had earned him many a ten-cents. When the nurse in the clinic was needed, when money had to be paid to the *obeah man*, the magician on the hill, it was Shad they called. And every night, when he lay next to his grandmother in her iron bed, she snoring so loudly he could hardly fall asleep, he would think about what errand he'd run that day and what problem he'd helped to solve. And decades later he would do the same, lying beside a sleeping Beth, thinking about the woman, the woman he'd thought was a goat.

The purple and red boat remained a puzzle to Shad even after a few discreet inquiries. Avoiding the fish market, where they gossiped too much for an investigation this subtle in nature, he questioned a few older fishermen who hung around the bar at night. But for all the complimentary white rums he provided, no one knew of the boat or a separated goat. It was just enough to intrigue a man who had to know.

CHAPTER TWO

A few days later and just before sunset, Shad eased down to the steps facing the island, pinching the creases of his pants between his fingers. He was waiting for the Red Stripe beer truck, which was late again. The beach below was empty except for the fishing boats, some at anchor in the water and others inverted on the sand.

His own small concrete house was visible among the other small concrete houses half hidden by coconut trees, some lining the road parallel to the beach, all with their colors softened over the years and only the tin roofs bright with rust. Most of the villagers were still at Saturday market in the town square, the women buying and selling vegetables and fruit, the men standing around Ezekiel's rum shop, betting on the boys playing cricket in the square. Away from it all, the island looked forgotten.

Suddenly, a blur of movement on the island caught his eye. The black dot, the goat, was clearly visible again, this time above the rocks on the western side. He watched it bobbing up and down, as if it was making its way behind the large boulders tumbling down to the water's edge. He craned forward to zoom in for a better view. The spot disappeared for a few minutes and reappeared on the western beach, elongating into a vertical figure. Shad leaped up from the step.

"A man, is a man!" he said, hitting his forehead with the heel of his hand. Not a goat, but a half-crazy loner who'd be hard to chase off. Now the boss would be vexed, had every right to be furious.

Equipped with binoculars belonging to Miss Mac, the bar's neighbor, Shad dropped to the back step again the next afternoon. From a cup beside him rose the steam of fresh mint tea, his remedy for the stomachaches he'd had since his first child was born.

After twisting the old lenses back and forth, he focused on a familiar mildewed wall in the center of the island and lingered for a few seconds on a faded mural. He panned from one side to the other. Everything looked as it always had . . . but different, alive even. Breathing heavily, he refocused and began a slower inspection.

The first clue: a coal pot, the country type with an iron basin with legs. The man had been cooking, had set up camp. In the bar, the phone started ringing. Snatching the binoculars away from his eyes, Shad leaped up and knocked over the cup.

Later, while Eric was pounding a nail into a shelf, humming a little tune like he did sometimes, Shad broke the news.

"A man? I have a trespasser?" Eric said, sitting back on his heels, his eyebrows two startled dashes.

"That's right, not a goat."

"Dammit!" Eric said and took a final swipe at the nail. "I guess I should go over." It was more a question than a comment.

"Suppose he chases you with a machete?" Shad said.

"You can come with me."

"Me? My children need a father." Shad grinned, rubbing his stomach.

That was the first day of a fruitless five-day vigil, the men alternating the task of sitting on the steps and peering through the binoculars. On the third day, while Shad was on watch, Eric had visited the Parish Council in Port Antonio to find out what to do about a squatter. They'd treated the matter lightly, he reported to Shad afterward, because foreign white men didn't have real problems.

"The man isn't bothering anybody. You're not using the island," Daphne, the Council's secretary, had said, laughing at him.

"Anyway," she'd said, "you can start with a trespassing eviction notice."

A lawyer had to do that, she added, walking away, her rear end swishing on high heels. Remembering, Eric had sucked his teeth almost like a local, and Shad had laughed—knowing Eric had been too polite to do it in front of the woman, like a local would have.

On the fourth day, Eric and Shad extended their weekly shopping trip to visit the legal chambers—a two-room office above a Port Antonio bread store—of Horace McKenzie, Miss Mac's only child, who would support her in her old age, according to Miss Mac.

Wedged between his desk and a window overlooking a back alley, Horace listened to Eric and Shad's story.

"An eviction notice takes a couple of weeks to file," he said.

"Who's to take the papers out?" Shad asked, remembering Horace in school, the teacher's son, always coming first, always having the last word.

Horace chuckled, mocha fingers caressing a lighter as he brought out a pack of cigarettes.

"No self-respecting policeman would take it out in a canoe to a vagrant, I can tell you that!" he said.

Eric leaned forward. "So I'm supposed to do it?"

"You could," Horace said.

"The man might be violent," Eric said, his voice rising. "What am I to do then? He's not going to leave voluntarily. We all know that."

"You have a lot to learn about Jamaica, Eric," Horace said, lighting a cigarette and glancing at Shad with a conspiratorial smile.

"The law takes the side of the squatter. If a person occupies vacant land for twelve years, they can claim title to the property. The onus is on the owner to do the legal work and tell the squatter to get off his land. That's just how it is."

The solicitor swept the cigarette to one side, exhaling to make his point.

"Jamaica is full of poor people and vacant land, Eric," he said, as if he were older, "and the idea is that it's better to have someone living on the land than to leave it unproductive. So if you manage to get this person off your

10

island, you should keep it occupied after that. That's my advice. On the other hand, if the man refuses to leave, you'll probably have to live with it—or take matters into your own hands."

Standing slowly, Eric gripped the arms of the chair, lifting the front legs an inch off the floor.

"Who do you think I am, Horace? A drug don?" he said. "I come from Shaker Heights, Ohio, man. We don't take matters into our own hands!"

He dropped the chair before exiting, leaving Shad to thank Horace for his time and to remember to have Beth look up the word *onus* when he got home.

"Remember, occupy the land!" Horace called after them.

The next evening the interloper came into view again. Seen only as a blurry stick from the step, the figure moved among the rocks. He was jumping from one to the other—too fast for Shad to focus the cranky old binoculars—and disappeared behind a bush.

Shad waited, stalking his prey, barely breathing, moving the lenses in a slow, sweeping movement, until he caught the figure standing still and gazing west. He made out the hands on the hips, the short, bushy hair, and beneath the flapping shirt . . . an undeniable pair of small breasts.

Shad jumped up, his pants catching for a second on a nail.

"Jesus, save me!" he moaned and smoothed down his pants with one hand. "But we don't need any police or eviction notice now."

CHAPTER THREE

Again, just when—after long, dark hours of listening to waves, trying to focus on the ceaseless brushing and surging, refusing to linger on ugly thoughts, turning to left and right on the mattress, throwing the sheet off, pulling it back on—she's been tricked into letting go, seeking black numbness.

On her back, she drifts off and finds herself trapped—pinned to the mattress—between wake and sleep.

The nightmare descends as usual with tiny, pointed pains in the abdomen. She observes it almost from a distance, unable to move. Her belly (the belly that's been empty, concave even, for nineteen years) expands to a six-month ripeness, the pains growing with it. With vague awareness of the irony, she hopes that this time it will progress, this visitation, to a normal pregnancy.

It's only a dream. Only a dream, a dream.

But it's out of her control, the way it always is, and the mass begins to engorge and contort, an alien fetus. Thick red veins grow inside her; cramps shoot from womb to chest. The distended belly stretches to its limit, sits on her lungs and makes her struggle for air. In a half daze, the breath rasping through her mouth, she wills her hand to stroke the protrusion she sees behind closed lids.

Shhh, shhh.

The demon inside can hear her thoughts. It responds only to kindness. The writhing starts to slow and the pains to subside. Her belly flattens to emptiness and she moves her foot to make sure she's awake.

Wary of the next dream, she rolls over and slides her hand under the pillow, and her fingers collide with the gun.

CHAPTER FOUR

Pulling up his shorts, Shad jumped over the side of *Jah Love*, borrowed from Minion, a man who didn't say much, but said yes to anything after two free beers. The old wooden canoe made a slurring noise as he hauled it farther onto the beach. Eric took the oars out of the oarlocks, laid them inside the canoe, and scrambled over the edge, flip-flops in hand. He could have swum over alone to the island, Shad knew, because he did it once or twice a year to prove something, but today he needed to look like an owner, dry, arriving in a boat with an employee.

"We get this over quickly, boss," Shad said, "with Sunday lunch and everything."

Eric had laid out the plan. They'd go together in a show of force and tell the woman she'd have to get off the island, that they'd be coming back for her tomorrow. Shad had suggested, and Eric had ruled out, taking a knife with them.

"The key is to catch her off guard, especially if she's crazy," Eric had said, like he'd done it before.

The two men stood on the little beach catching their

breath. Eric pulled a comb out of his pocket and swept it through his hair, then tucked the hair behind his ears.

"Your show of force is a comb, boss, good plan," Shad murmured and began the climb up the fifteen-foot cliff. The path's limestone dirt crumbled under his bare feet and he leaned forward for balance. Behind him Eric grunted, his wet feet slipping back on the sandals.

No one was in sight when they reached the top. It was only the second time Shad had come back to the island since the hurricane, and he hadn't been looking forward to the visit. He'd volunteered only because the boss needed support. Any other Sunday he would have been in church with Beth and the children.

Early that morning, he'd had to tell Beth about the woman while they were in bed, little Joshua curled in a ball between them, his bottom in the air. And when he finished, he'd sworn her to secrecy, knowing he could trust her.

Ahead of them lay a track between weeds and stalks of lemongrass. A fallen coconut tree lay in their path, a lone seagull sitting on it, looking at them. The bird flapped off as they approached, quickly soaring with the breeze. Eric's feet squeaked when he stepped over the tree trunk, a barefoot Shad padding behind. To their right, a long, roofless building paralleled the path, one wall half covered in love bush, the tendrils and heart-shaped leaves caressing a mural of angelfish and seaweed.

Under the lone tree, the cast-iron pot sat cold and empty over a fire pit, and a large bag of coal, enough fuel for a couple of months, leaned against the trunk of the tree. Food was stored in clear plastic boxes sealed against ants and cockroaches. Shad took a quick inventory. Tinned fish, bags of rice, a few vegetables, plantains, powdered milk. Off to one side sat cases of bottled water and a box with cooking utensils and silverware.

"She not starving, that for sure," Shad said.

"I bet she's sleeping over there." Eric stuck his chin out toward the largest building on the compound.

"You think we should go in? She might get frightened or something."

"It's still my property," Eric said, putting his hands on his hips.

Advancing toward the gaping opening in the two-story building, Shad looked around at the moldy walls and weed-tangled grounds. The place had decayed beyond hope since the last time, when they'd come out to salvage whatever they could. All they'd found were a few waterlogged mattresses and battered tables.

Sure enough, the familiar lobby—now a mix of cracked tiles and chopped cement—had been commandeered by the intruder. She'd moved into the corner where the receptionists had signed in guests at the front desk. Improvised furniture now lined the wall, everything arranged with the same precision as the kitchen under the tree. A foam mattress made up with blue-and-white-striped sheets lay on the floor in the corner. At its foot lay an expensive black suitcase, the airline tag still attached to the handle like a tourist's. Beside the bed, a scarf-covered table, probably a box, held a kerosene lamp, a few books, and an artsy-looking glass jar. Closest to them was a desk, wide planks over two barrels, the papers on top held down by pieces of coral. There was something genteel about the place, like photographs of a tasteful seaside cave.

"Look at that," Eric said, pointing upward.

Where once there'd been a wooden A-frame roof with colorful bird mobiles, there was now a low ceiling of steel wires supporting zinc sheets and a blue tarpaulin. Jute rope lashed the zinc and tarp to the crisscross of wires, the contraption clashing with the order below.

"Should hold up awhile, at least for dry season," Shad said.

Before them lay an open verandah about forty feet long and twenty feet wide. A wall ran from behind the woman's bed down the length of the verandah, the back of the old Orchid Bar. The bar where Shad had mixed drinks, washed glasses, read recipe books, and listened to drunken stories for seven years. Where he'd befriended people from New York, Barbados, Paris, whose postcards he'd stuck into the frame of the huge mirror behind the bar, creating a collage of his own imagined travels. Now a hollow wind filled the space.

Shad looked beyond the verandah's end. Ruffled water stretched toward the beach and the mountains behind, each range paler and bluer than the one in front until they disappeared into the clouds. The boss had told him, on that first day when he'd trudged out, fifteen years ago now, that Mr. Sommerset had had to chop a path with his machete.

"One look at the view was enough for me to buy," he'd said. He'd found paradise, he'd said. The mountains were the mossy green and the ocean the sapphire he'd dreamed of for years, dreamed of while staring at the gray concrete outside his office window in New York. Before he said that, Shad had thought New York was full of white stone buildings and men with fat wallets.

Suddenly a noise, a light shuffle behind them, barely audible above the breeze. Shad turned his head, slowly, slowly, keeping his eyes low. In the doorway was a pair of feet. They were dusty and small, brownish-yellow like an old photograph. The joints were swollen and the big toes angled inward—the shoe-trained feet of a city woman. Shapely calves rose to the knees, to the loose shorts, then the T-shirt, blood red behind the arms. The fingernails were unpolished, and she was holding a gun, resting it in her left palm like an evening purse.

Rubber bands tightened around Shad's stomach. He tried to swallow. Later, all he would recall was the gun, silver and neat, and his dry throat.

"Who are you?" The woman's voice was croaky, the words coming out in distinct syllables. The top lip was thin, the bottom lip thick and pouty.

Doe-like eyes encircled by gray looked at one man and flickered to the other. She had narrow shoulders and hair that formed a black halo around her head. Her face was oval and pointed at the chin, and her straight nose ended in wide nostrils. She was a pretty woman, forty-something, a *browning,* her skin the milky brown of a high-born Kingston lady, but her voice was different.

"That's what I want to know," Eric said. He turned

toward her abruptly, as if he didn't see the gun. "Who gave you permission?"

She tapped the gun once in her palm, held Eric's gaze, then glanced at Shad. There was no expression on her face, but the forehead had a little pucker, as if she was frightened and trying to hide it. Salt crystals clung to her arched eyebrows—a woman who'd never lived in the wilderness before.

"This island belong to him, miss," Shad said in a low voice. "You're trespassing."

He turned, enunciating each word the way he did for foreigners, leaving the patois behind, not sure if she spoke English well. She could have been from a hundred countries: Martinique, Haiti, Venezuela, Panama. Maybe she'd escaped from Cuba, like they did sometimes, and taken a boat ninety miles south to Jamaica.

"He should've had a sign," she said. The words were guttural but crisp—an American accent with some Jamaican underneath.

"A sign? I don't need one, everybody knows," Eric said.

Trying not to look at the gun, Shad thought of the knife in the kitchen drawer.

"What are you doing here?" Shad asked. He tried a small smile.

She cleared her throat and looked down. A gust of sea breeze tumbled a large almond leaf through the doorway and for a second they all followed its red and gold path.

"I'd like to stay awhile," she said. When neither man answered, she shifted to one leg.

"Name your price," she said, and looked up at Eric the way women did when they wanted something.

Eric's sigh sounded thick and impatient. "You can't stay here. It's too dangerous, probably not even legal, and I'd be responsible. I pay the taxes," he said.

The corners of her mouth twitched. "And I can pay those taxes for you," she said.

Eric looked at Shad, pretending reluctance, as if his claim for an exemption hadn't been rejected by the Tax Office. Shad raised one eyebrow in warning.

Eric looked back at the woman. "How much?"

"Eight hundred US a month," she said, stroking the barrel of the gun.

Rawtid, thought Shad, sixty thousand Jamaican dollars. That would be all the boss would need to hear.

"It's dangerous out here. Right, Shad?" the boss said. He was looking down the verandah at the view he loved.

"Not a good place for a woman," Shad said.

"Okay, one thousand," she said. "And I can take care of myself, thank you." A thud on the roof made her look up for a second, her brow wrinkled.

"You won't need that if I'm going to be your land-lord," Eric said, gesturing to the gun. He was covering his surrender with a weak smile.

She glanced down at the revolver and lowered it.

"What's your name?" Eric said.

"Simone."

"Simone what?"

"Just Simone," she said. She stood up straight and centered her head over her shoulders.

"I don't want a written contract, and I'll pay by direct deposit first of every month."

The goat, the crazed hermit, the criminal, began to morph before Shad's eyes. He saw a businesswoman in a nice suit and high heels, like the ladies in the bank.

"A local bank, right?" Shad said. The boss always got lost in Kingston unless he went with him, and they both hated Kingston.

The woman nodded and strode to the desk.

"And another thing," she said. "I don't want any more visitors." She put the gun down and wrote a note standing up.

"Your name?" She glanced up at Eric, like she knew she'd won, looking like one of those bossy women in soap operas, just the way she cocked her head to one side.

"Eric Keller. K-E-L-L-E-R."

"I'll make it retroactive to the first day I came. Plus one month's deposit."

Retroactive, nice word, whatever it meant, Shad thought, its solidity settling his stomach. Some words just made you feel safe.

The woman did some calculations on a piece of paper and wrote out a check. She placed it in an envelope, which she licked and sealed. The name and address of the bank was written in the middle in a square handwriting.

"How long do you think you'll be here?" Eric took the letter and pushed it deep into his shorts pocket.

She shrugged and led the way out of the room, leaving the gun on the table. Stopping just outside the door, she looked down to let them pass. She was shorter than Beth, with bony shoulders. And she smelled like seaweed. Her thick hair jutted toward them as they passed, the hair they'd thought was a goat's.

Halfway to the tree, Eric turned back, perhaps making sure she wasn't holding the gun.

"I'm not responsible for your safety, like you said," he called, his voice lighter than it had sounded for a long time. "And no drugs out here, no illegal business, if you know what I mean."

"No chance of that." She snorted. A few seconds later, her voice came above the whistle of the wind.

"What . . . were these buildings?"

Both men stopped. Eric stared at the mural in the old dining room.

Shad faced the woman. "It was a—," he said, the word stuck in his throat.

"An institution?" she asked.

A large brown pelican sat on the roof behind her. A hotel guest who'd asked Shad to sleep with her had told him the bird meant somebody was hiding something—*concealment* was the word she'd used.

"His hotel," Shad said. "The Largo Bay Inn, a nice place. It dead now, though."

The woman placed one hand on her neck and her face tightened.

"This wasn't always an island," Eric said. "Hurricane Albert—"

He turned and made flapping gestures with his hand. "Washed away the land connecting it to the town—made this end into an island."

A tremor rolled beneath their feet, a rogue wave hitting the north side of the island, and the pelican flew away.

"Had to swim to shore in the middle of it." A noise almost sounding like a laugh escaped from the side of Eric's mouth. "Almost drowned."

The water was calmer as they rowed to shore, rowed over the fragments of TV sets and champagne glasses that the boss had paid for in cash. Shad felt her eyes on their backs making sure they were leaving, and they both rowed without pausing, as if they knew what they were doing.

Ahead of them, the village was quiet. Everyone was in church. The only sign of life was two goats, broken away from the herd, nibbling thorny shrubs beside the road. Watching the bow of the canoe glide onto the sand, Shad remembered the gun and was glad she had it.

CHAPTER FIVE

A nighthawk like all good bartenders, Shad was getting the customers drunk enough to leave a decent tip. Perched on his stool, he pretended to listen to the chatter around him. He was thinking of the bar's new roof and his promise to help strip off the old palm leaves tomorrow. Weeding the vegetable garden would have to wait. He wasn't looking forward to telling Beth, because she could be cantankerous when she was crossed.

Leaning on the bar tonight were the regulars. Draped over one end was Solomon, the bar's part-time cook, who'd been sulking for seven years over his demotion from hotel chef. His companions were two local women and a fisherman named Tri, whose name—he'd announced unasked one night—was short for Triumphant Arch, a name his mother had been given in a dream.

"The only reason you come here is to catch a rich American man," Tri was saying to Janet, a seamstress who wore a different dress every time she came to the bar.

Janet pulled up the shoulder of her floral dress. "True," she said. "No fisherman can keep me."

Beth was going to be upset about the vegetable garden, but the new refrigerator should keep her happy for a while. It had arrived that morning strapped to the back of the store's pickup truck, standing upright for all to see. With only a small dent from the strap, the appliance had been bigger than Shad expected. His friend Frank had helped him throw the old icebox under the ackee tree and they'd set up the fridge in the living room, the kitchen being too small.

The fridge was a new addition to a growing collection of modern appliances in Shad's house. Although he told himself that the radio, television, and refrigerator were for Beth and the children, Shad's ambition was to fill every available space in his house with newness, knowing it meant he was a man of means, a man who took care of his family, a man who had value.

As soon as Frank and Shad had settled the fridge next to the dinette table, Beth had removed the Styrofoam from the shelving and wiped out the drawers. The smile never left her face.

"It's sweet, eh?" she'd said, her only comment. She was a woman who loved her home, a July woman.

Shad changed the CD in the stereo and calypso pulsed out into the bar.

I see you up dere in de dance hall,
Moving so damn fine,
Girl, I wanna know, wanna know,
How to make you mine.

Another lonely man looking for company, about to get into a whole lot of problems. Nothing like having one steady woman, good in bed and good with your children, a woman you marry one day, properly, in a church. Everything else, according to Pastor, was fornication.

Shad knew about fornication, had proved he was a man from his early teenage years, sometimes with two different girls a week. But Beth had been his only girl from the day he met her on the bus in Port Antonio, and eighteen years later he still reached for her when he got into bed late after work. And he knew he'd keep reaching for her, because she'd always believed he was a good person. Even when he lost the bus conductor work and become *a worthless good-for-nothing,* according to his grandmother. Beth had believed in him when she visited him every week in Kingston Penitentiary, her belly swelling under the school uniform with their first child. And since he wasn't a man to make a baby and move on like his daddy had done, and he didn't believe in dumping a child on the grandmother like his mother had done, and especially now that he attended Holy Sepulcher Baptist Church, Beth would be his only woman.

Sometimes, though, when she was hurt, she said things that hurt. The last time he'd disappointed her to run an errand for Eric, she'd thrown over her shoulder—

"You think the bar belong to you, nuh? And Mr. Eric is your partner?"

"I know I not his partner, girl," Shad had answered, quiet now that the arrogance of youth had left him. He stroked the razor around the back of his scalp.

"You see me, I is a man who believe that *loyalty* follow *gratitude*. Working the bar mean I don't have to fish. I is a man who like keeping my hands clean. I like being around people, and I like to work steady. The boss give me that, so I grateful." He'd rinsed the razor in the bathroom sink.

"Anyway," he'd added, "one hand wash the other. The boss need me as much as I need him. In Jamaica, he like a two-eyed man in a four-eyed country."

They'd both laughed so hard that Beth had had to hold on to the doorframe.

The boss had never liked the bar. He was a man living in the past, and to him the bar was just a run-down reminder of what had been. Half an hour earlier, needing to have a check approved, Shad had found him on the other side of the concrete wall, doing what he did every night. He was sitting in the solitary chair on his verandah listening to Radio Santiago de Cuba, easier to get than the Kingston stations, in one of his melancholy moods. And tonight he was staring into the darkness cloaking the island.

"You want me to turn on the light, boss?" Shad had asked after Eric resettled in his chair.

"No, thanks. I like it like this. They're playing sambas I used to hear in New York."

"Enjoy yourself, then," Shad had said, sure he was thinking about the woman, maybe imagining them dancing together.

"By the way," Eric called behind Shad, "I'm going over to the island tomorrow morning, in case you're looking for me."

"I thought she said she didn't want visitors."

"She might need something."

The boss was a good man, but he'd gotten weak since the hurricane. Shad had groaned mentally when Eric accepted the woman's offer, felt in his bones there was trouble ahead. But he had to admit she was an angel from heaven, an angel who'd put money into Eric's account. His overdraft would soon be lower, he'd told Miss Ferguson at the bank on the phone, because he now had a *tenant*. And there'd be money for a new roof and money to pay his taxes, he'd said afterward with a sigh.

"I hope she stay a long time, then," Shad had answered.

In all the last week since they'd met Simone, there'd been no talk between the men about the obvious, as if the question would drive her and the rent money away. It was Beth who'd cut to the heart of the matter.

"Why she on the island in the first place?" she'd asked that morning. She was sitting on the bed plaiting Rickia's hair, the baby squirming in Rickia's arms.

"She must have a good reason to live out there alone," Beth said. She rubbed Vaseline on Rickia's center part, making it shine.

"Maybe she just want a holiday by herself." Shad pulled up a little and threw a pillow into place behind him.

"What you mean? Living like that is no holiday," Beth said.

"I don't know. Maybe she stole money from a big company in America and she hiding away here."

"What if she murder somebody, and the police looking for her? You going to have to tell, you know. With your record and everything . . . ," Beth said. She snapped the clips shut at the ends of Rickia's plaits.

"I know, I know," Shad said, looking at the pink sheet and the roses dancing across his toes.

"Don't get mix up in anything, please." Beth stroked the back of her neck and the soft, fluffy hairs he played with when they made love. "You don't know where this one will lead."

"No, man, I always careful," Shad said.

"I hope nothing happen to her, though," she said, standing and taking the baby.

"Don't put your goat mouth on it, girl," Shad said. He held out his arms to kiss Rickia good-bye. A bad prophesy only led to bad luck, they said, as bad as a goat touching you with its mouth.

Thoughts of Simone had vanished an hour later when he got word that Job, the father he never had and the contractor who'd built Eric's hotel, had gone to the hospital the evening before. A childhood friend of Shad's grandmother, the toothless Job had hired Shad straight out of prison and never told a soul anything.

"Old Man Job, boss, he sick," Shad had announced as soon as he came into work later. "He have a stroke!"

"What happened?" Eric said. He looked up from the bill he was holding, his face stricken.

Shad twisted his mouth, hoping Eric would remember how Job had advised him to build a retaining wall, the wall he'd postponed to buy magazine ads. The wall that would have prevented the hotel's driveway from collapsing into the sea.

"He was fixing Ben's fence, and just fell down on the ground," Shad said. "Imagine, five hours it took the ambulance to get here! He could have died in the five hours."

Job, ever patient, who'd taught him and Eric—sometimes laughing at their clumsiness, his hand covering his mouth—how to drive steel poles down into the holes they dug, pour concrete into the holes, and slide the gray bricks down the steel. Job, who'd taken him and Beth to church because "your soul need saving."

A scurry overhead drew Shad's glance upward. The thatch roof had been Job's idea, the bar Shad's. It hadn't been easy to convince Eric. For a full year after the hurricane, Eric had spent hours every day sitting on the Delgados' verandah facing the sunken peninsula.

The solution to both their problems had come to Shad while he was nursing fresh gashes from fishing, the iodine bottle squeezed between his knees. He'd just wrapped a finger with a bandage and was about to move on to the cut above his wrist, when he thought about a little business he'd seen, and knew what he had to do.

"Boss, boss," he'd said to Eric, who was puffing on his pipe and rocking like an old man, "I think of something."

"Let me hear it," Eric had said, and kept reading his paper.

"Last Monday, me and my uncle went to deliver ten pound of snapper to a little restaurant in Port Antonio.

An ugly little place, but anyway, it there on a small piece of land next to the road—look like it making good money. And I start to think about a business you could start."

Eric had stopped rocking. "What kind of business?"

"A bar and restaurant," Shad said. "I went to see Job, boss, and we sat at his kitchen table, and we figured out how much it would cost to build a place on your land, you know, the little piece you still have over there." They had both gazed at the weed-choked driveway opposite, the driveway that had once led to the hotel and now ended at a cliff.

"There's not enough space," Eric had said.

"Listen to me, boss. We can do it."

"Even if I have the land, I don't have the money," Eric said, pulling in his chin. "I told you the insurance company didn't send me much. They said I was under-insured."

"I measure the land, and Job come up with some figures, boss. See if you can manage this."

Eric had promised to look at Job's sums—written in the thick pencil he always used—but he hadn't. It had taken Shad two more visits to persuade him to talk to Job.

Now this was where Shad worked and Eric lived, under a thatched roof that harbored lizards. The long rectangular structure beneath it was made up of Eric's apartment (a far cry from his hotel suite, he whined at first), a kitchen in the middle, and an open-sided room that served as the bar and restaurant, their lifeline.

Shouts rose from a table in the corner. Three house

guests of Roper Watson, an artist living on the eastern end of the village, were lambasting local politicians between slurps of Johnnie Walker Black.

"Talk the truth!" yelled one man. They'd leave a good tip, and Shad was prepared to stay until they stood up. Then he'd chase the locals away and lock up the kitchen.

Business was slow tonight, but the bar was the place to go when there was money in the pocket. It stood head and shoulders above the two rum bars in town. According to Bradley, a friend of Roper's from Boston, it was the Times Square of Largo. Shad hadn't known what Times Square was, but he and Beth had seen it on TV last New Year's Eve, and then he'd understood that Times Square, a place with more lights than all of Jamaica, was the heart of America. And then he understood that the Largo Bay Restaurant and Bar was the beating heart of Largo.

Part of the draw of the bar was Eric's personal story—the loss of the hotel and his refusal to leave Largo. Since the villagers liked a tragic story of rise and fall, Eric served as a constant source of speculation.

"He running from something, not true?" Old Man Job had once said to Shad.

The bartender always smiled and said nothing, knowing that Eric was a private person and that private people attracted the most attention. And while he thought of Eric as unfortunate—a man who couldn't hold on to a hotel or a woman—he also saw him as privileged. He might be as bland as ginger ale, but in Shad's mind a white man with a US passport had options. Options he didn't have.

It didn't worry Shad that the boss could go to America

whenever he wanted, because he knew that Eric wasn't going anywhere. The boss was a big fish in the small pond of Largo and liked it. Even though his navel string wasn't buried in Jamaica, his heart was. And after the boss promoted him from construction worker to bartender—to save money, Beth had commented—and with his fortune tied to Eric's, Shad prayed to his God on Sunday mornings that this man's dreams, whatever they were, would prevail.

"A strange man, eh?" Judith, a friend of Janet's and a newcomer to the village, was saying tonight. "A white man in a black man's country, a man from a big American city who live in a little Jamaican town. He even have a bar, but he don't stay up late."

"He have a hotel first," Solomon said, half drunk already.

"He married?"

Janet took a sip of Sprite. "He married once, and he have a big son who gay, a *batty man*." She crunched a piece of ice while Judith laughed.

"The son came out once and stayed in the hotel," Solomon said. "He name Joseph. He had two friends with him. All of them queer, used to wear pink and yellow shirts."

"And he have a baby mother," Janet said. "Nice woman, Shannon her name, but she gone back to Canada."

"True?"

"A photo—photographer," Solomon slurred. "Came out to photograph waterfalls. A sweet lady, tall and pretty, needed some meat on her bones, though."

"She used to come every month for a couple of years. Then she got pregnant and we never see her again," Janet added.

"Every year she send us Christmas cards with a photograph of her and the little girl," Solomon said. "'Love, Shannon and Eve,' she write."

Refreshing Judith's beer, Shad called to the group at the table. "So what you all think about the election coming up?"

"You mean, can they run a clean election? They too corrupt, man!" said one of Watson's friends, whose name Shad couldn't remember.

"The government should lose, yes!" said Tri. "Out with the People's National Movement! Time for them—"

"The whole culture of Jamaican politics is corrupt, man, not just one party," called out Bernard, a musician from Kingston.

"You not talking about my party!" Tri said, jumping up from his bar stool. There were general shouts for either side, a hand pulling Tri back to his seat, a call for another round.

Shad changed the music to a slow old Toots and the Maytals reggae to cool off the crowd. Eric would be going to bed around now. He'd sleep well tonight, knowing the work on the new roof would be starting tomorrow, but thinking about the woman might keep him awake. Preparing another round for Bernard and his friends, the bartender breathed a quick thank you to the strange lady.

"And don't let anything happen to you, please," he whispered over the ice bucket.

CHAPTER SIX

It was still early morning when she finished digging the outdoor toilet, only eighteen inches deep but adequate. After covering it with a coconut bough, she moved on to the next distraction—fishing.

Staying busy was vital. It was the only way to block her anxiety and fill the hollowness in her chest for a while. Last night she'd lain in bed and planned the next day's projects, and she'd decided that a fried fish or two would add variety to her diet, and she'd start fishing tomorrow.

Beginning her search for a stick, anything suitable for a fishing pole, she ventured through the old guest rooms off the lobby. She'd avoided them until now. With a knife in one hand, she advanced down the mossy corridor. Slightly bent over for fear of waking something, she peeped into the rooms where people had once slept and laughed and made love. But the rooms disappointed. All had been vandalized, and not a toilet or a broomstick was left. The only sign of life was a sleeping colony of bats clinging to a beam on a ceiling, making her shiver and tiptoe to the doorway ahead. Outside the breeze had dropped and she tilted her face into the sunshine.

"Yes, yes," she moaned aloud, working her throat in case she had visitors, in case Keller and his sidekick came back. A curious character, Eric, probably married, with stuff, like a sailboat. If he wasn't married, he had a local woman who fed him well enough.

Before her lay an old road out to the point, a storm shutter flattened over a pothole like a sagging ribcage. From the village came the soft braying sound she heard every morning, a sound she couldn't identify, that reminded her of cool mornings on the way to school.

The overgrown road was lined with a couple of small frangipani trees in bloom, each flower with its precise white petals meeting in a lemon-yellow center. Threading a flower through her hair, she continued her walk.

"The bride has to wear flowers," Rose had said, her small tongue wriggling as she struggled to tuck red hibiscuses into Simone's plaits. Rose was always the groom and chickens the guests. They had to shoo the guests away to walk down the aisle.

The road ended abruptly at the point, gray patches of asphalt clinging to a descending mound of rocks, Eric's sunken peninsula. On the opposite shore, an open building clung to the cliff, chairs and tables visible under a tattered thatch roof. A good earthquake should take care of it.

Nothing lasted here anyway. Life was cheap, and death was far more interesting. She'd learned that lesson at age four, when she'd been the first person to spot a corpse floating in the bay on the way to school.

"Marie, look! Is that man swimming?" she'd called to

her eldest sister. Her sisters had run ahead of her to the teacher with the news and hadn't told anyone Simone had seen the body first. It had been the excitement at school for the day.

Growing in a cluster of tall grasses near the cliff edge was a sapling, the narrow trunk straight and strong.

"It takes a good eye to find a good fishing rod," her father used to say whenever they went to look for a stem. "Patience is a virtue."

She glanced west toward her childhood home, fifty miles along the main road. She'd almost told the taxi driver to stop in St. Ann's Bay, but she'd felt compelled— even before the plane touched down in Montego Bay—to drive straight to the most isolated spot she'd ever seen, away from pitying eyes.

She started sawing the trunk close to the ground, the cheap kitchen knife pressing into her palm. No need for fishing rods after they moved to London. Her sixth birthday had dawned rainy and cold, and there'd been no birthday party at school. She'd spent the day looking out the window, hoping that a Jamaican sun would split the clouds and melt the ugly city and the ugly people.

Clapham had changed, they said, had become gentri- fied. No more cold-water flats or hairdressing parlors on the High Street smelling of burning grease and singed hair. No more immigrants.

Cutting away at the last strand of the plant, she straightened and held her throat. A scorpion was clinging to the stem a couple of inches below where her hand had been, its orange tail raised, ready to strike. She wacked the creature with the knife and watched it writhe in the grass until it lay still.

Later, with knee-high socks added to the sneakers, she sat on a rock facing north. The bait she'd dug out of the rock crevices just above the waterline lay beside her. Lucille and Marie loved to pull the little striped mussels off the rocks and watch them suck in their sticker pads, but they refused to do more.

"Let Simone do it. Sim, do this one for us," Marie and Lucille would call, and showing off, she'd smash the shell and hook the soft insides without a grimace, chasing them afterward to wipe her slimy fingers on their shorts.

Lining up the mussels on the rock, she crunched the first shell with a stone—her face screwed up as she separated the soft body—and threw line and bait out to sea. After washing her fingers, she wiped them on her shorts, no others to chase this time.

Her first fish had been the best.

"Hold steady, don't jerk it," Daddy said, and made her work the fish in slowly, hauling in the line hand over hand, until she could pull it up onto the low bank. It was a parrot fish, young and lively, swishing its tail back and forth as she marched home, awed sisters in tow.

Her mother, sitting on the verandah holding the baby, told her to take it in the back.

"Ask Sarita to cook it," she said.

The young Indian maid had clapped her hands.

"What a lovely fish!" she'd said, and heated up the outdoor coal pot, layering it with coconut oil. The three girls had squatted beside the pan watching Sarita fry the fish crisply with an *escoveitch* sauce of onions, slices of red and yellow Scotch bonnet pepper, and vinegar. After the johnnycakes were fried, they'd polished it all off sitting on the back step.

Lucille, licking her fingers, had made a promise. "I'm going to have fried fish at my wedding, not curried goat," she'd said.

The bait had disappeared when Simone hauled up the line. She picked up another mussel, smashed the shell, and reloaded the bait.

"Throw the line out farther this time," she heard Daddy say as clearly as if he'd been standing there.

CHAPTER SEVEN

Morning mist hovered over the mountain behind Eric while he rowed, sunlight warming his back. A mild breeze blew across the bow and curled into his ears. It was his favorite time of day—another reason for staying in Largo fifteen years.

"If you ever see me packing to move back to the States," he'd said, laughing with Lambert Delgado once, "you have permission to shoot me."

He affirmed the rightness of his choice daily by reminding himself why he'd left in the first place. He even created lyrics, more like mantras, celebrating his departure from the north, one of which he now hummed and murmured while he rowed.

"No more winter—no more cold—no more ice—no more snow," he broke out between hums. Last month it had been, "No air-conditioning—no stifling heat—no breezeless days—no subway seat."

Ahead of him, a flying fish leaped out of the water and skimmed the surface, followed by two and then three more. A bigger fish was probably behind them, scaring them to death. They disappeared into the low waves a few feet farther on, leaving no trace of their flight.

Half the fun of escaping New York had been select-ing his retirement spot, and in between working, fill-ing out forms, and conducting interviews, he'd started clipping articles from the *Times* travel section and taping them into a notebook. As the years rolled by, he'd visited one island after another, adding to the notebook until it was three inches thick. By a process of elimination, he'd decided that his haven would be warm, not hot, and rural, but not isolated. And since he needed people, the residents in this small, rural place would be honest and unpretentious—most of them anyway.

"One thing I'll never have to do," he'd said to Arnie, across from his desk, "is wear anything but sandals. I swear to God."

This morning, for the first time in years, he'd pon-dered what to wear, standing in front of the unpainted shelves in his closet. His briefs, shorts, and T-shirts looked worn and in need of upgrading. The uniforms of his earlier life had marched before him, the blazers for parochial school, the suits for work, the designer shirts for parties, every garment he brought given away to men in the village. Once he'd seen a shirt of his on a Rastafarian mending a fishing net, dreadlocks framing the logo, and he'd thought of sending a photograph to Ralph Lauren.

This is how your shirt looks on a Real Man, he was going to write on the back.

Letting the canoe glide onto the sand, Eric waited until the water beneath was shallow enough to keep his shorts dry. He hurried toward the almond tree, the toughened soles of his feet ignoring the stones and weeds, anxious to know she was still alive, that the nightly prayers he'd been sending up to Mary, Saint Christopher, the stars above his verandah, were working.

At the sight of a frying pan dripping water under the tree, he exhaled. He was unsure of the protocol for a landlord, and he folded his arms and waited, remembering the gun.

"Hello?" he called after a few minutes. "Simone?"

Suddenly feeling like an intruder, he kicked a stone away from the tree. She'd asked for privacy, would be annoyed in her sharp way. She might even change her mind and leave the island. If he left now, she wouldn't see him and he could come again next week with a better excuse. He turned toward the cliff path, his cheeks hot.

"Mr. Keller."

The woman strode toward him wiping wet hands on her shorts. Interruption furrowed her brow, her eyes hidden by large sunglasses. She stopped a few yards away from him, waiting, less prickly than the week before. Her crisp knee-high socks clashed with the baggy old shorts, two personas at odds.

"Please, call me Eric." His smile went unanswered.

"Your check cleared," he said.

She nodded, more tanned than he remembered her. The wind pressed her shirt flat against her breasts, the nipples little pimples, and he shuffled from one foot to the other. He should have worn shoes.

"Everything okay out here?" he said.

"Yes, thank you," she said, sounding like a next-door neighbor being polite.

"I just wanted to make sure you didn't need anything."

"I'm fine."

He held the hair back from his face. "You're sure? Mail, laundry?"

She turned her back to him, the breeze plastering the white T-shirt to her back, and he knew she was weighing his involvement against her need. When she faced him, he tried not to look at her breasts and instead focused on the wrinkle between her brows.

"Can you get me a regular supply of groceries?" she said, the brittle sound almost gone. "There's a man named Sam in Poco Bay who brings out my stuff, but he's not very dependable. I need someone to make sure he brings them every two weeks."

They got down to lists and quantities, Eric trying not to smile. He stood behind her while she wrote at her desk, and looked at the tight calves and thighs beneath the shorts. She'd been getting exercise, maybe swimming. She wouldn't know that sharks were sometimes sighted off Largo, the cry going up a few times a year and everyone rushing down to the beach to spot the triangle among the waves.

She gave him another check in a sealed envelope, and details of delivery to Sam.

When they stepped outside the door, he asked, "Do you want me to bring them out?"

"Sam can do it," she said, her eyes sweeping the shore. "He needs the money."

Quickly, he had to say it while she was in a good mood. "Maybe you should give me the name of a next of kin, you know—"

"I've told someone where I am. That's enough." There was Brooklyn in the mix.

"Just wanted to cover the bases."

"I've covered them pretty well," she said.

"You have a good reason for being here, don't you? If you—"

She glanced up at him, narrowing her eyes a little.

"I'm sorry, I didn't mean to pry." He brushed a mosquito from his arm and headed for the path.

He was almost to the center of the old circular driveway, where the fountain he'd dug out himself used to bubble, when he heard her not far behind him, her voice suddenly cool and smooth like a porcelain doorknob.

"Do you have children?" she asked.

He spun on his heel. "Two, a boy and a girl," he said, looking across at his bar. Shad was sitting on the roof.

"They're not here. One's in DC and one in Toronto."

"Don't you miss them?"

"You get busy, you know."

Midday sweat trickled between his shoulder blades on the return. He rowed normally, knowing she wasn't watching this time, the oars sometimes missing the water. He was glad he'd taken a minute before leaving to warn her about sharks, even if she pretended not to care, but he wished he hadn't sounded so lame about his children. She'd think he was a deadbeat dad or something.

CHAPTER EIGHT

The limestone pebbles in the car park made the low crunch of a luxury car rolling over them. It was three o'clock and Shad was wiping scraps of lunch from the wooden food tray, thinking about stretching his paycheck to buy Joella a new pair of sneakers.

The jet-black car crept in, the reflection of the red poinciana blossoms above sliding over its shine. A car like this would bring wealthy foreigners, and at this time of day the man would want an imported beer and the woman a fruit punch. Later in the day a scotch and a rum punch. A person's drink reflected his personality, his lifestyle, his history. If Shad could read the person right, he could nail the drink.

The limo's pitch-black windows allowed no view of the interior or its occupants, like the hearse that had carried Old Pastor's body. The car rolled up to the restaurant and stopped, the engine still running. No one emerged for a couple of minutes. Shad waited, his heart beating a little faster. When the driver's door opened, he let the tray clatter to the counter and gave a shout.

"Doughnut-Boy, is you?" He ran around the bar and

held out both hands to the towering man whose eyes were unseen behind sunglasses.

"Smiley? You, boy? Of all people!"

The two men embraced laughing, Shad only coming up to the visitor's shoulder. The black suit felt stiff and slick under his hands.

"What you doing here? And how you driving such a big car?" Shad asked.

"Is a Lincoln. You like it?"

"Yeah, man. You don't want to turn off the engine, though?"

"The air-conditioning running, Smiley," the big man said. "He like it cool."

"I see," said Shad, who didn't see. "Guess what? I not Smiley anymore, you know. Just Shad. That's my born name."

"Shaking off the old, right? I hear you. And I not Doughnut-Boy no more either. They call me Dollar-Bill now, Dollar for short."

"You must be making plenty money, then. You looking like a big shot," Shad said as he scooted behind the counter. "Whatever they call you, boy, is good to see you. Is a long time, not true?"

"Thank God." Dollar took out a crisp white handkerchief and wiped his forehead, throwing the odor of cheap aftershave across the counter. "Before we talk, you sell Heineken?"

"Of course, of course. How many you want?"

"Give me two. One for him," Dollar said, jerking a thumb at the car behind him.

Shad popped the caps of two bottles and watched them arc into the trash can at the end of the bar. He placed the bottles on the counter with glasses. The man poured one of the beers into a glass and carried it out to the car. A rear window slid down and a pale hand, the sleeve of a man's suit just visible, took the beer before the window closed.

Dollar returned to the bar, loosening his tie and opening the top button of his shirt. He slid onto a stool and took a slurp of beer.

"You ever think back to those days, boy?"

"Too often, man. I try to forget."

"I dream about it sometimes," Dollar said, and removed his sunglasses. He placed them on the counter, his nails shiny and clean. "I even smell that smell in my dream. I only been in there three times, but is like it living inside me."

Shad looked at the sunglasses and away from the brown eyes with the yellow rings.

"I dreamed the other night I was in a fight in the Pen," Shad said. "You not there, though. I had to fight by myself. Fifteen years and I still dreaming about the place!"

"How many times I save your skin?" Dollar asked.

"Every day, man, every day."

"Remember that time Dungeon grab you in the crotch?"

"And how you just lift him up and fling him in the dryer!" The two men could laugh about it now, Dollar giving out a ho-ho-ho, a rich man's laugh. He had fancy white teeth now, not his old crooked ones. Hard to believe they'd been like brothers once.

"Man, I owe you my life," Shad said. "I would be dead now if it wasn't for you. But I straight now, my friend, with wife and children. I not going back in there. Not for the rest of my life."

"You hear anything from Sassafras?"

"I hear police gun him down in Spanish Town last year. He was robbing a gas station."

"Damn, that could have been us, boy," Dollar said, an American twang surfacing for a second. "So, what you doing now?"

"Living quiet, wanting what every man want, you know. Good woman, little comfort for the family, children in school, ordinary kind of things." Shad ran a thumb over the scraggly nails on one hand. "And I a Christian now, boy. I content with work, home, and church. I done with stupidness. That's what I decide when I come back. I get a work building a hotel, then I learn the bartender business."

"Bartender business." Dollar glanced at the old bar stools the boss said he'd replace with the next check. "So, is here you work?"

"Head bartender, man, that's me. I can mix anything for you, fancy daiquiri and thing."

Dollar smiled like he used to smile at the guards sometimes, like he was patting them on the head.

"Glad for you," he said. He swung toward the island, showing a small ring of baldness at the back of his head. "Your boss own the island?"

"Yeah."

"What he doing with it?"

"I dunno," Shad answered.

"He not selling it or nothing?"

"No, no, he not selling," Shad said. He twitched his shoulders up and dropped them. "So, who's the star in the car?"

"Big man from foreign," Dollar-Bill said. "Run things in Ocho Rios."

"What kind of things?"

"He in business, you know," Dollar said, and ran a finger over one eyebrow.

"What he doing seventy miles from Ochy?"

The giant cracked his neck from one side to another. "Just taking a drive, coming back from Kingston the long way."

Shad's stomach started to rumble and he stroked it. "Nothing out here for him, man," he said. "Only fishing and country people."

"Even country people get a little action now and again," Dollar said, and laughed like sudden thunder.

"Not us, we quiet. Only thing coming up is the election."

Dollar-Bill took a swig. "Who you think the town voting for?" he said.

"Don't ask me, boy," Shad said. "I stay out of politics." He'd make a cup of mint tea as soon as Dollar left.

"You want to let these idiots get in?" Dollar pronounced the word *ee-diots*.

"They all the same, man."

Dollar drained the bottle and belched. "You don't know what happening, boy, or you'd change your tune."

Shad started reaching toward the bottle but then drew his hand back.

"How much I owe you?" Dollar said, standing over the counter, buttoning his shirt. He replaced the sunglasses and walked out to the car without waiting for an answer. The back window rolled down. The hand held out an empty glass.

Returning with the glass, Dollar placed a US twenty-dollar note on the counter, the pale pink polish glistening on his fingernails.

"That for you, youth," he said. "I coming back to see you sometime, you hear? Maybe we can do some business together. You never know." Thunder-laughing again.

The man pulled up his pants a couple of inches, as far as they would go.

"Walk good," he said.

Shad gave a low wave to his friend's retreating back. With the other hand he reached into his pocket and touched his good luck charm—the bag with his grandmother's grave dirt.

CHAPTER NINE

B ending back the first page of the journal, she wrote:

HOW TO SURVIVE ON A DESERT ISLAND

She underlined the heading. Underneath she added—
For the book I am going to write. After a minute she continued.

Reminder: Keep the goal in mind. Have some sort of deadline
for ending the process.

THINGS YOU ABSOLUTELY NEED FOR SURVIVAL:

1. Food and water:
    Packing food for a solitary island stay is more important
than packing clothes. Think of packing a carry-on bag when
flying—only the absolute essentials should be included. Food
should be chosen based on their nutrients and convenience.
A healthy diet should include proteins, starches, and fruits
and/or vegetables. Cans are wonderful and do not have to
be refrigerated, but they can be heavy. Hard baked crackers

are a good source of starch and are definitely preferable to bread.

Fruits are important, but no bananas or easily perishable fruit. Dried fruits are best, such as prunes and apricots. Certain vegetables like carrots and potatoes keep longer than others and should be purchased, rather than more fragile vegetables like lettuce and avocados. Snacks also help what would otherwise be a boring diet. Natural snacks are the best. One should also look around the area where one is going to live for food; for example, the fruit of the almond trees here.

Water, and lots of it, will have to be brought in bottles, unless there is a source of drinkable water available. All food and water should be kept in a cool place, secured against insects and animals, and stored in sealed containers.

2. <u>Protection</u>:
Survival on a desert island depends to a large extent on safety.

a) Residential safety: The dwelling should be protected from the elements. In all climates this means having its back to the wind and rain. In the tropics, there should be a good roof that can withstand sun and storms. In a colder climate, of course, the dwelling has to be kept warm, either with a fire or with insulation. Any of these might mean reinforcing the residence.

b) Personal safety: Depending on where the isolation occurs, the resident has to think of protecting him- or herself. There are wild animals in certain places and wilder people in others. It sounds extreme, but a gun or weapon is definitely needed. If possible, one should have backup, like a knife, that is easily accessible. Practice beforehand is important for ease of use when and if the time comes to defend oneself.

3. Clothes:
   Stick to the essentials.
   Hot-weather clothes
   Cold-weather clothes (a heavy water-resistant jacket for colder climates, plus gloves and hat; a raincoat in the tropics)
   Shoes and socks

4. Furnishings:
   Essentials—a good mattress that can double as a sofa, a table of some kind (to eat or write at), a desk chair, a kitchen area
   Luxuries—an easy chair, a regular bed

5. Extra things to pack:
   Books, both deep and shallow
   A journal to document one's process and to help achieve the objective of being alone
   Personal Items: mirror, comb, binoculars, manicure kit with scissors, sunblock
   Tools: digging fork and spade (small), hammer, nails, fishing tackle
   Weapons: machete and/or gun

She stopped and unwound her fingers from the pen. They were cramped, more accustomed to a computer keyboard. The intimacy between paper and hand reminded her of school days, the connectedness of pen to thoughts feeling odd but good. After shaking out her hand, she continued, her interest fading.

6. Pastimes:
   Stay busy—start and finish projects; e.g., building a
      latrine
   Learn something new, like hunting or fishing
   Write, read
   Exercise
   Pursue a hobby, like painting

7. Preparations:
   a) Shopping and packing before arrival (make careful lists)
   b) Setting up the dwelling: make the location habitable
      and safe; secure the bedroom from the weather and
      make it comfortable; create a kitchen that is basic but
      operational
   c) Sanitation needs: arrangements for brushing teeth,
      washing hair and body; toilet (very important for health)
   All of the above would be possible if one has transportation
   to the location, and if a person chooses to isolate themselves,
   for whatever reason. Should one be shipwrecked, of course,
   one would not have access to most of these items and would
   have to make do with what was found in the area.

She closed the book and placed it next to her. Her neck was burning—another spot she'd forgotten to cover with sunblock.

And praying, that had to be added. It would make a good discussion point for TV shows.

She turned to pick up the book and swung back. A fishing boat was approaching, unusual for midday, a modern outboard motor affixed to the rear. The two men in the bright yellow boat slid by a few yards away, a ganja joint hanging from the mouth of one.

She raised her hand and they waved back.

One man, his hand on the engine's tiller, called a lazy "Yeah, man," before they disappeared behind the rocks.

"Fuck," she said. Now the whole town would know. She dug a hand into her pocket. The gun was still under her pillow.

CHAPTER TEN

Maybe the moon wasn't right, but things seemed off-center to Shad, too many questions and too few answers. His stomach never lied, and his stomach had been unsettled since the woman arrived. They still didn't know why she was there, and it was only a matter of time before word got out that she was on the island. Then there was Doughnut-Boy, the most feared man inside the Penitentiary, a man with a history of doing anything for money, prowling the area with a rich man from foreign.

"What business you think his boss have in Largo?" he asked Beth a couple of days after Dollar's appearance. They were having lunch at the dinette table, Beth nursing the baby while she ate. A soap opera was playing on the television by way of Brother Simpson's handmade satellite dish on the roof.

"He looking to start a business?" Beth said, dragging her eyes away from the TV.

"Largo Bay too small for anything but a tourist business. We too far from the airport or the wharf."

"Maybe he just like to drive around in his big car."

"True," Shad said, and took another bite of fried plantain.

"What I don't like is that Doughnut-Boy know where you are now," Beth said.

Shad rubbed her plump arm. "Dollar-Bill. Nothing will happen, pudding. Don't worry your head about it."

"You think he going to forget that you owe him?" Beth sucked her teeth and turned back to the blond woman on the screen.

By the end of lunch, he wished he hadn't told Beth and worried her, but she was the only person who knew everything about him now that Granny was dead. When he first came out of prison, it had shamed the old lady so much that neither of them had said a word about it, and when his former schoolmates asked him where he'd been, he'd talk about Port Antonio and being a bus conductor. Beth, a newcomer to Largo, had had her hands full taking care of the new baby and his grandmother, and she'd kept her mouth shut. And Eric had been none the wiser. He didn't seem to care about his own past, much less Shad's, but there came a time when a man had to talk the truth.

That morning Shad straightened his shoulders and approached the table where Eric was reading the paper. It was always best to approach the boss with a plan. He could have an unpredictable temper sometimes, being an August man, but when he was drinking his coffee he could take almost anything.

"Boss, something I have to tell you," he started, not sure what he was going to say. He had thought he should say something, in case Dollar came back and talked about the Pen.

"If you have a minute," Shad continued, feeling the sweat spreading under his armpits, dampening his shirt.

Just then Solomon emerged from the kitchen and shuffled up to the table, his toes hanging over the front edges of sandals two sizes too small.

"Good mahning, Mistah Eric," Solomon said. As usual, Maisie had dressed her tall, skinny husband in white pants, shirt, and apron. He no longer wore the crisp chef's hat of his glory days at the hotel, the hat that always crumpled from collisions with the doorway, especially when he was too drunk to duck. But with the help of quick swigs from a pint bottle, the man still cooked like the Montego Bay chef he'd once been, and everyone loved his roast pork and his gingered chicken.

"Eggs again, or some nice saltfish and ackee?" Solomon said, breathing early-morning fumes of toothpaste and white rum at Shad and Eric. Just then the phone rang and Shad ran to snatch it up.

"Largo Bay Restaurant and Bar," he said like a mulatto in charge of an office.

"Boss, the chicken lady can't come tomorrow," he called when he hung up.

"What's the problem now?" groaned Eric. They both knew it meant buying the chicken in town and bringing it back in ice, melting in the open tray of the Jeep.

"She going to the American embassy to interview for a visa," Shad said, picking up a mop.

"Why does she want to do that?"

"Remember she tell us her husband live in New York and she going to join him?"

"She'll end up in a little apartment in Brooklyn, wishing she was back in Largo," Eric said. "I bet she'll regret the day she married the man."

Eric closed his eyes and squeezed them with his fingers. He was thinking of Shannon, Shad was sure, who hadn't come back because he hadn't asked her to marry him.

The end result of the morning's busyness was that Shad had said nothing about his teenage career stealing handbags in Port Antonio with a guy named Crew Member. He didn't mention how he'd had a gun, which he'd carried in his pocket sometimes because it made him feel strong, and how he'd caressed it sometimes but never fired it. He didn't say anything about how he'd cursed the policeman who arrested him and ended up in a six- by six-feet cell with no toilet, the filthy walls covered with beach scenes from magazines. Nothing of the biggest, meanest prisoner, who'd dragged Sarge off Shad once and knocked him out cold.

His stomach queasy, Shad lay down after lunch for a nap, pushing baby Joshua gently a few inches toward the wall, hoping he wouldn't wake up.

The next morning found Shad driving Eric's car to Manchioneal, a town big enough to have a small supermarket. His instructions were to give a shopping list to

Miss Chang of Chang's Emporium and to deliver the groceries to a man named Sam in Poco Bay.

"Say nothing, *absolutely nothing*, to anyone about this," Eric had said. "Nothing about Simone, period." That's how he'd said it, with a period, not a full stop, like a Jamaican would have said it.

On both sides of the road, the green walls of banana plants rose above the Jeep, blocking out the light. Blue plastic bags covered the young fruit. It would be harvest time soon, Shad's favorite time of year, when pickup trucks full of cash-rich workers would stop at the bar—beer for the hourly workers and white rums for the supervisors—after the daily cutting and packing.

Swinging the Jeep wide, Shad overtook a man riding a mule, baskets lashed to each side of the animal. The man waved, his bare feet dangling beneath the mule's belly in the rearview mirror.

The boss thought he knew everything, but he didn't understand people all the time. This Simone woman acted tough, like she could rough it, and the boss believed her. But you couldn't stay on an island by yourself for months and not go crazy. It was like being in prison. Sometimes you wanted to scream yourself dead with loneliness. And you lived with fear in every pore of your body, the fear of being attacked, the fear of going mad, the fear of yourself. You got so used to the fear that you forgot how it felt not to have it.

If the woman stayed on the island too long, she'd end up like crazy old Hector outside the village in his mountain shack, dirty and talking to himself. Even if she could beat the loneliness, she was inviting trouble, sitting out there by herself, because if she thought that no one in the village would notice her, she was really crazy.

"People in Largo poor, but they not stupid," Granny used to say.

Simone would be big news when word got out. It was only a matter of time, and the space between now and that time was exactly what she needed to do whatever she had to. She might not realize it, but she was buying time from Eric, and he was trying to keep her a secret because he was giving her time in exchange for rent money. Shad sighed and changed to a lower gear. She better work fast.

Two hours later, the vehicle squeaked to a stop along- side a wooden house on stilts.

"Oy, anyone home? Mr. Sam?"

Hearing only waves hitting the shore, Shad walked around the side of the house. An elderly, barefoot man was hosing down a purple and red canoe on the beach in front. The words *Lion of David* were painted on the prow in uneven and increasingly larger letters. A small dog, a *mongrel dog,* with a white patch around one eye, jumped up and started barking.

"Sam? You they call Sam?"

The man looked up and turned off the hose, hushing the dog. Sweat stuck his clothes to his body, still sinewy after a life of pulling nets. He wore a beret of red, yel- low, and green on top of gray dreadlocks that ended at his waist.

"Yes," the Rasta man said. "Me is Sam."

61

"I work for the American man who own the island off Largo Bay, the man with the bar," Shad said. "I have some groceries for the lady Simone. You know her, right? She want you to row them out to her."

Sam nodded and pointed to the steps leading up to the house. "Put them down."

"I going to bring groceries for her every two weeks from now on. Okay?"

The fisherman frowned and shook his head. "*I* is supposed to buy her groceries, so she tell me."

"Don't worry yourself, man," Shad said. "I'll take care of that. All she want you to do is row the groceries out as soon as I bring them."

Still frowning, Sam bent down beside the boat and turned on the hose again while Shad, followed at a safe distance by the dog, brought the bags of groceries from the Jeep and placed them on the back step. When he finished, he approached Sam, staying far enough away to keep his sneakers dry, but close enough to smell fish coming from his pores.

"That everything. So, tell me, star, you know the woman long?"

Straightening, Sam turned off the hose. "What you say?"

"You know the woman from before?"

"No. She just come in a taxi and ask me to row her over to the island."

"You know where she coming from?"

"She say she coming from Alta—Atlanta," Sam said.

"Atlanta, Georgia." Shad scratched his head. "I wonder why she want to live on the island. What you think?"

Sam shrugged. "She say she need to forget," he said.

"Forget what?"

"I never ask and she never say." Sam turned on the hose, making the little dog jump and ending the interview.

CHAPTER ELEVEN

All she can hear in the darkness are the waves, pushing in and out at the end of the verandah, washing toward her, pulling away, wanting her, rejecting her. She needs to know the water is there, that it will come back, needs the gurgles and pauses to stay in the present and calm the dreams.

It never rests, this water, always surging, never tired. It ebbs and flows with the moon, like her womb, constant as the blood flowing through her.

She places a hand under her breast, feels her heart beating low, pushing the fluid through her veins and arteries, her own tide of life, a faster tempo than the waves hitting the rocks. Four beats to one splash, she counts.

Reaching out in the dark, she feels for the vase, rubs her hand over its round coolness. Then she places her hand on her belly, the smoothness of the vase still safe with her, and rubs her abdomen in circles, slower and slower circles.

A hand, a tiny hand with curling fingers and little nails, curling around her pinkie finger. A brown arm and a body resting on her stomach, the chubby tummy in rolls, the belly button protruding out of the chubbiness, and little legs pedaling a bit, the toes long.

But the face, she has trouble seeing it now. The eyes were big, that she remembers, and the hair, black and curly, lots of it. Someone said it would fall out, but it didn't. And so she floats off to her dreams, with the infant on her belly, kicking every now and again and clutching her finger.

And in her dream she is a statue, a statue in a church she'd once been to in England, a stone church in Kent. She's a statue holding an infant clutching her finger, and her eyes are looking up to heaven and her heart is hollow and round with pain, and she knows how it feels to be a statue on a pedestal at night, holding an infant and feeling unspeakable sadness, with only darkness around her and the smell of stale incense.

CHAPTER TWELVE

A bee circled Shad and he ducked and shooed it away. High overhead a cluster of yellow and green mangoes teased him, and he pushed the long stick toward it. Hooking the bent nail around the stem, he shook the mangoes loose, one by one, and caught them as they fell. He placed them in a jute sack at his feet and tied the string at the top.

"Miss Mac," he called to the woman a few yards away, "I done for today. The rest not ripe yet. We can leave them until next week."

"Thank you, son," Miss Mac said. She put her book down and stood up on the verandah. Behind her, the sea's blue and aqua stripes stretched far into the distance. The crashing of the waves on the beach had a hollow, curling sound, louder than that beneath the bar.

She stood erect, as she always had, and Shad was reminded of her nickname in school. Errol Bailey had once said it to her face by mistake.

"Yes, Country Queen," he'd said, bending over a puzzle, and she'd ordered him to stand in the corner and tried not to smile.

"Take enough mangoes for the family," Miss Mac said. She still looked like a mother hen, the top-heavy torso balancing on spindly legs, still wore the same plaid cotton dresses and sturdy shoes she'd worn in school.

Shad removed six mangoes from the bag and placed them in his pockets. He carried the sack to the steps and swung it onto the verandah.

"I want to know," Miss Mac said, "how you can pick mangoes and your clothes still look nice and fresh."

Shad turned on the garden pipe and stood away from the spray. "Cleanliness next to godliness, yes. I know what it feel like to be dirty all the time, ma'am, so now I try to stay clean. Nobody want a dirty bartender, right?"

Miss Mac laughed, showing all her teeth, the back ones solid gold. "Well, you're looking sharp today. Beth taking good care of you, nuh?"

Shad turned off the pipe and shook his hands out. "Yes, Miss Mac. She give me a fresh ironed shirt every day."

"How the children?"

"Joshua have a little colic so he not sleeping so good," Shad said.

"The girls doing well in school?"

"I checking homework, trying to remember everything you taught me, ma'am," Shad said. "Joella starting to watch the boys, though. They passing the gate and calling her name. It make me a little nervous, you know!" They both laughed, Shad remembering Beth in her uniform at the bus stop.

"You a parent now, you have to keep a close eye on your property," Miss Mac said, waving a finger. A mongoose scurried from one bush to another a few feet away, its long tail straight and parallel to the ground.

"Speaking of property, Miss Mac, you ever thinking of selling this land? Like how, it spread out so nice along the beach?" Shad said. "Horace, he don't want it?"

"Boy, Horace has his nice house in Port Antonio. He not coming back to little Largo. My mother left me this land and she got it from her father. It used to be a long stretch, twenty miles along the road, but my brother got his and I got my nine acres. And I know what it worth, you hear me? It too valuable to sell for nothing. So I'm thinking one day somebody going to offer me good money for it, and I'll just take it and retire to Horace's house, like he always asking me." Meredith MacKenzie had always been a bright woman.

"Miss Mac," Shad said, "I have something to ask you. You read the papers and you know everything about Jamaica. You're a *knowledgeable* lady."

"I like how you say it." She chuckled and tucked in her double chin. "What you want to know?" She sat down and took off her glasses, the way she used to when she listened to a student.

"What you know about a rich American man in Ocho Rios?"

"Like a sugar estate owner?"

"Nah, I don't think so," Shad said, thinking of the pale hand reaching for the Heineken. "This man look like he never walk a piece of land in his life."

Miss Mac's eyes rolled upward. "Big American businessman, let me see, other than the Indian shop owners—"

"No, ma'am. A white man who have racehorses and a private plane, that kind of person."

"He could own a hotel," she said.

"I thought all the hotels were owned by Jamaicans," Shad said.

"Not all of them. Some are owned by foreigners. They have Americans, English, even Spanish people with big hotels on the North Coast. The owners live abroad, never come out here. The managers live in the hotel."

"I don't think this man is a manager, but he live here. He have a limousine, a big black car," he said. "He come around here sometimes."

"Maybe he owns a chain of hotels, not only in Jamaica."

"Maybe he looking to build another hotel," Shad said, folding his arms. "Like how Largo is pretty, hotel people with any sense would want to put one here."

"Or he could own a factory in Ocho Rios."

"Why would an American have a factory here? It wouldn't be worth his time," Shad said, leaning against the verandah wall. He chewed on his cheek for a second and turned to Miss Mac. "Factories make a man rich, Miss Mac?"

"If they're in the Free Zone, they do," Miss Mac said.

"The Free Zone?"

The elderly woman eased back in her chair. "The government started them back in the seventies or eighties. Foreign companies can put up factories in areas called

Free Zones—I think we have two now, in Kingston and Ocho Rios."

"What's so free about them?"

"The owners don't pay taxes on their profits for a certain number of years. They don't pay customs duties neither," Miss Mac said.

"Sounds like a sweet deal for them." Shad was back at school, looking up and counting the moles on her face.

"A scam, you mean!" Miss Mac hooted. "They cut the garments in America and send them down here to sew up in the factories, then they send the finished goods back to the States without paying us taxes. A sweet deal, yes!"

Shad frowned. "What the government get out of it, then?"

"It give them votes in the election, because people get work. But they say that some of the big government men get paid off for giving out permits to the American companies."

"That don't seem fair," Shad said.

"Fair? It's illegal."

"Why they don't arrest them?"

"Nobody can prove it. The whole thing is a shame," the old lady said, throwing up her hands. "They pay a little better than the Jamaican minimum wage, but it's still low, way lower than they pay in America. The worst part is how they treat the workers, like they have a whip over them."

"Maybe that help them to work hard. You know how Jamaicans can be lazy," Shad said, grinning.

"Working hard is one thing, but it's like they're in the army."

Shad pushed off from the wall, his mouth twisted. "I think I hear of this place. Not the same place they call *South Africa*?"

"Same one."

"My cousin work there, then," Shad said. At his uncle's funeral, Agnes had smiled in a bitter kind of way when she told him what they called the place where she worked.

"Your cousin? Ask her, nuh?" Miss McKenzie said, picking up her Bible and putting on her glasses.

CHAPTER THIRTEEN

O n the low rock in front of her reading bench lay a
fish, stranded by a wave. Clutching a journal and
pen in one hand, the gun in the other, she bent over
to examine it. About six inches long, gray and unpretentious, the fish struggled, gills and tiny chest pumping.

The dog sniffed the fish and started barking.

"Cammy!" she called and set down the gun. The animal retreated a few feet, its eyes never leaving the fish.

She watched the creature gasping, mouth agape,
death approaching. It would make good bait. The mussels hadn't worked. The eyes were starting to glaze over,
bruised by the raw air, not much time left.

She scooped up the fish and tossed it into safe water,
squatting down, willing it to swim. At first it stayed
still, lying on its side an inch below the surface, looking
larger than it had on land.

Then it started to transform, the dull grayness turning the iridescent blue of returning life. When the meta-
morphosis was complete, it righted itself and wiggled
away.

A small smile on her face, she sat down, almost forgetting the throb in her thumb where she'd cut herself the evening before. She'd been peeling potatoes and thinking of the men in the yellow boat.

She opened the book, a new one smelling like fresh paint in the salt air. She bent back the first page and wrote with her bandaged finger sticking out.

Dedicated to my daughter Celeste.

She turned the page and squinted into the glare bouncing off the waves, unsure of the date.

This journey is about my quest for myself, to remember who I am.

She chewed on the pen for a minute. Writing had never come easily. There'd been other things she did well—get scholarships for college, strategize campaigns, do whatever was needed. She looked at her bunions, turning her toes up. Maybe she'd try toenail polish when she got back. Her toes would be looking better; she'd be able to show them. The last time had been with Rose, sitting on suitcases at the end of the bed in Brooklyn.

If I am anything, I am a chameleon, I adapt. That is what immigrants do. They pack, they move, they adapt. Then they do it all over again.

A row of boxes stretched into the distance, brown boxes, always brown, never overstuffed, double-taped—

the contents, her name, and her new address written in black marker in the middle of the top and on two sides.

I have lived in three countries, four cities, and easily twenty-five homes.

The first home she remembered best, the cottage in St. Ann on Mahogany Road. There were gingerbread lattice openings at the tops of the doors, and you had to be careful the old sash windows didn't fall on your hands when you pushed them up. After that there were damp flats in Clapham, Rose's bedroom and four, five apartments in Brooklyn, a dark house in the Bronx, apartments in Queens and the Bronx, a larger place in Manhattan near Columbia University, a rental and the house in Atlanta, homes on streets she couldn't remember, homes that felt stranger than some hotels.

You eventually learn how to leave without a tear and live without friends. When I was a little girl, my best friend was Mary Simpson. She was the same height as me and was missing two teeth in front where her brother hit her. I shared a desk with her, and we promised to be friends for the rest of our lives. Miss Mills was my teacher and I loved her crinoline dresses. When I was five she came to my birthday party to say good-bye and I cried.

Marie had told the woman they were going to England "to seek our fortune."

Then there was Praveen, the fat boy in the flat next door in Clapham. We ate curry chicken in their kitchen when our parents worked late, and he helped me with my sums.

My best friend was my cousin Rose. She knew how to do everything.

Rose, stretching out her eyelid and taking forever to apply eyeliner, painting it on Simone and her other bridesmaids in those ridiculous pink dresses. She'd missed her so, so much when she and Bertram moved to Oakland.

Jeff was my best friend for a while. When he tried to carry me over the threshold, he could not get my legs through the doorway and we fell down in the corridor laughing until we cried, and I pulled him inside.

The last time she'd seen him, he'd hugged her and her hand had touched his silky handkerchief. She'd pitied the woman who'd paid for his ticket to Atlanta and bought him the beautiful suit.

A drop of salt water landed on the page, smudging three words. She blotted the page with her T-shirt and closed the journal. When she got back to the tree, the dog was lying in the shade, eyes flickering in a dream.

CHAPTER FOURTEEN

J ust as Shad had suspected, the woman on the island
became a hot topic among the villagers. From her per-
spective, she may have been cut off from the world by
a moat of seawater, but she didn't understand the power
of the grapevine in a place where half the people couldn't
read. It wasn't only the men in the yellow boat who'd
seen her. Dozens of fishermen lived on the sea at night,
throwing out nets and checking on lobster pots. A few
had seen the flames under her cooking pot, seen her pro-
file in the lamplight as she bent over a book.

Shad blamed himself for the outcome because he'd
confirmed the villagers' rumors. It had all started, he told
Eric, with an innocent betrayal—and not by Beth.

"Tell me, nuh," Frank had asked him while helping
load lumber into the Jeep, "is true that a woman living
on the island?"

"Why you want to know?" Shad had asked.

"Because Wally and Abel say they see a woman when
they passing the island," Frank said in his slow way. "And
if it not so, it nearly so, sound like to me."

Grateful for Frank's help, Shad had answered, "Don't

tell anybody, and is not me saying this, but a foreign woman living out there. I have to buy food for her and take it to Poco Bay. The boss swear me to secrecy, so don't tell anybody, you hear?"

A few nights later, Frank admitted to Shad, he'd told three friends playing dominoes, and within three weeks of Eric and Shad's first trip out, the whole village was able to confirm the fishermen's reports that there was a woman living alone on the island.

Foreigners were always a puzzle to Largoites, who thought Kingston was as good as foreign. Everybody was suspect. People who didn't fish or farm were unusual, like the artist man and his friends. Men who liked to have sex with other men were devilish perverts and should be chased out of town. And a *woman* who lived by herself on an offshore island had to be a lunatic.

Eventually the story of the mad woman got to a young layabout nicknamed Tiger and his friend Sharpie from out of town, Shad reported to Eric.

"Who?" Eric asked. He wasn't good with names.

"You met Tiger already," Shad said. "He's the son of Miss Armstrong, the lady who rents out the boat, you know the one, the green plexiglass boat? Well, Tiger is her boy. He actually a man, little younger than me, but nobody think of him so. He's good-looking, a tall, skinny guy, brown-skinned with the little scrawny beard, always sitting under the big tree on the corner, selling a few mangoes and a little weed."

"And who's the other guy?" Eric asked.

"Sharpie? He start coming around here about a year

ago, and he and Tiger hook up, they tight. He never here long, come for a couple weeks and then disappear. They say he from Spanish Town, but nobody know for sure. He walk right past you when you meet up. Nobody like him. They just don't take to him because he don't talk to anybody and he don't seem to work. Maybe he supply Tiger with weed, we don't know.

"One thing for sure—he never smile. I never see him smile yet, like he don't have a funny bone in his body. That a dangerous kind of man. You never see him? He dark like me and he squat." Shad spread out his arms like a weight lifter. "He not tall, but he fat with a round face, like a chocolate bulldog. Big, sad eyes. Always wearing a sweat suit and a big gold chain with a cross. A cross, you can imagine? Jesus's cross on a man's chest, and he never come to church! You don't think that is blasphemy?"

"Get back to the story," Eric said, buttering a piece of toast.

"I think the whole thing was Sharpie's idea," said Shad, resting his head in his hand, his fingers splaying up his cheek. "I know Tiger from a little boy, and I don't think he could have plan it himself. He too simple."

"Plan what?"

"The trip. They got the idea when they were lying in Frank's old canoe smoking some Negril weed—well, so Frank say—and they decide to check out Simone."

Eric stopped chewing and stared at Shad. "What you mean, 'check out Simone'?"

"They went to visit her," Shad said.

"What!" Eric shouted, pushing back his chair. "When was this?"

"Last night. They row out in Tiger's mother boat." Shad looked off at the island, saw Tiger in his baggy shorts and NBA T-shirt, Sharpie in his sweat suit, the crosses on their gold chains flipping up and hitting them in the face with the breeze.

"What happened? Did they hurt her? Did they have a gun?"

"No, no, she okay. And they didn't have no gun, just a bone they took for the woman's dog," Shad said.

"She doesn't have a dog."

"She have a dog now. Everybody know she have a dog."

"I've never seen a dog," Eric said. "Anyway, go on, go on."

"So they smoke some weed and row out to the island. Tiger can't row anyway, so it must have took them a long time to get out there." Shad shook his head and a smile started wrinkling his lips. "I can just see them trying to get up the cliff, the way Sharpie so big and Tiger so stupid."

As a man who enjoyed telling a good story, like all Jamaicans, Shad playacted the whole scene for Eric. Lowering his voice, Shad mimicked the two men whispering at the tops of their voices, grabbing each other as they struggled to mount the cliff. At the top, they'd crept along the path.

"Where the dog?" Shad became Tiger, peering ahead into the darkness, no moon out. A few more feet and they'd heard barking.

"Dawg!" Shad called in a trembling Tiger voice.

The bone was still in the boat. Tiger had rushed back down the cliff and retrieved it, while the other man had waited.

Eric felt for his coffee, eyes glued to Shad's face.

Armed with the bone, the two men had walked toward the buildings, looking from side to side. A noise made them stop, said Shad, then the dog barked again, closer this time. Tiger had tiptoed in front, Shad announced, waving an invisible bone before him.

Tiger had spotted the fallen coconut tree and stepped over it. Behind him, his companion tripped and fell facedown across the tree and into weeds, his new shirt ripping on the tree trunk. Shad became Sharpie, getting up cursing and brushing himself off.

"Then all of a sudden—*BADD-EYE!*" yelled Shad, clapping his hands.

Eric jerked forward. Coffee slopped onto the table. "What happened?"

"The woman fire her gun and the bullet whizz right past Sharpie's ear!"

Shad, in Sharpie's deeper voice, sprayed Jamaican curse words between his wide teeth. "*Raas claat!* What the *bumba* the mad-ass woman doing? She goin' *raas* kill us!"

According to Shad, the men had turned around, pushing each other aside, and raced back to the cliff. They'd fought, Shad breathing hard, to see who could get down the path first. Tiger pushed the boat off and jumped in. His companion waded out and threw himself onto one side, capsizing the boat and spilling Tiger into the chest-high water. Shad laughed, a whinnying laugh, and spun around on the spot.

They must have cursed each other's mothers while they pulled the boat upright and climbed back on board, Sharpie soggy in his sweat suit. Shad described the men shaking with fear, their clothes clinging to them and their oiled hair dripping in their eyes—as if he'd been there.

"How d'you know all this?" Eric asked.

"When they got back they see Minion—he was pushing off to go fishing—and Minion help Tiger turn the boat over and put it back on the logs. Sharpie went off and left them, he so vex. And Tiger still so afraid, he tell Minion the whole story like he need to live it again. Then Minion come straight to me and knock on my bedroom window."

"And you're sure she's okay?" Eric said.

"I telling you, nothing happen to her. If anything, she win that round."

"Thank God." Eric sighed. "But shouldn't we call the police?"

"And tell them what? Nobody going to witness or talk what they hear. They 'fraid of Sharpie."

Eric was silent and Shad walked to the pole nearby. Across from him, the island looked morose, the rocks under the clear water like dark jigsaw pieces.

"I glad she use the gun," the bartender said. "She get in some good target practice."

CHAPTER FIFTEEN

The journal entry for the morning, scrawled under the tree:

I fired the gun. Scared shitless, but I fired and they left.

I don't know who they were, but it sounded like a bunch of them. Could have been the men in the yellow boat, maybe with others. I could hear them cursing and running. It was too dark to see.

Cammy started barking and woke me up, thank God.

Keep me safe. Please, please.

had recrossed his legs and smiled at the receptionist. The smell of incense seeped under the door of
Brother Zachariah's office. This was Shad's first visit
to the new *obeah man*, who liked to be called "Doctor" instead of Zachariah. The obeah man before him had died,
a man with bad teeth and a bad temper.

Picking up an old *Good Housekeeping*, Shad turned the
pages, thinking of what he'd tell Beth when he got home.
She wouldn't be happy. Obeah isn't something to meddle
with, she'd say. Why you want to go against Pastor Mc-
Clelen? You heard him when he said the obeah man does
the devil's work, right? Even if it work.

He would answer her plainly: Somebody had to do
something. And the best way for Simone to live in peace
and keep paying rent, keep paying his salary, was with
the obeah man's blessing. Everyone said the Doctor had
powers, that his spells could give a man a new boat or
stop a woman from having a child, right? Even Maisie
said that, and she was a Baptist and still believe in
ghosts—*duppies* and *rolling calves*—and obeah men. And
his grandmother used obeah once, when she couldn't find

her mother's bracelet, and she found it after she sprinkled the oil around the house.

Drastic times call for drastic measures, Miss Mac said in history class, and it was the only solution he could think of. Besides, if Simone wanted to stay on the island, she had a right to stay, the boss had said. Shad had agreed because living in a place where you could be at peace was the best thing in the world, and the woman needed some peace, anybody could see that.

Eric had been in a bad mood that morning. He'd said nothing about the woman, nothing about a plan to protect her, and after asking for a couple of hours off, Shad had walked to the house everyone avoided if they could, the white house on the hill where the obeah man lived.

The man kept to himself, didn't go out much. He'd come to the bar only once, for his daughter's wedding reception, and nodded to Shad and Eric from a distance. Many bottles of rum and curry goat platters later, he'd slipped out without making a speech. A happy Mrs. Zachariah had paid the bill in cash—crisp Jamaican one-hundred-dollar notes, laid on the bar, one on top of the other with the faces up.

Zachariah's house clambered room by new room up the mountain south of Largo. Panting after the steep walk and three flights of stairs skirting the house, following the signs that said PRACTISE, Shad had found himself on a verandah that served as a waiting area. Lining one wall were straight-back rattan chairs and a table full of old magazines.

"The Doctor is busy with a client," the young woman

at the desk had said. "I see if I can fit you in." She was dressed in a brown pantsuit and spoke like a receptionist in a dentist's office. But instead of asking for his insurance card, she'd told him to have a seat. Within the house there was silence, the only sound a wind chime somewhere.

Half an hour later, Brother Zachariah opened the door to his office and ushered out a sniffing woman, head down, kerchief dabbing at her eyes. He patted her arm and told her to come back next week. The woman slipped him some folded banknotes. Her eyes lifted in quick contact with Shad's before she went off down the steps. The Doctor smiled at Shad and beckoned him inside.

Putting down the magazine, Shad almost felt like Zachariah was a regular doctor, like the one he went to last year when his stomach acted up. The only thing was he didn't look like a doctor at all. Although he'd worn white to his daughter's wedding, today Zachariah was dressed in red from head to foot—red patent leather shoes, thin red nylon socks, red pants, red Cuban shirt, and a red-and-white-striped turban.

The office he showed Shad into was a large open room with sliding glass windows on one side overlooking the town. The other three walls were lined with shelves—bottles large and small filling one wall, and books the other two. In the middle of the shelves were a sink and a long table holding glass vials, mixing bowls with mortars, and a tall glass jar with the dry bones of a small animal.

After they were seated on red velvet chairs, Zachariah

peered at Shad through the metal-rimmed glasses on his wide nose. Then he clapped his hands and leaned forward as if they were old friends.

"Nice to see you again, son. Myers, right?" The Doctor smiled, one gold tooth gleaming on an incisor, a star cut out of the middle. He looked like a white-rum-and-red-wine man.

"Yes, sir. You have a good memory."

"I have a dream last night you coming to see me," the man said, "but it didn't tell me why. Somebody do something to you?"

"No, no," Shad said, wondering if he'd brought enough money for the fees. "It's about a woman living on the island. She—"

"I know. I hear she have . . . a little unpleasantness with some visitors," the older man said, mixing American English and patois. Like he'd worked with foreigners or lived abroad.

"That's right." Shad nodded.

"Why's she there?" Zachariah, suddenly serious, raised his eyebrows. His hands, the color of twelve-year-old rum, lay in his lap, the long fingers intertwined. On his right hand he wore a gold ring with a snake's head.

"I don't know." Shad looked at the man, not knowing how to ask for magical favors.

"She need a shield, I think." The obeah man glided to the table next to the sink. He reached up and brought down two large brown jars, using a funnel to pour a few drops from both into a small bottle. Then he added a couple more drops of something, his back to Shad. After shaking the vial once, twice, three times, he licked a label and attached it.

"Tell her to sprinkle this around the island at night," he said. "That's all she need."

Shad took the glass bottle, wrapping his fingers around its cool label.

"That will be twenty dollars, US." Zachariah nodded, extending his hand. Shad deposited Dollar's tip in his hand and placed the bottle carefully in his pocket.

Later that afternoon when he came into work, he called Eric into the kitchen and pointed to the bottle lying on top of a dusty chamois cloth.

"What's that?" Eric asked, squinting at the label without his glasses.

"Brother Zachariah, he sending it to the woman on the island."

Eric burst out laughing. "I like how you think, man. Nobody will touch her."

"Afraid of retribution," Shad said. They both knew what happened when the doctor put a spell on someone, for good or for bad.

"Remember Sister June?" Maisie had said in the kitchen a couple of years back. "She go to live with that fisherman who had obeah on him, and the two of them disappear from earth. Nobody ever see them again." The plain face of the woman had lit up with the horror of nothingness.

"How much do I owe you?" Eric said, picking up the bottle.

CHAPTER SEVENTEEN

The dog rushed forward and circled him, barking at first, then falling silent to sniff his shorts pocket. Jittery, it backed away.

Eric squatted down and held out a hand. "Here, boy."

"It's a girl," said Simone. "She's a bit nervous." The dog started barking again, ignoring the woman's attempts to hush it until she raised the book and stamped her foot, a small cloud of dust rising around them both.

"Where'd she come from?"

"Sam brought her out," she said with a slight softness to her voice. "Said she'd be company."

"I brought you some mangoes," he said, standing slowly, trying not to hold on to his knees. "They're in season."

Simone took the bag he held out. "Thank you." He could hardly hear her above the wind.

He swung his arms, clapped his hands together. "So, how've things been going?"

She looked up at him and down at the bag.

"You heard, didn't you?"

She gestured to the fallen coconut tree. They sat on

the trunk, he first, holding his pocket, and she sitting a couple of feet away, her shoulders wider but bonier. In front of them the dog sat alert, ears twitching.

"What did you hear?" she said.

"The version I got was that two guys came to visit a couple nights ago. You chased them off with a gun, tried to kill them." He could feel the corners of his mouth twitching.

"My story is always different, I guess." She rested her chin on a fist, a new scab on one finger. "They were sneaking up on me."

Reaching down for a yellowed leaf trapped under the trunk, she ran her finger over the vein.

"Reminds me of the magnolia tree in my yard," she said, and for a second he thought she'd finished with the men, until she looked up at him.

"What were they up to?"

"They were just being mischievous," he said. He sighed and stroked his jaw. "They were probably going to rape you."

"Oh, my God," she said, holding her throat. "Who were they?"

"Two men with nothing to do, petty criminals. We know who they are. I didn't call the police because they'd make you move. And they might charge me with renting an unfit property."

"Why me?" she asked.

Eric took off his sunglasses. He left them dangling from the string around his neck.

"Are you from here originally?" he said.

"Yes, we left when I was five."

He drew a line in the dirt with the toe of his sandal. "You probably remember Jamaica as some kind of Eden. You had friends and family who loved you, memories of good times, right? And you're right, it's a beautiful place. What you wouldn't remember is that the flip side of beauty is ugliness. And the flip side of paradise is poverty and ignorance. There's a lot that's wonderful here, but there's a lot that's pretty raw."

Eric stared at his feet, his toes spread wide in the sandals. "Children are beaten, girls get harassed. Gays never know if they're going to live another day."

"I'm not bothering anybody," she said.

"When people are poor and don't have much education, they're only interested in their own survival. What they don't understand, they want to get rid of. To the villagers, you're—well, like a grain of sand in the shoe."

She half smiled and shook her head. "I was kind of hoping the grain of sand would become a pearl."

"I'm going to be honest with you—they don't really care what happens to you. They can't relate to you, they can't control you. You get in the way of what feels normal to them. That's how you become a scapegoat. They hang all their problems on you and chase you out into the desert, like in the Bible."

He put his glasses back on. "I'm just trying to say that you're real vulnerable out here."

"I need more time," she said. "Can you do that for me?" She looked at him, a sweet look he could feel in his chest.

"If you're sure you want to stay, I'll try. That's all I can promise."

"I have something to do, but I haven't done it yet," she said, the leaf forgotten in her hand.

"You're staying, then. You're sure?"

She nodded.

"You'd risk your life to stay?"

"I'm not leaving," she said. "I have nowhere else to go."

Eric scratched both calves and frowned at her.

"What part of Jamaica are you from?" he asked. "You don't have to answer that if you don't want to."

"St. Ann's Bay. My father was a printer there."

"Hey," Eric said, pulling back. "My father was a printer too, in Cleveland. Worked one of those old Heidelberg presses."

She threw down the leaf and looked toward St. Ann's. "I can still smell the ink."

The silence was easier. Her legs were unshaved, black stubble starting to show. His legs beside hers looked old and dry.

"I've been thinking," he said, rubbing his knees. "Maybe I should get you a boat and leave it here, in case you want to row over."

"Thank you, no," she said. "I want it this way, with no escape route."

"Aren't you afraid?"

"Of course. I'm always somewhere between scared and terrified."

"You put up a good show."

"I know I'm in danger, especially now, but it's the loneliness that gets to me most," she said.

"I promise I won't ask again why you're here," he said, and looked at the forgotten leaf. "But why here, in a bombed-out hotel, of all places?"

"I wanted to be close to water. I've been too far away from it since we left. When I saw the island, it was the only place I could be," she said, shrugging, her voice almost shy. "There's a—I don't know—a connection."

He looked at the top of the almond tree. "I know what you mean. It's just a bunch of rocks, but—"

"I had a dream," she said, "just before I left Atlanta. I was walking in a wood somewhere, somewhere cold, and there was a castle on top of a mountain. Then I went inside and there was no one there. I was afraid, but it was all right, you know. That's how I feel here."

"It's not quite a castle, but it'll do, I suppose."

"I love the old buildings. They're so . . . ruined . . . they're almost spiritual." She laughed a little, like she was embarrassed to say the word. The word *ruined* echoed back at Eric.

"Are you going to do anything with it?"

"I doubt it," Eric said, and scratched his chin. "I've twisted myself into a pretzel thinking of how I could reconnect it with the land. Even with one of those wooden bridges, you know, the ones with trestles that rattle when you drive over. I once asked this road engineer who was eating lunch with his family, I once asked him about the price of a bridge. I'll never forget. He didn't answer until he finished chewing. He wiped his mouth and said, 'Millions, in US not Jamaican dollars.'"

She said nothing, and the silence of dead possibilities drowned out the noise of the wind for a minute.

"What about you? Why Jamaica?" she said, like she was talking to her hands.

"Simple, really," he said. "I hate winter. Maybe the dark more than the cold."

He laughed and swept his hair back with his fingers. "Sounds weird, right? A guy from Ohio hating winter. It got so bad in New York, I'd lie on my balcony in the summer soaking it in, figuring I could only last out till retirement. I had this funny thing that got me through the winters. I heard about solar panels about, I don't know, twenty, twenty-five years ago, and I started seeing myself as a human solar cell, storing up sun on my balcony to keep me through the winter."

He wanted her to look at him, willed her to look up. "I'm kind of like an old battery now—have to recharge daily."

"A solar cell? I like that," she said, eyes still on her feet. "Where'd you get the idea of a hotel?"

"In a hammock in Ocho Rios, back in eighty-nine. I was leaving the next day. All I could think about was the winter up north. I was staying in this cute little inn, and I'd gotten to know the couple who ran the hotel—he'd been a salesman in Chicago—and I thought, My God, if they can do it, I can. Running a hotel couldn't be any harder than human resource management—that's what I thought, anyway. So after that, I just started working to make it happen." He looked at the moldy building on his right and his voice shifted down a notch.

"I guess I did."

Clearing his throat, he drew the oil from his pocket and held it in his closed hand.

"Do you have a license?" he said.

"For what?" She looked up at him.

"The gun," he said, gesturing with his chin to the bulge in her pocket.

"Do I need one?"

She sighed in response to his nod. "I only bought it to feel safe, not to hurt anyone."

"How'd you get it?"

"A taxi driver got it for me in Ocho Rios," she said. "Had me stay in the car and just appeared with it." He saw her sweating in the backseat and the man handing her a brown paper bag.

"I know somebody who can get you a license, if you want," he said. His heart was beating faster. The nipples of her breasts were standing up, and she'd tucked her hands under her legs.

"In the meanwhile, I have something for you." He opened his fingers and showed her the clear glass bottle dwarfed in his palm.

"Take it," he said, holding it out to her. She took it from the bottom, not touching his fingers, and turned the label around.

"Oil of Protection?"

"Gift from the local obeah man."

Her mouth opened wide like a teenager's. "You've got to be kidding! What am I supposed to do with this?"

"Sprinkle it around. At night," he added. "The important thing is that the whole village knows he's protecting you. They think they'll be dead if they touch you. Between the gun and that, you should be fine for a few weeks."

Simone shook the bottle and turned it on its side. "You really believe in this magic stuff?"

"Hell, don't ask me. I was an altar boy for five years. One week a month I prepared communion wafers that turned into Jesus's body when the priest held them up. I filled holy water basins so people could dab on some water to protect themselves from the devil. What do I know?"

He leaned back and slapped his knees. "I remember my grandfather taking me hunting for four-leaf clovers in our backyard. He used to put them between pages in the family Bible, for good luck, he said. He'd done it as a boy in Ireland. Even after he died, I'd look for one, just for him. If you ask me, it's not about magic. It's what you believe in."

They both looked at the bottle and she nodded her thanks. "I'd like to meet him one day," she said.

"My grandfather? He died back in sixty-three."

"No," she said, "the obeah man. I'd like to meet him."

CHAPTER EIGHTEEN

"What you mean Tiger don't live here no more?" Shad held the door open with his foot in case Miss Armstrong tried to close it.

"The police come for him?" he asked.

"No, no police come," she said, her voice sounding older than she looked.

"Then what happen to him?"

"Two days ago, he left Largo," she said. "He never say where he going." She tilted her moon face upward, the jaw set.

"You his mother, and he don't even tell you where he going?" Shad said.

Turning back inside, Tiger's mother returned to the armchair in front of a large television, her haunches rolling with each step. On the screen, a man at a podium was stuttering.

"Who . . . who . . . is an astronaut on the first Apollo flight?" Thunderous applause greeted his answer.

"Miss Armstrong," Shad called from the door, "you see him with another man?"

She looked at Shad, and then back at the television.

"Thanks for your help." Shad closed the door just loud enough to let her know how he felt, but not so loud as to be disrespectful, and walked down the front steps. Miss Armstrong had gotten used to hiding things over the years, and she wasn't going to start talking now. She was protecting her son, like any parent would. He wasn't a bad man, Tiger, everybody knew that, only weak and lazy. Even as a child, he was the one who'd be dragging through the village after the school bell rang.

Across the wire fence from Miss Armstrong's, a yard full of junk surrounded a rotting house, three scrawny dogs sprawled on the steps. A toilet without a seat and an old sofa lay in the shade of the tree spreading across the property. Mother Mason needed help to clear out the yard. He'd ask her on Sunday at church.

A rooster crowed at the side of Miss Armstrong's house. Bad luck, the old ladies said, a rooster crowing in broad daylight. About to close the latch on the gate, Shad let himself back into her yard. A new addition had drawn his attention—a shed made of shiny zinc sheets. Shad walked around the house, tucking under the windows, to get a closer look.

The interior of the shed was lined with wire shelving and chicken boxes. A handful of chickens and a rooster were pecking at an empty feeding trough. In the far corner, still standing in its pine crate, was a brand-new outboard engine. It was the kind that every fisherman wanted, the kind they gawked at when they went to the boat show at the Kingston arena, the kind that cost eighteen or twenty thousand Jamaican dollars. The unscratched helmet of the black steel engine threw out the words *Mercury* and *60 HP* in bright white lettering. Beneath the motor a chicken sat clucking, about to hatch an egg, like the dot in the exclamation point made by the long shaft.

Shad walked slowly to work, the path concave under his sneakers. A soft-drink truck tore down the middle of the road toward Port Antonio, and Shad flapped his hand at the dust. Tiger would have to be hustling more than a few joints to make that kind of money, and someone had to know where the money was coming from.

LaSharee was wearing a blue chiffon negligee over a slip when she opened the door, looking like she'd just woken up with a bad headache.

"Is you, Shad?" she said under the tousled honey-blond wig. "What you want?"

Shad followed her inside the tiny living room and squeezed between the coffee table and the love seat. The sheets covering it were still rumpled.

"I want to speak to Tiger. You know where he is?" Stale perfume wafted up from the sheets. The girl fit easily into a small side chair, and Shad pictured her sleeping on the love seat, curled up like a baby.

"Don't ask me." She looked around the dinette table beside her and found matches and cigarettes. "What you want him for?"

"Just checking on something."

"Tiger come and go, no explanation, like all you men." She looked at him hard over the cigarette, mucus still in the corner of one eye.

"He working for somebody?" Shad asked.

"Maybe."

"He must be doing all right, anyway."

"About time," she said.

"He moving around with anybody special?"

"Why you asking all these questions?" she said, exhaling a cone of smoke in his direction.

Shad shrugged. "He always say he want to be a bartender. I might have something for him."

"Bartender?" she said, smiling, the mischievous teenage look still there.

"I look like a woman who go with bartender?" The room was getting foggy with smoke.

"Just tell him I want to see him," he said.

"I tell him."

"You know where to find me," Shad said at the door, cigarette smoke curling up his nostrils.

CHAPTER NINETEEN

Curious man, Eric. He's deeper than he looks. He uses his vague way to distance himself from people. I'm not going to ask if he's married. He doesn't wear a ring, and he talks like a single man.

I like when he visits, and I like when he leaves.

Two days ago he brought some oil from an obeah man to protect me. That night I walked the whole circumference of the island and dribbled the oil every few steps. It was dark and hard to see, but I managed.

At the end I sprinkled a few drops on Cammy and myself. I had to laugh when we both sniffed the oil at the same time. I don't know what it smelled like to Cammy. To me it smelled like the geraniums Mama used to leave too long in the white vase shaped like a shell.

Mama and Daddy hated Ouija boards and fortune tellers. They made us swear we'd never use obeah. And here I am with Oil of Protection the only thing between me and harm!

Stretched out on the rock behind her, the dog barked at a swooping seagull.

Eric is different from Jack and all the others. More like Gary in Creative, easy and sexy with long white hair. Good thing I'm not here to think about that. I just need him to let me stay here and to keep me safe.

Thank God for the oil. I can finally sleep.

CHAPTER TWENTY

"Red Stripe, please," the man said—in a nice American accent, Shad thought—as he settled onto a stool.

It was that silky time of day before sunset, and the man had driven up in a rental car, the *R* clearly visible on the license plate. He was in his midforties, about Shad's height, with a sallow brown complexion that came from staying indoors. He looked refined, a college man with pressed jeans and a baseball cap. Shad had watched him scanning the place as he approached the bar, his expensive sandals crunching on the concrete floor, and guessed his drink right.

After placing the beer in front of him, Shad straightened the glasses next to the sink. It usually took a couple of sips for customers to say what was on their minds.

The visitor put down the bottle. "A man named Eric around?"

"Not here, but he soon come."

"I'll wait," the man said, and looked at the island.

"You come from far?" Shad asked, wiping menus on the counter.

"I'm from New York."

"On business?"

"Just visiting," the man said, cool, hiding something, like a man on his way to rob a gas station. His face was smooth and boyish. "Drove from Montego Bay."

"What team is that?" Shad asked, pointing to the man's cap.

"A baseball team, New York Yankees. Ever hear of them?"

"No. Ever heard of our team, the Reggae Boys?"

"The soccer team? Yeah, I heard of them," the man said.

"They good, man," Shad said, and leaned on the counter. "But you know what I would love to see in real life? An American football game!"

"You know American football?" The man's eyebrows disappeared under the visor.

"Yeah, man," Shad said. "I watch it on Sunday afternoons sometimes. I have a television, you know, and at first I used to laugh, watching them run into each other and fall down. They looked like children playing. I understand a little better now, but I can't find anybody to tell me the rules." Eric didn't even have a TV.

"It can get confusing."

"Tell me something," Shad said. "Before they start to play, the team bends over in a circle. What they doing? Praying?"

The visitor smiled, his teeth pretty.

"That's a huddle, man. They're planning the next play." In the growing darkness, the men continued to talk, an occasional burst of laughter shooting out from Shad.

Suddenly the light over the bar snapped on, interrupting a sentence. Shad turned to the doorway, looked at Eric, and tipped his head toward the guest. Eric introduced himself while the bartender placed a glass of ginger ale in front of him.

"Cameron Carter," the man said, shaking hands with Eric and Shad. Cameron, a good man's name.

"Eric."

"Shadrack."

"From the Bible, right? Shadrach, Meshach, and Abednego, the three young men who survived the fire," Carter said.

"Yeah, man, that's right. Where you learn that from?" Shad asked, glancing at Eric, who'd never asked about his name.

"Sunday school, man."

Eric was looking at Carter with his head tilted, like he was thinking of the last salesman who came by, the one trying to sell him insurance that would take him to Miami if he got sick. He should buy it this time, Shad decided, popping the top off another beer. The ambulances around here might never show up.

Carter frowned at the fresh beer on his coaster. "I'm looking for a woman named Simone Hall. I was told you could help me."

Eric took a sip of his drink and licked his top lip.

"I don't know anyone by that name."

"A couple of folks said she was over there." He stuck a thumb toward the island without looking at it.

"What folks?"

"A man in Poco Bay named Sam and his wife."

Shad wondered how much Carter had paid Sam. Eric was toying with his glass, his head lowered like a ram goat defending its territory.

"Why do you want to find her?"

Carter pulled out his wallet and laid two photographs on the countertop. Shad and Eric leaned in, their heads almost bumping across the bar. In one picture, two women in sweaters and jeans stood in front of a Christmas tree. There was a family resemblance in the mouth and eyes. Simone, plumper, with hair pulled back away from her face, wore a tight red sweater, and the younger woman had on a white shirt, open at the neck. A beautiful girl with a wide smile and wavy black hair, one of her earrings lying flat against her cheek.

The other photograph was a family portrait with an elderly woman sitting on a formal dining room chair, a fur collar encircling her neck. Carter and four women, Simone and the young woman among them, stood behind the chair. They were all staring straight into the camera, lips curled, following the photographer's instructions. They looked like they had money, unhappy black people with money.

"She's my sister."

Eric looked at Shad through his eyebrows. "She's there."

"I want to see her."

"She doesn't want any visitors." Eric said, reaching into his pocket for his pipe.

"Did she tell you what happened?"

"No," said Eric.

"My mother's worried about her."

"She's fine. She's not going to hurt herself, if that's what you mean."

"That's good to know." Carter shifted his weight on the stool and looked at the darkening cluster of rocks. "Anyway, I need to go see her."

"I wouldn't suggest it. The last man who tried almost got shot."

Carter's face froze. Then he threw his head back and let out a hoot, showing manicured teeth.

"That's my girl!" he called to the ceiling, and Shad laughed a little with him.

"Tell you what," Eric said, shrugging his shoulders, "I'll go across tomorrow and tell her you're here."

Cameron exhaled slowly. "I'll take what I can get. I'll come by in the evening to hear how it went."

When a sleepy Beth turned to Shad that night, he kissed her and said, "Guess what? The woman brother in town now, staying at Miss Mac's. And I feel the boss like the woman."

Shad grinned in the dark. "Excitement come to Largo, girl, better than *Young and Restless*!"

CHAPTER TWENTY-ONE

Her head snapped back, eyes wide. "My Cameron, my brother?"

"He has the photographs to prove it," he said.

"Where is he now?" She averted her eyes, struggling to keep her voice calm, he could tell.

"In Largo," Eric said, and scratched his arms. She had a life, she had a family. One day she would return to them, abandoning the home she'd created in the ruins of his. A distant rumble of thunder interrupted their thoughts, and they both looked toward the sound and the dark clouds over the mountains, she with the furrow between her eyebrows.

"Did he come alone?"

"I think so."

The dog barked from the shade, shifting from one paw to another.

"Cammy, shut up," Simone called.

"He said your mother was worried."

She chewed on her lip. "Didn't you tell him I'm fine?"

"Yup," said Eric. "He's determined to see you."

Her eyes darted back to her room. "You didn't tell him about the obeah, did you?"

"Of course not."

"Or about the two guys who came over?"

"Nope."

"And you're caught in the middle, aren't you?" she said, and pushed her hair back with both hands. "I'm sorry, Eric."

"What do you want me to tell him?" he said.

"I guess I have to see him," she said. "Let's do it on—what's today?"

"Monday."

"Give me till Sunday."

"Sunday, then," he said, starting a slow turn. "Since I'm coming back, do you need anything?" Anything, anything.

She blinked and looked straight at him, as if she were seeing him for the first time. "Funny you should ask that. I've been thinking of June plums recently, you know, the big yellow plums with the prickly seed. My cousin Rose and I used to eat them when we were little." Her eyebrows kept lifting and lowering in time with her words.

"We'd climb onto the roof of my uncle's chicken coop and pick them from the tree, and the juice would run down our chins." She was smiling.

"I'm surprised you didn't ask for something American, like a hamburger."

"Why would I do that?"

"Oh, I dunno," he said, and looped his hair back over

one ear. "Soon after I moved down, I started having this craving for a New York hot dog, you know, those big, thick ones with the mustard. About the only thing I missed—that and the music."

"The music," she said, and beckoned him to follow. They walked along a path she'd created between the long grass, her rhythmic buttock muscles making his groin tingle.

"I miss my music too. What kind of music did you miss?" she said, as if she just wanted to talk, about anything. They were sitting on a flat stone shelf at the water's edge, the salty smell penetrating their pores.

"Good old rock and roll," he said. "You can't get it here. I used to sing to myself just to hear it. Miss Mac, my landlady, used to laugh at me.

"I played bass and sang with a band once," he said, and twiddled his fingers. "Four of us practicing in my parents' garage. Another guy and I used to harmonize."

"Sing something for me," she said. Here, in the middle of the Caribbean, a surprise request.

Speckles of foam landed on his feet from a passing wave. He started strumming the air, trying to think of something. He cleared his throat and sang a couple of bars of "Born to be Wild," laughing every now and again when he forgot a phrase. He broke off and leaned on his knees. The sea was turning gray, the rain getting closer.

"One day my father said he'd had enough. That was that. You didn't mess with my father." He was hiding under David's bed again, seeing the faded brown belt dangling between his father's legs.

"You have a good voice." The comment everyone had to make.

"Thanks, I'm terrible." He laughed. "I was a better guitar player than a singer. I finally bought some records and a real nice stereo when I went back. Of course, they're all gone." A wave gurgled among the rocks and sucked out.

"You get over the cravings, though. You get used to the patois and the rain and the people, and one day you realize you're looking forward to mango season."

Her thin brown feet were lined up parallel to his large yellow ones. If he wanted, he could cover her whole foot with one of his.

"I don't know if I'll be here long enough," she said.

The rain was coming. He'd have to go soon. "How've you been doing? Any new discoveries?"

She made two fists and rested her face on them, the breeze wrestling with her hair. "I'll never be the person I was, that I know."

He scratched his shin, half facing her. "Who do you want to be?"

"That's the thing." She shut her eyes tight. "I've spent my whole life following my family from one country to another, going to school, working like the devil. This is the first time—"

"What kind of work do you do?" Safer ground.

"I'm in advertising, account executive with Belding and Belding. Used to be in New York, then I helped open the Atlanta office."

"I bet you're good at it."

"My boss calls me his *house whip*," she said, and raised her eyebrows.

A few minutes later, Eric pushed the canoe into the waves and jumped in. The bow of the boat rose and fell while he struggled to place the oars in the oarlocks. He started rowing. A broadside wave tipped the canoe. He plunged the oars deep to stay upright, started rowing again. A few yards out the current sucked at the boat, making his rowing useless. He was being pulled west, around the island's point. There'd be no reaching Largo before the rain blew over. He rowed hard with the current, toward the tiny beach on the western side of the island. When he got close enough, he leaped over the side, holding the bowline, water slapping at his thighs.

He waded ashore just as the rain started falling in large drops and wrapped the line around a rock. A small overhang of the verandah projected out north of the beach, offering just enough shelter to keep the worst of the rain off, and he scrambled onto the rocks beneath it.

After wringing out his T-shirt, Eric leaned back and hugged his knees. Simone was probably sitting on her bed not more than twenty feet away, waiting out the downpour like him. Maybe she was wondering if he'd made it to shore yet, or had seen him make a detour.

Above the droning of the rain, he heard the sound of clanging metal, the sound of pots being set out on tiles. She was catching water to drink or to wash her hair.

"Singing in the rain." She was singing, her voice sweet and melodic. He ducked lower under the shelf, hiding from his off-key voice.

"Just singing in the rain, what a glorious—

"What the fuck?" she cried, almost drowned out by the breeze whistling through the wires of her roof.

Eric peeped over the edge of the verandah, shading his eyes from the rain. Water had collected in a pool on the tarp and was pouring down the wall next to her bed. Simone dragged her mattress away from the wall, her stomach muscles slack, while the dog peered around a barrel under the desk. She pushed the mattress toward a drier spot in the middle of the room. Out of the box beside the bed came a plastic sheet, which she tucked around the edges of the mattress. She sat down with her legs under her and gazed out above Eric's head.

A minute later, as if doing a dance for an invisible lover, she wound up from the mattress in slow motion, and in the same movement she removed the gun from her pocket and threw it on the mattress. She pulled off her wet T-shirt and dropped it on top of the gun. Her breasts glittered in the rain, brown fruit dangling as she bent to tug at her shorts sticking to her legs.

Turning his head but not his eyes away, Eric watched her drag her shorts off, followed by pink panties, which she threw on top of the heap. He pulled down a couple of inches just as she turned. Squishing puddles on the wet tiles, she walked out from under the tarp and into the rain. She stopped about ten feet from the edge of the verandah. Completely stark, baby naked.

Eric turned his back and slid deeper under the verandah, looking out to sea. The sky was beginning to clear over the mountains. The southern wall of the lobby would give her privacy, thank God, save her from prying village eyes.

A happy shriek came from above, a Simone unknown.

"I've always wanted an outdoor shower," she said, maybe talking to the dog.

"Yes, yes," she moaned, almost an orgasmic moan.

To his right, a shaft of light shone through a hole in the tile floor. With some adjustment for his knees, he tipped his head back and peered through the hole. He was looking right at her.

She was standing with eyes closed, arms at her sides, and head tilted back. Her small breasts sagged a little, the nipples like raisins. The triangle of hair between her legs was black and almost straight. Rainwater ran down her forehead and nose, caressed her neck, her bare shoulders and back, licked her breasts, her belly and legs.

A thunder clap startled her and she opened her eyes. She straightened her head and a smile spread across her face. Her skin glistened and water dripped off her fingers and nipples. The tongue came out and licked her lips, came out more and licked the flesh around her lips.

"You know what they say about salt, Cammy? The Greeks traded it for slaves. That's what she read to me." She wiped her eyebrows.

"They use it in African folk magic, for cleansing and for protection from evil. Imagine that."

Water was pouring now through the hole and down Eric's neck, seeping into his briefs like a punishment.

Raising her arms skyward, Simone looked up to the

clouds, the stubble in her armpits reaching for the wiry bush on her head.

"You know what?" Her lifted voice seemed aimed at him. "We never played in the rain, not ever. It was always about staying dry and covering up, about umbrellas and raincoats."

Thunder rumbled far out at sea. She tilted her head up.

"Is that you, C?" she shouted just as the rain started to slow.

CHAPTER TWENTY-TWO

Cameron is coming soon and I have to finish whatever I came to do. I must open to an end and a beginning. I must surrender and have faith. I must let go.

I surrendered to the rain today. I know how it feels to be one with the circle of water falling from the clouds, draining into the sea, evaporating up into the clouds, falling again.

Why have I never done this before? Every man and woman should be made to stand naked in the rain at least once. I've never felt so free. I offered myself up to whatever was in store.

There was such power and truth in the rain that I felt closer to being spiritual than I ever have. Religion has never meant anything to me, but just standing there alone with the water and nature embracing me, cleansing me, healing me, told me that there is so much more to life than the things we see.

If there is a God, I'll be provided with whatever I need, the people or the events that will answer my every need.

I am not alone, I know it. Celeste is here.

CHAPTER TWENTY-THREE

"You don't get a lot of tourists here, do you?" Cameron said, sliding onto a stool. He was wearing a sleeveless T-shirt for the first time, looking more like a local.

"We used to," Shad said, "but not now." He looked around from counting liquor bottles on a high shelf, a pad in hand. Beside him, Eric was scanning the shelves above the fridge.

"We get a few passersby during tourist season," Eric said. "Mid-December to April. But at this time of year, hardly any."

"Why not? The bay is awesome." All three turned and looked at the view, dimming after sunset. Waves were rolling in, slapping the beach below.

"Nowhere for them to stay," Shad said crisply, and jotted down *3 bots vodka* with his new pen.

Eric patted the top of the fridge. "Most of them stay in Ocho Rios. Port Antonio gets a few."

"Somebody is going to come along soon, I'm telling you," Cameron said.

Shad introduced him to the other customers, Tri

and Janet, who'd stopped their chatter to examine him. Tightly encased in a red and blue dress, Janet turned her cleavage to Cameron and smiled.

"That is your sister on the island?" she said.

"Yes."

"And you let her live there alone?" she said, swishing the ice in her drink.

"Leave the man alone, nuh?" Tri said, and another question died on the woman's lips.

Eric straightened with a checkbook and rubbed his back. Holding some bills in one hand, he climbed onto the stool beside Cameron and put on his reading glasses.

"You got used to the driving yet?" he said.

"I've never seen so many potholes," Cameron said. "Why don't they fix them?"

Shad laughed. "No money, the same old story."

"Because of party business, man," Tri chimed in.

"That's not true," Janet said. "All of you against the government say that, but it's because you don't want to work."

Cameron leaned over the counter toward Shad.

"Let me have a rum, not with coconut water this time, thank you. I don't care how much you love it, man." He laughed. "Give me ginger ale with it."

Over his shoulder, Shad called to Cameron, "You sell real estate, right? Like houses?"

"Malls mostly, what we call strip malls. Like your shopping plazas."

"That's big, man!" Shad said, pouring the rum. Eric examined Cameron over his glasses.

"My clients are mostly African Americans and West Indians, believe it or not," Cameron said.

"True?" Shad's voice raised an octave. He placed the rum and ginger on the bar and a soft drink for Eric beside it.

"They're professionals," Cameron said. "Doctors and lawyers, businesspeople who make a lot of money and need to invest it. It helps with their taxes." He took a sip of his drink.

"What kind of places they like?" Shad said.

"I sold five malls in Queens and three in the Bronx in the last two years." He checked off the malls on his fingers, Shad widening his eyes with every mall.

"The market's soft now, at least in my areas," Cameron ended, and made a funny mouth.

Shad turned to the locals. "You guys want to get comfortable at a table?" In less than a minute, Tri, pulling Janet with him, had shifted to a distant table, understanding there'd be a free round for the favor.

Eric lit up his pipe, opening his mouth in small gasps to make it catch. He waved the match.

"What's that?" he said, and motioned with his pipe to the visitor's arm. Shad followed Cameron's glance to the scar on his bare upper arm.

"Fraternity brand," Cameron said, showing his pretty teeth. "Three seniors held me down in a basement. It almost killed me for a couple weeks, but it was worth it. The girls liked it."

"They brand you like a slave?" Shad stopped counting whiskey and winced, feeling the heat on his own arm. They'd branded runaways, like cows.

118

Cameron nodded and put down his drink. "That's the idea. To show you can take it, you're a survivor." Shad and Eric looked at each other.

"Hey, there's something I've been meaning to ask," Cameron said. "What's the story behind the island?" He swung his eyes from Eric to Shad and back to Eric.

A crumb of ash popped out of the pipe's bowl and fell on the wooden countertop between the glasses. Eric put it out with an index finger and Shad wiped it up.

"Tell us what happened to your sister first," Eric said. Cameron's face slid downward, his mouth looking like Simone's.

"Her daughter died three months ago. Her only child." The words hung in the air for a second.

"How'd it happen?" Shad asked, opening a can of Coke for Janet, who'd winked at him from the table.

"She was at university in Gainesville, and she was coming back from some boy's house at three in the morning. The brakes failed when she went round a corner." He tapped the counter and stared at the sound. "She used to drive too fast."

"I'm sorry," Eric said. Shad nodded.

"We thought Simone was getting over it. She'd gone back to work."

When Shad returned from serving the drinks, Cameron was still frowning at the counter.

"Wouldn't talk about her daughter, wouldn't open the door to her room, this bright red door. It stayed shut the whole time, like she was still in there. She didn't talk much, anyway. She was like an iceberg at the service.

Leading up to it, she'd stayed in bed, never cried, just lay there with her eyes open, scary kind of. And as soon as the service was over, she went back to her house and got in bed with her clothes on. We had to make excuses to the guests downstairs. My mother acted as the hostess." Shad saw the old lady in the photograph sitting in the same chair, shaking hands, looking grim.

"What was your niece's name?" Eric said, the scent of maple tobacco spreading across the bar.

Cameron closed his eyes. He inhaled and opened his eyes.

"Celeste—I can see her in front of me. Beautiful girl, tall, funny, great sense of humor. And a straight shooter, you know. She always spoke the truth, but she didn't hurt you with it."

He tilted his head and looked at Shad. "You know how some people can just be full of love, man? That's how she was, even though she saw people for who they were, it never stopped her from loving people." He shook his head. "She had this little birthday book, and she wrote down everybody's birthday. Then she'd call you and sing 'Happy Birthday' on your birthday. She couldn't sing worth a damn, but you'd look forward to it, you know."

"What about her father?" Shad said, knowing Eric wouldn't ask.

"Nice guy, not one for hard work, you know. Everybody likes Jeff, but you can't count on him when it comes down to it," Cameron said with a weak smile. "My mother wouldn't let him give the eulogy. I did it, wrote it on the plane, mostly my own memories. I should have written it for the young people, though. A lot of her friends from high school came. They sat at the back and cried the whole time."

"It must have been tough for your sister, man," Shad said, thinking of the woman on the island with her unhappy face, lying on a bed in a black dress, the covers twisted over her and a hat thrown down on the floor.

Cameron shook his head. "I thought she was coming down here for a couple of weeks, hole up in a hotel until her head cleared, you know."

Eric placed the pipe and its dying embers next to his glass. "We all react differently to grief," he said.

After a minute Cameron stretched his arms above his head and then brought them down in a swoop.

"Now let's talk about the island," he said.

"What about it?" Eric said.

"You mean the buildings?" Shad asked.

"Yeah. How'd they get out there?"

"It used to be a peninsula, connected to this piece of land here with a driveway," Eric said. He pointed into the darkness in the direction of the island. "I built a hotel on the point at the end of the bay, and dammit, if a hurricane didn't come along and—"

"Are you kidding?" Cameron said, his eyebrows twitching at the island. "It wiped out the land between the hotel and the town? You mean, it's a new island? Damn, that's a great story."

"Depends on who you talking to," Shad said.

CHAPTER TWENTY-FOUR

Solomon stared out the passenger window, his head slouched to prevent it from hitting the roof of the cab. He looked into nothingness, ignoring the aqua bays around each bend and the bamboo arched high over the Jeep.

Shad pursed his lips. "Okay, okay, I apologize. But you know I meant well."

"The road to hell is paved with good intentions," Solomon replied in a monotone, still glaring at the view.

"I just meant that if you didn't drink so much liquor, you wouldn't have to go to see a doctor in Ocho Rios."

"One drink every now and then never hurt a man."

"Speak the truth, Solomon. Several drinks a night."

"See what I mean?" Solomon said, sucking his teeth at the side mirror. "Just because he taking me, he think he can insult me."

"You going to have liver problems, man," Shad said.

"Is just a little indigestion," Solomon said.

"Not from what Maisie told me." The woman's protruding eyes had protruded more than usual that morning when she'd begged Shad to take him to the doctor.

Solomon refused to answer. The miles dragged in silence as the Jeep raced along the North Coast, through Port Antonio with its gingerbread two-story shops around the square, past the steep road that led up to the red and white hotel on top of the hill, past the fields of sugar cane, over the flattened stalks dropped from cane trucks, through the ancient Annotto Bay, abandoned by a fickle spice trade. Around dozens of bends and over hundreds of potholes, under guinep, pomegranate, orange, lime, and tamarind trees, Shad sped west until the narrow roads and heavy traffic in Port Maria forced him to slow down.

"Imagine," he said, more to break the irritable silence than anything, "must have been plenty carriages coming to this church long time ago." They were passing an old Anglican church, the year *1861* carved above its stone entrance.

"You ever hear of Tacky?" When Solomon shook his head, Shad pointed to a stone monument in front of the courthouse. "He was a slave, you know, leader of the 1760 Easter Rebellion. That statue thing is to him. They call it an *obelisk*. Nice word, eh? It just lift you up."

Shad swung around a corner, looking for a shortcut. "Days gone by, Jamaica was a country with men who were honorable, you know what I mean? They stood up for something. Too many people just greedy now, just interested in money. We becoming a country of selfish people." He blew the horn at two taxis that had stopped in the middle of the street, the drivers chatting side by side.

"You see what I mean? Selfishness." Shad sucked his teeth. "What make people different, Solomon? What make some people selfish and some people, like Tacky, risk everything, even his life, to fight the planters? He knew he would die."

"When a man not free to dream, he ready to fight, he ready to die," Solomon said, and grunted. "No man should take your dream away from you."

"Dreams," Shad said, overtaking a big man riding a child's bicycle.

"I have a dream," he said, and turned to Solomon with a grin. "I want to own a bar one day. I will pretty it up, you know, and play nice music, and let people dance. And I'll have good food, sell it for a little profit, like curry goat and *escoveitched* fish, nice local food. Nice environment, you know, everything. Make it like a house party every night."

Outside of the town, Shad sped up again, Ocho Rios only twenty miles away. "You have any dreams, man?"

The older man looked out of the window again. "Chef."

"What you say?"

"I want to be a chef again, with a good kitchen, good stoves, good knives," Solomon said, and the two lapsed into silence.

"Maisie have dreams, you think?" Shad asked after a while.

"She used to want children, but she all right now. We too old for that."

"I know what Beth want. She want a bigger house.

She say one bedroom not big enough for six. She want a bedroom for the girls, say they can't keep sleeping on the sofa."

"Make sense," Solomon grunted.

"I can't afford a bigger house on what I making, man," Shad said, and sighed. "God will have to provide, yes!"

"You can add a room on the back."

"A room on—," Shad said, and frowned at Solomon. "I could add a room on. Solomon, you brilliant, man! I never thought of that. Good idea, thank you," Shad said, changing gears. "When Job get better, God willing, I going to chat with him."

The older man was dozing when they pulled up to the hospital emergency room.

"Wake up, man," Shad said, patting Solomon's shoulder. "We arrive." Solomon looked at him with bleary eyes.

"I'll be back in a couple of hours. If you not out here when I get back, I come looking for you, you hear?"

Solomon nodded and fumbled with the door.

"Just don't forget me," he said.

Outside of Ocho Rios, Shad drove uphill on a road furrowed by ruts, trying to remember where Agnes lived. He stopped on a corner where two men sat on upturned packing boxes.

"Najib Terrace? Up so, then left," one man said, waving his Pepsi can.

With each mile, the roads got narrower, the potholes larger. Shrinking in size, the houses jostled each other until there was barely room to walk between them.

Agnes greeted Shad at her door with a shout. "Smiley? How you never tell me you were coming?" She steered him to her new porch swing.

"You like it?" she said. "Is my gift to myself last Christmas."

"Nice, man. Beth and the girls will love to swing on it next time they come."

"How they doing? I have coconut cake to send for them." Agnes crossed her thick arms over her belly.

"What you doing in Ochy on a Saturday, boy?" she said.

"Came to drop Solomon, our cook, at the hospital. He been having stomach pains that stop him from sleeping."

"Still running errands for people, eh?"

"As long as I can help——," Shad said.

"You mean, as long as it make you happy." Agnes laughed. "Since I know you——"

"Every man have his purpose, right?" Shad said.

Under the verandah rail, milk-can pots overflowed with pink and white flowers, *ram-goat roses* like his grandmother used to grow. A guest had called them *primroses*, the same identical flower that God had created without a name. And he'd reflected that Jamaica had made its flower sound crude and uncivilized like a goat and America had turned its version into a well-behaved, tight little flower.

"I love your flowers," he said. "You always good with them."

"They my children," she said, "when I have time for them."

126

Shad glanced at his watch. "How the work going? You still at the garment factory?"

"Yes, still at the factory. Love it and hate it, you know?"

"Why you say that?"

"Is the only place I can get a work," Agnes said. Her chin disappeared into the folds of her neck. "You can't get work in the hotels unless you have training, and I never like to serve people anyway."

"Why you hate it, then?" asked Shad.

"The factory managers treat you like children, man. You must come at an exact time. Twice late and you out. Thank God, I always early. My nature, you know. Then you have one hard seat you must sit at all day—you have to bring your own cushion—and all you can do is sew, no talking to your neighbor. You have to sew a certain number of garments every day. If you go over it, they don't pay you extra, but you can't go under."

"Sound like pressure to me," Shad said, thinking of the easy chatter of his customers.

"Pressure, yes. Even when you want to go to the bathroom, you can only go at certain times. When you sick and you have to go more, you must bring a letter from the clinic. They don't trust you. Is like they expecting you to do wrong."

"Why they think so?"

Agnes waved a fly away. "The women steal, yes. I don't take nothing, because is nothing I want to take, anyway. Men's drawers is what I sew," she said, laughing. "I don't have no man to give it to. If I did, I'd probably steal—since they expect you to anyway."

"How the women get away with it?"

"They search you when you going to the bathroom and leaving the building in the evening. You have to open your bags and show them. The women put the drawers in their bra and panty, quick while they sewing. Then they say they mess up the sewing. You allowed up to four errors, or seconds, a day. No more. So they sew careful, careful, and only have two seconds, and stuff two in they bra."

"The owners don't catch them?" Shad asked.

"Of course, they know," she said. "The supervisors doing the same thing, though. Everybody hate the factory and the owner so much, they all in it together."

"Lord, have mercy," Shad said. It all sounded disgusting, low-life, like his old scams.

"The supervisor say the owner 'write it off him taxes.' Is like they don't lose money on it, you know. Only make money."

"You know the name of the owner?" Shad asked.

"American man name Manheim. Milton Manheim. He own four factories now. He came down a couple years ago and buy out the owners from before. We don't see him much."

"He have a long, black limousine?"

"You know him?" Agnes said.

"No, but I might know his driver."

His cousin's mouth dropped, showing a yellowed row of bottom teeth. "You mean the big, fat guy?"

"Yeah, yeah."

"Where you know him from?"

"Long story," Shad said.

Agnes crossed her arms tighter. "Not a good one, right? All I can say is, stay away from him now."

"Why you say that?"

"He just look like evil. You don't think so?" Agnes said, and started toward the narrow door.

"Come, I get you some cucumber juice. It nice, with ginger and brown sugar, just made."

CHAPTER TWENTY-FIVE

Water to cross, deep water, dark blue.

It's Africa, a compound with other women, all busy doing things. She knows them but doesn't know them. The women are bare breasted. They wear long skirts and elaborate necklaces, some with colorful beads and toys. One woman has a necklace with a horse doll and a tiny cup, perhaps for the horse to drink out of. She reaches out to touch the necklace, but the woman turns and walks away.

More water to cross, this time a pool of dirty water, and she has to get to the other side. The women know how to cross, but she's never done it before, and none of the women will tell her. They're too busy.

A man is on her right, an old friend, and she asks him for help. Before he can answer, a cave appears, with a red door. A woman opens the door and other women go inside. The man disappears to wherever people go in dreams.

She enters the cave with one of the women, holding on to the woman's thin skirt, the color of amber. Inside the cave is an elder, a wise woman who sits surrounded by other women, in dim yellow light.

The old woman looks at her and raises her eyebrows, asking her—without saying a word—what she's learned. She stands alone and says nothing, has no answer to give, knowing she'll find the answer when she wakes up.

CHAPTER TWENTY-SIX

Sunday mornings had always been the bane of Eric's life. Either someone was getting him up early to go to mass—his mother, his wife—or something was preventing him from sleeping. Since his arrival in Largo, he'd been clanged awake every Sunday at seven thirty by the rusty bell of the Holy Sepulcher Baptist Church, a little way east along the main road, which made up for its small congregation with its loud bell. And he'd come to know, as he did this Sunday, that he had another thirty minutes of sleep before the second bell and the low moan of the opening hymn.

Snuggling further into his pillow, he tried to fall back asleep, tried not to feel the throb in his temples from too many glasses of wine. But sleep evaded him and he lay and listened to the waves below his open shutters. He could tell from the sounds and vibrations that the water was as calm as it ever got, that it would have small crested waves and be a good day to row across.

She'd be expecting them.

He stretched his arm across the empty side of the bed and looked at the island, awake already, the top of the almond tree coated with sunlight. He wondered what she was doing now, maybe having breakfast. She'd have no idea she'd been the focus of attention at a dinner party last night.

The party had been held by Lambert and Jennifer, in the same house Eric had pushed toward when he came ashore during the hurricane, naked, his clothes dragged off by the waves. It was on their barred front door he had thumped, kneeling on all fours to stay out of the way of flying branches, his hair plastered to his face, and through which Lambert had dragged him as the gale howled into the house.

Once opposite the hotel's entrance—and now facing the windowless wall of Eric's apartment—the home's driveway wound up past mango trees to a one-story plantation house with a view of the bay. Surrounded by Jennifer's artwork, the couple entertained monthly and Eric was always invited. The dinners gave him an opportunity to enjoy their housekeeper's roast beef, and the political scraps offered by the guests.

Politics hadn't entered the conversation last night, however. The group of six—Roper Watson and his girlfriend, Sonja; Watson's visitor, Bradley Cunningham; Eric; and the hosts—had had plenty of local gossip to mull over. Simone was the subject, of course, and Eric was to be the source of the news.

"Give us the scoop, man. Why'd she move to the island?" Lambert said, his thick black mustache just missing a dunking in his soup spoon.

"Don't ask me," Eric said. "She pays her rent and wants to be left alone."

Jennifer passed the rolls. "Maybe she needs some time for herself," she said, and laughed. "I could take a couple weeks away from the kids." Her blond hair shimmered in the candlelight. An interior decorator from Florida, she'd taken to upper-class life in Largo like a fish to water.

"I think she's crazy," Bradley said. "No one would do that unless they were certifiable."

"She could be an artist," Sonja said. "If I didn't have a day job, I'd love to find a place like that just to write, maybe paint." Eric saw a group of artists sitting at easels, painting on the island. They probably wouldn't want to pay rent.

"The brother wouldn't have come out, though, unless something wasn't right," Roper said.

Bradley jumped in. "Maybe he heard about that drug guy's visit—what's his name?"

"Tiger," mumbled Eric.

"At least Brother Zachariah is on her side," Lambert said, lifting his wineglass to Eric, who took too big a gulp of wine and coughed behind his napkin. Speculation about Simone lasted through dinner, only ending with the brandied guavas.

The second ringing of the church bell brought Eric back, and he eased his legs over the edge of the king-size bed, his headache now bearable and the tiles under his feet grounding him. Pushing open the doors to the porch, he stood in front of his chair and took three deep breaths. The sun was flickering through the bougainvillea, its warmth on his cheek as he launched into the exercise ritual he'd promised himself he would start today.

He lifted his arms up high and took a breath. After

everything got back to normal and she'd left—because she would leave—he'd go down to the Parish Council and name the island Simone. Simone Island. Swinging his arms in wide circles, he felt embarrassed at the thought, as if he'd announced it aloud in the bar.

He lifted his right leg to touch his left hand, missed by a couple of feet, and switched legs. His knees wouldn't straighten and he was breathing hard, an aging man with a hangover doing aerobics—the first time in years he'd done anything more than walk or row. This was for his health. His birthday was coming up and his goal was to lose ten pounds by the time it came.

This wasn't for Simone, Simone standing over him with drops of water glistening on her breasts and thighs. He stopped lifting his legs and took a breath. She didn't look old enough to have a big daughter. A daughter who was dead, who deserved to be grieved.

Doing side bends, feeling his stomach flopping to each side, he hoped she didn't have binoculars, wouldn't see him in his old boxers.

"Am I too early?" Cameron said, standing in the empty bar, his aftershave cutting through the stink of Saturday night and cigarette butts. Eric placed two cups of coffee on the table and sat down with a thud.

"You understand you may not be welcome, don't you?" he said.

Cameron sat down the instant a wave beat hard against the cliff, sending a shiver through the cups.

"I've thought about it," he said.

"I don't think she's going to leave," Eric said. "And you can't force her."

"She can't stay out there," Cameron said, reaching for the cup.

"I just want to warn you, she asked to be left alone and I agreed," Eric said, holding his hair back to take a sip of coffee. "You're on your own here."

Carter's jaws expanded and contracted as he looked at his cup. "I thought you—"

"I'll row you across, but I'm not going to interfere," Eric said.

The two men finished their coffee, avoiding each other's eyes.

On the beach, they rolled Minion's canoe off the logs and turned it over. Cameron looked over at the island, his voice flat.

"I could sue you for reckless endangerment, you know," he said.

"What the hell do you mean?" said Eric. A pulse of heat throbbed through his chest as they dropped the boat onto the sand.

"You own the place. You let her live there, and you know it's not safe. I bet you don't even have permission."

They dragged the boat to the water's edge. Eric went back for the oars.

"News flash," Eric said, throwing the oars into the boat. "We're not in America, friend."

CHAPTER TWENTY-SEVEN

S he'd been thinking of Otaheite apples when she woke up, and she'd lain in bed thinking of the last time she'd eaten one. It had been while walking home behind her mother, the cries of the market women still in their ears. Her scrawny four-year-old ankles had been scratching since they'd left the market, and she looked down to examine them. When she saw the fleas, two on one ankle and one on the other, she'd screeched and dropped the apple.

"Stop that, girl, it's just two little fleas. You're such a crybaby," Madge had yelled.

Cameron wouldn't know about Otaheite apples—he'd been too young. There he was on the beach opposite, pushing off with Eric in the canoe, a giant cigar with two stick figures. In her room she replaced her bathing suit with clean shorts and a T-shirt. The hair she left as it was—to give him the shock he needed.

When the canoe touched the beach, her brother, a hater of boats, jumped out and hauled the boat onto the beach, following Eric's instructions. Eric waved at her and stayed where he was, leaning his arms on the oars, ready to push off at any time. A man who hated an argument.

Cameron picked his way across the rough pebbles on the beach. At the bottom of the cliff, he looked up, his face more beautiful, more tanned, than it had ever been, his teeth even and white like Celeste's. They'd compared teeth one day in the hall mirror, Cameron and Celeste, each insisting his or her teeth were straighter. They'd laughed, hugging, and asked Simone to be the judge.

"Imagine meeting you here," her brother said, and started up the path, arms balancing. He was wearing Bermuda shorts, pressed and starched in New York and wrinkled in the boat—"City Slick," Celeste's name for him, who'd started out for Sunday brunch and gotten lost.

The dog beside her barked once, and she gave her a pat, feeling the dog's heart beating hard like hers. At the top of the path, Cameron opened his arms. Brushing his cheek with her own, she pulled away, suddenly smelling her own staleness, deodorant forgotten.

"It's good to see you, Cam," she said.

Out of his shorts he pulled an oval yellow fruit. "Eric said to give you this."

"Thanks," she said, and rolled the June plum between her hands. "How did you find me?"

"Not easily, let me tell you," he said, his arm around her waist as they walked. "Your message didn't say much, but I had a feeling you'd come to Portland. I knew you loved it on your honeymoon. I remember you talking about it, saying you wanted to come back one day, so I went everywhere and asked."

"And you drove on the left," she said.

"It took me a while, I can tell you. I was lucky to find you."

"Mission accomplished, as they say."

He nodded, taking in the ruins. "Interesting place," he said.

She said nothing, waiting for him to get it out. He looked at her, his head to one side.

"You can't live out here by yourself," he said. "You know that, right?"

She shook her head, kept a smile on. "I can, and I'm going to stay. It's what I want to do." She patted his stomach. "Stop worrying. I have Cammy to protect me. I even named her after you. And I have a gun." They both laughed a little, the same laugh, nervous this time.

"If you want, I could come and—"

"I need to be alone, Cameron."

They sat down on the coconut tree trunk, he pulling his shorts up a few inches before sitting.

"What are you eating?" he said. "You've lost weight."

"I'm eating well. Eric sees to that."

He stretched his legs out slowly. "I'm not leaving Jamaica without you."

"Do what you want," she said.

"I tell you what," he said, his voice firm. "I'll give you a few more days, till next week Monday—"

"Wait, wait, wait. Hold it right there. What are you

trying to do, be the man or something?" She heard her voice rising and tried to hold it steady.

"I'm not trying to be the man. I'm worried about you, that's all."

"I've been here more than a month already, and I'm still here," she said.

Cameron looked at the improvised kitchen, everything low to the ground, and back at her.

"Did you bring the ashes with you? Is that why you're here?" he said.

"It's none of your business, Cameron. Leave me alone." She hoped she sounded capable under the body odor and coarse hair.

He spread his hands, looked at her hard. "We have a right to know, Sim. We're your family. What am I going to tell Mama? She's worried!"

"Mama?" she said, and stroked her legs.

"She loves you, Sim."

"Loves me? She's never mentioned it. Do you love her?"

"Yes," Cameron said, his nostrils flaring the way they did when he was four and she'd accused him of eating the marmalade.

"Mama," she said, slapping her calf. "Mama and love, now that's an interesting combination. I don't remember any love. She ever told you she loves you?" Cameron blinked.

"She made our lives bitter and dry, Cam, you know that. You didn't even like to come home. Remember we used to call you 'MIA'—Missing in Action?"

"She did her best, Sim."

"Did her best," she said with a snort. "Did her best by telling Lucille to study nursing because her looks would never get her a man?" She lowered her voice, remembering Eric below. "She's a control freak, you mean. When Marie wanted to marry that Liberian doctor, she said she wouldn't have a 'jungle man' in the family, remember?" She saw the two women glued together—one tall, one wide—in their house in Throgs Neck, everything blue and orderly.

"She's not going to control my life ever again, I can tell you that," she said.

He leaned back a few inches and studied her.

"Why so judgmental all of a sudden?"

"Because I finally get it," she said, throwing out her arms. He cringed a little.

"It's always been about money, Cam, not love. She pulled us out of Jamaica because she wanted more money. Daddy was never happy in England or the States—you know that. He had to take all those awful jobs, work night shifts. He drank himself to death he was so unhappy. Did she care?"

Cameron frowned. Beads of sweat lay in a fold across his cocoa-butter forehead.

"I don't know about you, but I'm glad we migrated," he said. "Look how these people live."

He stabbed a finger into his palm. "Half of them can't read or write. The electricity and water are off half the time. Most of the people are"—he closed his mouth for a second—"poor as dirt. I'm better off, that's for damn sure."

There were small lines around his mouth she'd never noticed before.

"You miss the point, Cameron. 'These people' as you call them are poor but they come from their gut, they look you straight in the eye, and they live life true to themselves. What do we—?"

"What are you talking about? It's one of the most violent countries in the world, Simone!" Cameron said, and threw his arms up.

"I know it's violent," she said. "There's a lot of anger but—"

She looked toward the village. "It's about the past, the violence, the injustice. They're not through with that yet, but there's a kind of honesty about it that we don't have in America."

"You've idealized Jamaica, Sim," he said, "and demonized everything American. Take your blinders off."

His voice was getting louder and his gestures bigger. "If we'd stayed," he said, "we'd be living just like Mama and Daddy when they left. But because they left, we all got an education and we're all professionals."

"Mama and Daddy weren't that poor, Cameron. Stop being dramatic."

"Poor enough that they couldn't have brought us to where we are now," he said.

"You live in a Manhattan apartment the size of a closet," she said, "and you work 24-7. Is that where you want to be?"

"For now," he said, his voice cooler.

"What about the rest of your life?" she said, the Capricorn thrusting headfirst. "You haven't had a decent relationship since Nancy."

He stood up, the linen shorts more wrinkled, and looked away.

"I shouldn't have said that," she said. Nancy, sparkling in her flight attendant uniform the last time they'd all had lunch together, just before she left for the Brazilian man.

"Let's see," he said, pivoting to face her, the sibling rebutting. "Let's talk about decent relationships. You've been having an affair with Jack for how long? Fifteen, seventeen years? Left your husband for him, followed him to open the agency in Atlanta?" She couldn't speak.

"You took Celeste away from her school, her friends, and her family to be with a man who had no intention of marrying you. You took her away when she was a teenager, uprooted her, dragged her to the South, and hardly ever brought her back to the city to see us." His face was turning dark purple. "The only grandchild. My only niece or nephew."

"She liked Atlanta."

"She hated Atlanta and you know it. But you didn't care that you'd taken her away from her teachers and her activities and her sports at the height of her life—when she was thirteen. Thirteen! It took her years before she made friends in Atlanta, you know that. That's why she was running around with the wrong crowd, dating too early. You said that yourself. And all because of—" He broke off.

She looked toward the shore, the waves getting choppier.

"What fantasy world are you living in," he said, "thinking Jack was going to leave his wife for you? Leave the country club life for you?"

Sucking in her breath, she stood up. "We've all had to pay a price, Cam."

He looked away and folded his arms. "Maybe your husband and daughter paid the price."

She felt her cheeks getting hot, blood surging into her eyes. "That's it, we've done enough damage for one day." She started toward the lobby, the June plum warm in her hand.

"Please leave," she said, walking backward, the words falling out like bitter beads. "And *do not come back.* I don't need to be saved."

"You could die here, Simone," Cameron said, pleading again, the little brother.

"Let me die here, then!" she yelled.

She stalked off toward the doorway's cavity, anger planting its feet with each step and Cammy trotting happily beside her.

In her room she threw herself backward onto the bed. She covered her eyes with her arm, blocking out the image of Celeste waiting for an answer. Pain crawled down her shoulders and ribs, along with her brother's question—

"And when last did you tell anybody you loved them?" he'd shouted at her back.

CHAPTER TWENTY-EIGHT

The wooden porch floor shook under a man big enough to take it in two strides.

"Anyone home?"

Shad slid on some shorts. Doughnut-Boy again, Dollar-Bill, whatever his name was, the limo right outside his house. He sat down on the bed for a second and took a deep breath. The visit had come sooner than he'd expected.

Dollar filled the small living room, the low ceiling of the house only a foot away.

"Sorry, I don't have no beer or anything to offer you," Shad said.

"No problem, man."

"So what bring you here?" Shad said, hoping Beth wouldn't get back to find Dollar in their home like a giant cockroach in a tight suit.

"Just passing through, have to look up my friend. You know how it go," Dollar said, about to sit on the only armchair in the room. He stood up again without touching the seat, blocking the light.

"I was wondering if you need a little extra money," he said, "what with times tight and having a family."

"Everybody need a little extra," Shad said, his smile getting heavy. "What kind of work you thinking of?"

"Light work, man. No big thing."

"Like what exactly?" Shad said.

Dollar swung his arms. "The man I work for, seen, he just want to know what happening around here, with the election coming up and everything."

"Why me? I not into politics."

"You know everybody, man. You on top of things. You always know what going on—from Penitentiary times." The yellow rings around his brown eyes were saying more.

Stomach twinging, Shad sat down at the dinette table. "What kind of things he want to know, your boss?"

"Like I tell you, no big thing. He just want to know which way the election going around here."

A rooster crowed in Master John's yard next door, the only sound other than Dollar's breathing. Beth should be home soon.

"Boy, I don't know. I never interested in politics. Too much confusion and quarreling, you know," Shad said.

"Easy money, man. I come through couple times a week and check on you. I don't even have to come to your workplace. I can check you right here. And once a week I bring some cash for you."

Dollar peeked through the wooden louvers into Mas John's yard, two-tone shoes gleaming on the largest feet Shad had ever seen, then or now.

"I put in a word for you already with the big man." Dollar turned and smiled, showing the new teeth again.

"Why he want to know about politics around here? He American, right? He can't even vote."

"He doing a little work for the party," Dollar said. "They ask him to check on what happening on the Coast."

"He working for the government, for the prime minister?"

"Not working for them, just good friends, helping out a little," Dollar said, smiling again. He'd never smiled in the Pen.

"I drive him up to the prime minister's house all the time," he said.

"So how come the regular party workers don't do the work, don't check out what going on around here?"

"Everybody know them. People not going to say nothing around them. We need somebody fresh."

"And I fresh," said Shad. "They wouldn't think nothing of talking to me, you mean?"

"Right. You is a key man around here, and like how you hear everything at the bar, if you hear anything against the party, you know. . . ."

"I see," Shad said. What rock was the man hiding under? Nobody around here liked the party. They complained to one another every day about the cost of electricity, the state of the roads, the water lock-offs—every week a new complaint.

Dollar pulled at his collar. "What kind of money you looking for?" he said.

"I never said I was looking for any money," Shad said.

"You said everyone need a little money, right? So, how much?" Dollar-Bill said. A drop of sweat was trickling down the big cheek.

"I tell you, star. Thanks for thinking of me, but I don't need the money right now."

Dollar sat down on the armchair, making the plastic cover shriek. His legs stretched halfway to the front door.

"Tell me, how's the woman on the island?"

"Good," said Shad. "She have a gun." His hands were shaking a little and he interlaced the fingers.

"So I hear," Dollar said.

"You happy now," he said, his big voice lower. "Remember times going to get tougher. Tourist season not going to start for another five, six months, and hurricane rains coming. And things not going so good abroad. Fewer tourists coming out next time, you know what I mean?"

Shad tilted his head to the side and smiled. "You always a good salesman, boy."

"I just reminding you, you a family man now. A little money come in handy to put some food into the fridge there," Dollar said, pointing at the dwarfed refrigerator in front of him.

"Truth, man? I don't feel good reporting on anybody," said Shad. "When people come to the bar, they need to relax and speak what in their heart, you know? They need to trust me, seen?"

"They don't need to know."

"This a small place, man. They soon find out."

"How they going to find out?" Dollar picked at a tooth with a pinkie finger.

"They see you visiting me. You don't think they not going to ask me?" Shad said.

"We could meet somewhere else. Just name the place."

"I don't know, man. Anyhow, even if I did it, and tell you who don't like the party, what your boss going to do about it? Nothing he can do."

Dollar made a grunting sound back in his throat. "You be surprised. We can make people come around," he said. "Just give me the names."

"And then what?"

"Have a chat with them, make them see the light."

"Oh, so it go, eh? Nobody free to make up they own mind?"

"Some people just need a little *information,* you know?"

Shad stood up and rubbed his chest. "Yo, brother man, I have to go work now, you hear? I think about it, but I kind of busy right now."

Dollar stayed seated. "Even for old times' sake?" he said.

"Hey, man, I have to live here after the election, you know?"

Dollar took a deep breath and stood up. "Think about it. I come to check you again."

At the door, with only a few inches to spare on each

side, Dollar turned and said, as if he'd just thought of it, "Tell the wife hello. Beth she name, right?"

Shad closed the door behind Dollar, turning the key without making a noise. He climbed back into bed and pulled the sheet up to his chest. He was trying to remember, then was sure, quite sure, he'd never mentioned Beth's name to Dollar.

CHAPTER TWENTY-NINE

Why am I here in this silence? I should be home with a family around me. Why wasn't I one of those women who have three children who are still alive, and whose husbands sleep next to them every night?

Why was I different? What choices did I make that took me down this path, to a point where I have no one, feel so little, am so insignificant?

There is an emptiness that has lived inside me for almost as long as I have known myself. It started when I was a little girl, when I left Jamaica, and I've watched it grow into a hard nut of loneliness over the years. I stay busy so I don't have to think about the emptiness that opens only to fear or anger or pain.

I remember when Celeste was born and they handed her to me, there was this sudden warmth in the middle of my chest. It struck me then that this was love, and for a fleeting moment I knew what love felt like. But it went away right after, when parenting became late-night feedings, a messy living room, and teenage stubbornness. It never returned.

I remember feeling pride when she scored a goal for her soccer team one time. We were still in New York then. And I felt comforted when she took such good care of me when I was

151

sick in bed with the flu, after we moved to Atlanta. I remember feeling satisfied when I had a seventeenth birthday party for her, and so many kids showed up. But I don't remember the feeling of love, the warmth in the middle of the chest, the knowing that this is the ultimate feeling, I don't remember feeling it ever again.

That last time I saw her, there was no surge of love when she arrived in the house back from school. There was only anxiety about her grades, fear that I'd have to pay for extra semesters, shame that she'd drop out.

And after that, there was the stab of terror when I heard, and then numbness and constant pain after the service. And a dismissal of Jack and fifteen years of . . . what? Not love. Addiction perhaps, addiction to power and excitement and sex.

And now there is a sadness that fills every cell in my body, every minute of the day, sadness that wedges itself into my chest until the pain makes it hard to breath.

There has to be an end to sad emptiness. I want to be brought back to life. I want to release the pain, or as much as I can. Some pain will stay forever, along with the old photographs, will settle into the corners of my heart, reminding me of her until the day I die.

But even while I learn to live with the vestiges of sadness, get the courage to open her red bedroom door and go through her clothes and her mementoes and her albums, I want to be alive again, to feel my heart jump and to know this is how love feels.

I need to create space for that to happen. That's what being here is about, creating space to fill with peace, and one day with love.

CHAPTER THIRTY

"Computer?" asked Meredith McKenzie, glancing from her new boarder to Shad over the top of her glasses. She was standing in her kitchen wielding a rolling pin over a slab of dough, strands of gray hair clinging to her face.

"I need to get onto the Internet," Cameron said, "check with my office—"

"No, sir, I don't have one of your computers. They cost too much and I wouldn't know how to use it!

"Technology," she said, in the preachy voice she'd used at the blackboard, "will never take the place of writing. I'm just grateful to the Almighty that little of it come to Largo."

"I just wanted to—," Cameron said.

"When I was a student," she said with a thump of the rolling pin, "I received a lot of prizes for my handwriting. It sloped to the right, the way they taught me. I never brought the pen off the page, you know, until the last letter." She smiled to herself.

"So I never understand why a fountain pen and a typewriter with good oil and a fresh ribbon, you know, aren't enough anymore."

Her cinnamon arms speckled with flour, she waved toward the corridor.

"There's a phone in my bedroom, if you want to use one. Ten US dollars for ten minutes. I have to keep the price up because I never know where people are calling and how long they talk. If you want a cheaper call, you have to go to Port Antonio."

She started talking to the row of dumplings beside the board.

"Everybody who come here too tense, if you ask me," she said. "They should just enjoy the sea breeze and don't worry about all that computer business." She broke into laughter underlined by the gold fillings, and the rolling pin thudded down again.

Cameron and Shad threaded their way back through the living room with its heavy mahogany furniture. On the wall above the sofa, a spear slanted over a triangular object.

"Ever hear of a boomerang from Australia?" Shad said, and stopped in front of it for a second. "Miss Mac said a man who stayed here sent it. Imagine, all the way from Australia—*a boomerang*."

Out on the main road, traffic was light and the men walked down the middle of the long, straight road that paralleled the beach. It had been Eric's suggestion that Cameron should learn to row and Minion should teach him—so he could go out to the island himself if he had to—and Shad had volunteered to take him to Minion's house.

Shad pointed out Solomon and Maisie's cottage and the larger home of the head teacher.

"Are all the children in school?" Cameron said.

"Days gone by, only a few children stayed in school. When I was ten, my uncle took me on to work in his boat, and I had to stop school. Most of my friends had to do the same thing. Things better now, though. Most of the children go to school, learning all kinds of things. They even have a computer in the school." Shad laughed.

They were passing a woman hanging clothes on a line.

"Miss Isabel, how Job doing?" Shad called out.

"Holding his own, thank you," Isabel said, staring at Cameron. "You have a new friend?"

"Yes," Shad said, and tipped his head at Cameron. "The brother of the woman on the island."

Isabel's eyes opened wide and she nodded to Cameron. "Good night."

Cameron murmured to Shad, "It's not even six o'clock. What's with the 'night'?"

"Any time after work becomes night to us."

When they finalized the transaction with Minion, they headed back.

"How long you been gone from Jamaica?" Shad asked Cameron.

"I was six months old when we left for England, never been back. My parents came back a couple of times, and Simone came back once on her honeymoon, but not me."

"You have a lot to catch up on, then," Shad said.

Cameron looked down at his feet and shook his head. "You live in New York and you think you know everything, right?" he said. "And here I am, forty years old no less, doing all kinds of things I've never done before, driving on the left, learning to row—and wearing flip-flops."

"Good experience, man. Learning to walk in some-body else's shoes, right?" Shad said, and they laughed.

"I've always thought of myself as a Jamaican, you know," Cameron said. "We ate Jamaican food at home, oxtail and stew peas, and my parents and their friends were always talking about the island, always following the politics. My mother still speaks with an accent even."

A sports car was approaching and the men hurried over to the side. Two blond tourists flew by. "But here I feel like a foreigner. I don't know this place at all."

From inside the window of a house, a boy with pointy ears stood staring at them. Cameron waved at the child.

"You see that little boy? I feel like him. I'm just looking at the passing scenery, listening to what's going on—trying to, anyway, because I can't even understand patois."

"You think you could come back here to live?"

"I doubt it. I'll come back to visit, sure."

Shad was about to answer when they heard a scuffle behind them. A huddle of children ten feet back was whispering and pointing to Cameron. One bold boy ran up close to him, smiling from ear to ear.

"What's your name?" asked Cameron.

The children halted behind. They giggled and looked at each other, then one little girl, her hair in cornrows, shouted to the boy—

"Tell him, nuh?" she said.

The boy's mouth opened and closed.

"Talk up, man. Tell the gentleman your name," Shad said, laying his hand on the child's head.

"Elijah," the boy said so softly Shad told him to repeat it. His big eyes bounced down to the ground and back up.

"Tell me, Elijah, why are you following us?" Cameron said.

The boy looked up at him for a second and ran back to join his friends, who started screeching at each other in patois. When the two adults shrugged and started walking again, the children followed for a short distance, chattering, before running away.

"What was that all about?" Cameron asked.

"They're curious, just being children. They don't see tourists walking on the road, and you look like them. They not used to black tourists, black people who speak like Americans. You don't have children?"

"No time for that, man. Life in America has you going all the time, know what I mean? Anyway, my wife—ex-wife—didn't want any."

"Children are good for the soul, that's what my wife says. They ask questions, make you think." They were approaching the bar.

"You should try it sometime," Shad said, and waved to Tri, who was coming in the opposite direction.

CHAPTER THIRTY-ONE

C ammy had fallen asleep already on the rock behind her, one paw over her nose. It was that kind of afternoon again, not one for writing. She put the pen down next to the journal and the gun. Behind the clouds, the sun was streaking the sky with pink. Other colors were appearing, lavender and gray-blue and orange, the clouds outlined with gold auras.

A circular cloud blocked the sun. A few months back, a client, a well-oiled, older woman who knew how to intimidate, had told her what it was called. They'd been sitting outside of a coffee shop on a spring day.

"I want cumulus clouds, not those mean, thin ones," the woman had requested for her airline commercial. She'd exhaled a puffy cloud of smoke to show the shape she wanted. And, awed, coffee cup in midair, Simone had held her breath until the smoke disappeared. When she told Jack, he'd laughed about it, had stopped massaging her to throw back his head, his weight shifting on her bottom.

That was before she'd promised Stephanie she'd feed her cat and had to go all the way back to the office because she'd forgotten Stephanie's keys in her desk. Before nodding to the night guard and taking the elevator up fourteen floors. Before hearing voices coming from Jack's office (the woman's teasing, full of pheromones). Before knowing his low laugh, ending with a question she couldn't hear. Before tiptoeing along the corridor, her heart beating so hard she had to hold her throat. Before seeing Arlene's bare feet crossed at the ankles on top of the coffee table—the red toenail polish like cherries in whipped cream. Before nodding to Arlene, whose young hand was wrapped around a martini, her jacket thrown onto the sofa. Before her lover, her partner, her boss looked up at her, his smile stuck, his hand on Arlene's thigh. The first loss.

It was the first blow, the surprise right jab, Jack's infidelity, the knowledge that she was now too old, that she was at last just a cog in the wheel and had to come into the agency every day pretending that all was normal and she was in charge. She'd even felt some pride that she could carry on regardless, that she could survive this indignity and the accompanying gossip. It was the first blow that hit her, crumpled her over, leaving her injured—and still standing.

But it was the second blow, the sledgehammer to her stomach five weeks later, the knockout punch of Celeste's accident, that brought her to her knees, had her, over a period of weeks, slowly collapsing to the ground (still walking around the office in her black suits with back erect), until she felt like her forehead was on the ground, until she cared not one fig what others thought. And it was this that made her say to Don Amarillo, their biggest client, in her calmest, steeliest voice:

"Will you fucking make up your fucking mind about the fucking ad, because it's been six fucking months already and I'm goddamned sick of your dithering, and as for that fucking assistant of yours . . ."

It was the second blow, the death, that had brought her down, brought her to this place. It was the knockout punch that minimized Jack and their affair, that reduced what had been between them to a footnote on a page of screaming pain.

She leaned back against the rock. It would be sunset in Atlanta or wherever he was, and they'd be working late no doubt, surrounded by glass, locked in a square bubble floating away from her. She saw her former colleagues, now in irrelevant bubbles, eating in restaurants and sitting at computers and speaking on cell phones, connecting with other bubbles, meeting, talking, making love, feeling at the center of the universe.

What would they, Jack, Arlene, the woman with her elegant cigarette holder, what would they think of her living alone in this primitive place with her hair sticking up on her head and grown out under her armpits, looking like Africa? The renegade vice president gone crazy.

A slight sea breeze tickled her cheeks and neck, almost a lover's kiss, smelling nothing like the fumes from the I-20 expressway that reached her house when the wind was wrong. She closed her eyes, a smile on her mind. The resignation letter would be addressed to Jack (*CON-*

FIDENTIAL on the front), with terms and conditions written by her lawyer.

Late-afternoon sun bathed her eyelids and her cheeks, her neck and shoulders. The braying sound came again from the village, later than usual, a distant, ghostly music. It called forth a sudden sensation between her breasts, a prickle of new growth that felt warm and pure. With each beat of the waves at her feet, the tingling spread deeper into her chest.

If one could be like this forever. No past, no future, no fear—a scary new feeling.

This must have been what Dorella felt at the yoga center, a place with mechanical waterfalls and harp music that made your shoulders drop when you opened the door, and why Do exhaled, moaning, as soon as they lay on their yoga mats. Not her. As soon as she entered, she'd dread the meditation for the first five minutes. And when all the yoga poses were finished, she'd waste a half hour sitting with legs crossed, pretending she was deep in contemplation, but thinking only of work and Jack and Celeste and the chocolate cake on the kitchen counter, a tumble of thoughts, and wish she were somewhere else. And what made it worse was Dorella just loving it, drifting away into some kind of never-never land, and being all dreamy on the way home.

And this place that didn't even have a name was forcing her to sit, to do nothing but be—to feel this reaching down into the depth of her own silence while the sound of the water enfolded her.

There was nothing to do but feel grateful for the sun's

weakened arms, grateful for Cammy snoring lightly behind her, grateful for feeling one with the waves and their churning foam as they raced toward shore.

Nothing to think about, no need to go anywhere or feel anything but the warmth outside and the prickling inside, and the motion of the water in every one of her cells, filling the numbness.

CHAPTER THIRTY-TWO

Visiting the Largo Bay Restaurant and Bar every evening had become Cameron's habit, and Elijah, now his only fan, started waiting for him every evening outside of Miss Mac's, becoming the bearer of village news.

One evening, Cameron—at first shocked and then just angry—described to Shad the events leading up to that evening's revelation. While Shad put down the change he'd been counting, Cameron playacted the scene, almost as if he was a Jamaican.

The first night Elijah had followed him, Cameron reported, he'd kept at a distance, but the next night things had changed.

"What they call you, sir?" Elijah had asked suddenly, running soundlessly on bare feet to catch up.

"Cameron. And you're Elijah."

"You remember me?" the boy had said.

"Of course I do. You're a bright boy. How could I forget?"

The boy had grinned, showing his missing tooth, still in his dirty school uniform, the shorts too big.

"How old are you, Elijah?" Cameron asked.

"Seven," Elijah had said, shrugging. "Or eight. You going to Mistah Eric's bar?"

"Yes. Why aren't you home with your family?"

"Only my uncle. He playing dominoes in Mas Ezekiel's bar." They'd walked in silence the rest of the way. When they came abreast of the red and white sign of the Largo Bay Restaurant and Bar, Elijah had run away without a word.

Again tonight, when Cameron emerged from Miss Mac's, Elijah had been waiting, squatting on a stone beside the gate. Cameron mimicked him jumping up to walk alongside. He'd probably had to skip every now and then to match his steps with the man's, Shad knew.

"You going to see your sister, suh?" he'd asked.

"Yes, I am."

"You going to row across? Minion teaching you to row. I see you rowing yesterday."

"Did you?"

"Yes." The boy had squealed with his hand over his mouth, Cameron said. "You look funny, rowing round and round. Minion look vex. I see you."

"I'm getting better, though. When I learn to row, I can go see my sister."

"I want to see her, but I can't go," Elijah had said, shaking his head.

"It's a long way for a little boy."

"No, I can row, and I can swim too," the boy had told him.

"Then, why can't you see her?"

"Because the obeah man protect her," Elijah said.

Cameron had stopped walking his pretend walk in front of the bar. "The obeah man?"

"Yes, sir. He send Oil of Protection for she."

Shad pictured Elijah smiling uncertainly and running off, the pale soles of his feet disappearing into the night, leaving Cameron with his mouth open.

At this point in the story, Cameron circled the bar and whispered, almost spat the words into Shad's ear, although there were only three customers seated at a far table.

"Obeah, he said! Whose idea was this?"

Shad smiled without his eyes smiling. He'd been expecting this. "It was my idea," he said.

"Are you crazy? Obeah? How could you do that to my sister?" Cameron said, his eyes popping out of his head, an artery in his neck pumping hard.

"Sometimes a man have to take action."

"Put a spell on her?" Cameron waved the beer Shad had handed him earlier.

The door to the apartment creaked open and Eric emerged, damp hair tucked behind his ears.

"What's up?" Eric asked, his freshly showered smell reaching them first.

"He find out about the Oil of Protection," Shad said, "and he vex with us."

"Hey, man," Eric said, "two men tried to rob your sister, maybe worse! We had to do something."

"Oh, my God," Cameron said, throwing his arms out and slopping the beer. "Two men attacked her? I thought

165

you were joking when you said she'd shot after the last man. What else are you hiding from me?"

Shad looked at the pool of beer. "Two men rowed over one night and the dog wake her up, and she fire the gun and they run off. Nothing more."

"Oh, my God." He stared at Eric. "I told you she was in danger. Do you know who they were? Did you tell the police?"

"We know, but they gone," Shad said. "And the police wouldn't come from Manchioneal for a little thing like that."

Cameron slammed the bottle down on the counter. "When were you planning to tell me this?"

"Do you think we'd have used obeah if it wasn't for a good reason?" Eric said.

Cameron shook a finger at both men. "That obeah is crazy stuff, and you know that, right?"

Eric shrugged and eased past Cameron. "When in Rome . . ."

"My family doesn't want any part of that."

"We had to do it. It was the only way to keep people off the island. Believe me, we had your sister's best interest at heart," Eric said, and opened the fridge.

"We wanted to protect her," Shad said.

"With mumbo jumbo?"

"Nobody has touched her since," Eric said.

"Well, we don't believe in witchcraft," Cameron said, and crossed his arms.

Shad steered him to a bar stool on the other side of the counter.

"Have another beer, on the house," he said while Eric wandered off toward the kitchen with a bottle of tonic water.

"I still don't like it."

Shad reached into the fridge and pulled out a Heineken. "You don't know anything about obeah," he said. "How can you hate something you don't know?"

"I know it's all superstition, spells and shit."

"Sometimes superstition has something behind it," Shad said. "Ever thought of that?"

"You know what a con artist is? That's what obeah men are. All those fortune tellers, people like the obeah man? They're con artists! They take people's money and twist up their minds."

"Maybe you should check into it, before you twist up yourself," Shad said, pouring the beer into a glass.

"Who is this man, anyway? What kind of oil was it?"

"Tell you what," Shad said, placing the glass in front of Cameron, the way he handed the baby a soother, "I'll explain everything to you if you give me a minute to get a mop."

CHAPTER THIRTY-THREE

It was a choice, not a compulsion, visiting her, he'd told himself. It made sense to check on her every week or so, even if he thought of her a hundred times a day. The truth was he'd never been good with temptation, had had to go to confession almost weekly when he was a teenager and *Playboy* had just come out. His friend Rich used to sneak him a copy from his father's stash, and he'd turn to a favorite page in the bathroom when his parents were out and go for it.

Eric swung the bags of groceries to the ground. The image of a naked Simone was imprinted on his brain now—the small breasts drooping, with nipples curved upward, the black pubic hair only a few feet from his head. He might as well have photographed her and pinned a giant poster at the foot of his bed. Seeing her last Sunday with her clothes on, greeting her brother from the top of the cliff, had done nothing to erase the picture of her body dripping rainwater above him, guilt making him stay in the canoe.

"Simone!" he called. "Simone?"

Eric crossed his arms. He slapped a mosquito dead, a

female trying to feed its eggs by risking its life. Problem solved.

She emerged from her room, head down, as sleepy as the dog trotting ahead making muffled woofs.

"Sorry, didn't mean to disturb you."

"What's the problem?" she said. The baggy clothes did her body no justice.

"Just delivering your groceries," he said. "Thought I'd give Sam a rest."

She ran a hand over her head, patting down braids that kept popping up.

"Thanks," she said, and yawned. "I hadn't even noticed I was running out."

There was no invitation to sit down.

"Laundry?" he said, and put his hands on his hips. "Anything I need to take back?"

"No, I'm good for another week, thank you."

"Mind if I sit down a minute? Got a bit winded from the rowing and carrying the bags. Not as young as I used to be," he said, laughing, feeling the blush spreading.

"Sure," she said a little too politely.

He squatted down where he was, and she sat on a rock under the tree, the dog settling beside her.

"Guess what?" he said. Her eyebrows went up at him.

"Your brother found out about the Oil of Protection."

She murmured something he couldn't hear above the breeze.

He fell back onto his bottom. "I guess somebody in the village told him."

169

"At least I won't have to hide it from him anymore. How did he react?" She leaned over to pat the dog.

"Not well," Eric said.

"I'd think so. Our family looks down on that kind of thing."

"He let us know," he said.

"I think my parents were afraid of it."

"Most people here avoid it," he said. "They believe in it, but they avoid it."

"Has he said anything about when he's leaving?"

"No," he said, and hugged his knees. "He's learning to row, though. I think he's planning to come out at some point."

"Oh, God, no," she said, and winced.

"He's pretty bad, so it should take a couple weeks for him to get it right," he said, smiling, trying to bridge the distance.

"I hope it takes him longer." She looked back at her room.

He scratched a foot. "Cameron told me about your daughter. I'm sorry."

He'd debated telling her he knew. He'd thought about it while he drove into Port Antonio for her groceries, while he selected almonds and dried apricots from the imported shelf.

She was silent, looking down and nodding, the way she had when he gave her the oil, and he had to will his hand not to reach out. He waited until she looked up, one corner of her mouth tugged outward.

"I guess I couldn't keep that a secret either," she said.

"There aren't many secrets in a village."

She stroked the dog's fur from neck to tail. "She wasn't a high achiever, you know, which used to irk me. When she was—before, I always saw her faults. I could list them in my sleep and I let her know that I knew. She was lazy, she was unrealistic, not academic enough, she drove too fast," she said, her voice going up, down, into valleys of self-torture.

She shrugged, staring straight ahead. "Everybody loved her, and she loved them back. And she was funny, God, she was funny. She had this sense of humor that picked the tiniest thing out about a person, never mocked them, just found something you hadn't noticed about them and made you see them deeper, tickled you inside, so you'd smile for days thinking about what she'd said.

"And she knew just how to make you feel good about yourself. You'd walk away from her feeling better than when you came, remembering her smile." She passed her hand in front of her mouth, her eyes glazed over. "She had this wicked smile, ear to ear, full of teeth. She liked her own teeth—it cost me enough to have them straightened. And she would smile suddenly and just brighten everything. My sister said she knew how to turn a gloomy day into sunshine. That's what she said."

She looked up at him and her voice went flat. Her hand moved mechanically, stroking the dog's fur up and smoothing it down.

"I remember the last time I saw her. I can't get it out of my mind. It was early in the morning and I was rushing to work. I had a frown on my face, I remember that, and my voice sounded just like my mother's, impatient, irritated. I was standing at the kitchen counter drinking coffee, and Celeste was draped across two chairs at the breakfast table."

"Was she in college?" he said.

"Yes, she was in premed," she said. "I remember it like it just happened. I said something like, 'The only way you'll get into medicine is through nursing. I'm tired of paying good money for bad grades.' Something like that. And then I said, 'I'm really disappointed in you.'"

She picked up a stick and made a circle in the dirt. "Those were the last words I spoke to my daughter."

"What did she say?" he said. Tears were pricking at his eyelids and he blinked a few times.

"Typical. She just laughed and said, 'You'll be proud of me one day, Mom, don't worry.' I'll never forget. She walked toward me, wrapped her arm around my shoulders—she had these long limbs, you know, a tall girl like her father—and she kissed me." She touched her left cheek.

"Then she told me to 'chill out' because I'd look like Dracula's bride at my meeting, and she made me smile," she said. The corners of her mouth curled up. "I was rushing out to a big meeting at work."

From the end of the stick a heart emerged in the dirt.

"Then she told me she loved me. Those were her last words. 'I love you, Mom.'"

She raised her eyes, dry, cavernous eyes. "My last words were 'I'm disappointed in you' and her last words were 'I love you.' Can you beat that?" she said, tipping her head to one side.

"And I remember passing her old car in the driveway and thinking—this is the hardest part—I remember thinking, 'Damn if I'm going to buy her another car. Let her father do it this time.' I hear those words, even though I didn't speak them. I hear them over and over again."

Eric looked at his feet, the toenails needing to be clipped.

"That's tough," he said.

"It's—" She stopped with her lips parted.

"You're in a good place for—whatever you call it— healing, I guess," he said, the words alien, words a woman would use.

She nodded.

"I hope it's going well, then," he said, straightening his back. "The rainy season is coming. No guarantees what could happen."

She threw the stick into the bushes.

He rocked, hugging his knees, and stood slowly. "How much more time do you think you'll need? I'm not rushing you, just asking."

He'd liked from the first that she'd loved his island and found a use for it, and she'd forced him to live in the present, to focus on it here and now. When she refused to leave, he wished he'd done that himself, had the guts to endure, but this worrying about her had to end one day.

Standing, she stretched overhead, the way her brother had.

"I'll know when I'm ready," she said.

CHAPTER THIRTY-FOUR

"You never hear that Jamaica means 'Land of wood and water'?" Shad said, signaling Cameron to turn the car right.

"That's in Arawak language—*Xaymaca*," he said in his best tourist-guide voice.

Eric was giving him a *brawta,* extra pay for taking Cameron around to see the local sights, and Shad had spent yesterday afternoon with Miss Mac, boning up on what he should tell him about Jamaica.

The Arawak Indians were here first, Shad reminded himself. Jamaica was one hundred and fifty miles long and fifty miles wide. Blue Mountain Peak was the highest point, over seven thousand feet high. The weather was tropical, and there were only dry and wet seasons.

"Not like America that goes from cold to hot and back to cold," Miss Mac had said in her teacher voice.

"You mean cold, like on top of Blue Mountain Peak?" Shad had asked. He'd frozen half to death on a church outing to the peak.

"Colder," Miss Mac said. "Like the freezer in your fridge."

No wonder Americans liked Jamaica, Shad had thought. How could they stay warm?

The original plan, as Eric had explained it, was for Shad to be driver and guide using his Jeep. Shad had reminded him that although he drove the Jeep some-times—had been the one to drive the other workers home just before the hurricane and park the vehicle in Lambert's garage—he had no driver's license. Shad had suggested another plan. He would act as tour guide if Cameron would drive his rental car.

After they got the details down, Eric had suggested it to Cameron one night.

"That's kind of you," Cameron said, sounding formal, still irritated. "I'll pay Shad, of course."

"No, no," Eric had countered, his right arm stretching generously toward Shad. "It's on me."

There was awkwardness all around, Shad had told Beth that morning, because Cameron hadn't said much to him or Eric since he'd found out about the obeah.

"I thought him and his sister were from Jamaica. He don't understand the Doctor helping her?" asked Beth, who'd never had much patience with ignorance.

"No, he think it stupidness. His people don't believe in it," Shad said.

"Pastor don't like it, but it work," she answered.

"I not even sure myself, tell the truth."

"They don't have obeah in America?" Beth had stopped plaiting Ashanti's hair to look at him.

"I don't think so. I never hear Americans talk about it."

"Well, we know in Largo that obeah work." Sucking

her teeth, Beth had bent to her task, the baby hairs on the back of her neck still fluffy under the new perm.

Shad had shaken his foot under the sheet. "Anyway, Cameron still vex with Mistah Eric, you can see it. The touring business is a peace offering. The boss don't like anyone vex with him too long."

And this, the first trip, was to take in Reach Falls, a waterfall and deep pool that Shad had swum in as a boy and where he brought his own children. The drive took them east of Largo, Sam's house flashing by as they drove through Poco Bay.

Shad put his arm out the open window and let the breeze run up his short-sleeve shirt. This was living, he thought, grinning, inhaling the new-car smell—better than any cologne a woman wore. He'd have to tell Frank he'd been riding in a brand-new Mitsubishi, and he'd been practicing saying the name.

"How many children do you have, Shad?" asked Cameron.

"Four. Joella is the oldest, almost fourteen, pretty and brown like her mother."

"Oh, boy," Cameron said, and winked. "What about the others?"

"Rickia is the bright one, says she's going to be a doctor." Shad looked out the window. "Ashanti, she's quiet— we have to take her to a doctor—and Joshua, six months old. All of a sudden, Beth got pregnant. We weren't planning on it, but we have a boy now."

After parking, they hiked the rest of the way to the falls. A few local children and a tourist family were swimming when they got there. Shad sat in the shade of a tree, the way the tour guides did, watching Cameron strip down to his bathing suit. Bearing a nut-brown tan, Cameron waded out and swam toward the falls, swinging his head from side to side above the water like a novice.

With cool air drifting off the falls and the roar of water in his ears, Shad dozed off. In what felt like minutes, a shake on his shoulder roused him. Cameron was standing in front of him, dressed in damp clothes.

"You finished so soon?" Shad said, and stood up unsteadily, holding on to the trunk of the tree.

"We've been here a couple of hours already," Cameron said, his old smile plastered on his face. "Some tour guide you are! You've been sleeping the whole time."

"I promise not to fall asleep on the job again," Shad said, and grinned. Next thing, Cameron would cancel the tours, and there'd be no money coming from Eric. No money for the stove to surprise Beth with this Christmas.

"I'll drink a cup of coffee next time," Shad said.

The trip back to Largo was interrupted by a stop in Port Antonio where Cameron wanted to use a cyber café he'd seen. A wall of the shop was lined with four computers, and while Cameron clicked away at one, Shad browsed the sunglasses and straw hats near the front steps. Next door, a shop owner called to a couple of passing tourists.

"Come, check out my T-shirts, nuh?" she said. The tourists, a tall woman and a short man, laughed nervously and moved on, and the shopkeeper sucked her teeth.

Across the street, dance-hall music blared from an appliance store, washing machines lining the sidewalk.

After a word to Cameron, who kept his eyes on the computer screen, Shad started down the steps to examine the stoves opposite.

Two seconds later, he froze with one foot on the bottom step. Coming out of the appliance store were two men wearing sunglasses, an odd couple, one in a tight suit, big enough to fill the doorway, his companion short and stout, dressed in a yellow track suit, a thick chain around his sweating neck. Together they walked along the sidewalk, the big one doing most of the talking, the other glancing into store windows, a sulky pout to his mouth. There was something familiar about the way they strolled, the big gorilla in front of the little gorilla, one talking away, one not needing to reply.

"So, the Blue Mountains tomorrow?" Cameron said, jogging down the steps.

"Yeah, man," Shad answered, his foot still on the bottom step and his eyes following the two men around the corner where they'd just disappeared.

"It should be interesting, driving up mountain roads on the left. I've heard about it, lots of curves and cliffs."

"We don't have to do it," Shad said, frozen to the spot.

"Heck, it'll be good for me, kind of a survival test," Cameron said.

"We good, then, no problem." Shad stroked his scalp hard and they turned toward the car, Cameron talking and Shad following, feeling no desire to respond.

ometimes—like today—her meditation didn't go well. Nothing helped, not even the sound of the waves, or breathing deeply, or trying to think away the whirling images.

She'd feel the tallness of the girl behind her shoulder, twisting a springy tendril of hair between two fingers. If she looked around, she knew, she'd see the long legs with the knobby knees, the bony hips under some dress bought on sale, and the big eyes always reminding Simone of Jeff.

And she'd hear the ring of the early-morning phone call and her own shrill voice. (*An accident, my daughter? What do you mean an accident? Is she okay, where is she? WHERE IS SHE?*)

And she'd drive again that numb and silent trip with Do at the wheel, and see the two fucking idiot policemen in Gainesville—one with a mole on the side of his nose— and she'd smell the hospital morgue's terrifying anti-septic, watch the attendant pulling the tray out slowly, fearful of hysteria, and stare at the curtained vehicle all the way back to Atlanta, the hearse driving too fast in front of them.

She'd stand at the funeral home's door after the service, kiss and be kissed by faceless mourners, inhale Jack's aftershave when he bent down to her, hear again Suzie murmuring sympathies beside him, their wedding rings dull with age and bruises.

And she'd see the orange-red door at the end of the corridor, see the horseshoe on the right side, the souvenir one from the Kentucky Derby that Uncle Cameron had sent her, and the small brass plaque in the center with her name, the plaque they'd searched catalogs to find, because Celeste wasn't a name you found in souvenir stores.

And she'd know there'd be no meditation today. There'd be only the chatter of the memories and a nausea of the heart.

CHAPTER THIRTY-SIX

S had knotted the string on the new bottle opener. He measured its length with his arm before cutting it.

How did they know each other? They weren't related, and they didn't come from the same town. Sharpie was from Spanish Town, people said, the old capital, with some of the meanest drug gangs in Jamaica. But nobody knew for sure because they avoided him if they could. When he was in Largo, he lived in a small house on the outskirts of the village, a house that stayed empty most of the time, and as far as Shad could remember, he didn't have a car. Maybe he didn't even have a license.

He tied the string to the hook above the trash can. Dollar was a Kingston man. Gang members in sunglasses would show up on visitors' day, standing at the counters behind the bars, next to Beth with her bread pudding and soap. Dollar's visitors never brought gifts. They always spoke in low voices and left early.

"Long time no see, man," said a chirpy voice across the counter.

Shad started. "Jennifer, good to see you!"

"You were far away," Jennifer said, and pushed back

her hair. Gold bracelets on her wrist clinked and winked in the bar lights.

"How is Beth?" she said. "I hear you have a boy now!"

"Yeah, and we all spoil him rotten, you see?"

"I'd love to see him." She looked around. "Where's Eric?"

"He had a doctor's visit in Ochy." To Jennifer's raised eyebrows, he added, "Just a checkup."

With the bar between them, the two chatted with the politeness of friends separated by the class divide, still uncomfortable to the American woman.

"Bring the kids up to the house one day, and I'll give them some ice cream," she said.

"They'd love that."

She swung around to glance at a group of people advancing toward the bar, the men looking like Scotch drinkers who liked to talk.

"I almost forgot," Jennifer said. "There're going to be eight of us for dinner. Doesn't Solomon cook on Saturday nights? Our cook is off. We weren't expecting guests—"

Shad set up chairs around the large, circular table closest to the bar. Lambert called for a round of drinks. A tall woman with a bass voice sat down across from him, her Asian-straight wig mocking a face with heavy features and bad skin. She'd take a beer, she said. Next to her, in a polyester pantsuit, was another woman, very young, very quiet, who asked for a Coke. The other four were men in shirt jackets, the tailored, short-sleeved shirts that politicians often wore. All requested whiskey, except one with a large Adam's apple who ordered a vodka tonic with lime and bitters.

Solomon, shaken from a doze in the kitchen chair, took the food orders while Shad prepared the drinks.

"So, what's the score in Largo?" Lambert asked the table after they'd ordered.

"We stand a chance," one of the men said, taking off his glasses and wiping them.

A man with a long, straight nose chimed in. "The government's ignored Largo so long, we think we're going to win it this time."

The group reeled off the problems in the area, from water lock-offs to overcrowded schools.

"And why, why can't the government fix the pot-holes?" Jennifer moaned. "We've written letter after letter to the newspaper."

"They don't have to," a plump man said, wiping his forehead. "The whole parish of Portland always supports the People's National Movement, so a little place like Largo doesn't matter to them."

"So why would it make a difference to you, then?" Lambert asked while he took the glass of wine Shad offered him.

"We need every vote we can get," the tall woman said.

"The only problem is stopping the old-school poli-tics," the vodka-tonic man chimed in.

"Meaning what?" Jennifer asked.

"Meaning that, although we have a chance now because everyone is so unhappy with the government, they might still get back in. They're going to use every trick in the book, from bribing people to distributing groceries. You might get your roads paved then!"

On the way back to the bar with the empty tray, Shad turned around, his sneakers squeaking on the concrete floor.

"What about spying?" he said. "They ever do that? Pay people to tell on other people?"

"I never heard of that, but they might try anything," said vodka-tonic. "Why? Have they been coming around?" The man's Adam's apple jumped up and slid down.

"Just asking, just asking," Shad said, and scooted behind the bar.

"If they're willing to have their toughs beat up people outside of polling stations, you better believe they'd be capable of it," the big woman said.

"But we've never had anything like that in the past," Lambert said. "We've always had peaceful elections here."

"Up to now," the fat man growled. "But these government people have their ways. They're changing the rules. They haven't needed Largo before. Now they do."

He leaned forward. "I was up in Vineyard Town on Thursday, and they were saying that a new kind of politics is happening there. They call it *politricks*."

Amid the laughter, Shad heard Dollar's words: *We can make people come around.*

Refilling ice trays at the sink, Shad called out, "What kind of tricks?"

"The first thing they been doing is targeting an area that needs to be 'persuaded,'" the man answered. "That's what they call it. Then they start paying people to talk about how good the party is, and to start recruiting party loyalists, paying their food bills, rent, lights, and so on. They go for the low-hanging fruit, you know, people they think would be easy targets. They give them promises of more money to come, and work when the party gets back in."

The man leaned back with his glass, which would need refilling soon at the rate he was drinking. Shad reached for an Alka-Seltzer box under the bar. The tall woman smoothed down a few strands of her wig that had been blowing in the breeze.

"Next step," said the Adam's apple, "is for them to plan a road-paving job, a real good one, not just to fill potholes but to repave the whole road. They hire big bosses from Kingston, organizers, and those bosses hire people who are party loyalists or people who promise to vote for the party. It's a whole racket."

"They have anything to do with the drug gangs?" asked Shad. "Sounds like gang business to me."

The man with the long nose leaned forward. "You're absolutely right. I heard that they're making arrangements with gang leaders to use their men. Makes sense, when you think about it. The gang bosses work for the party, have their best men working in communities recruiting, pressuring, and so on. Then, when the party gets in, the party owes them favors."

"Oh, my God," said Jennifer. "The government would be able to protect them from extradition or—"

"Or even from being charged in the first place," Lambert finished.

A shiver went up the back of Shad's neck. He could feel the roots shift under his scalp. If he'd had hair on his head, it would have been standing straight up.

The rattling of the kitchen's bead curtain announced Solomon's entry, his tray of food filling the bar with the aroma of thyme, scallion, and Scotch bonnet pepper. He distributed the dishes, confusing two of the dishes' owners and switching them without apology, before shuffling back to the kitchen to get another load.

While the group ate, the regulars arrived. Janet entered first. She waved at Jennifer and smiled at the men on her way to the counter. Tri recognized the vodka-tonic drinker, a former minister of government who had represented the area, he whispered to Shad.

The talk went back to politics, Tri complaining to the politicians about the local situation. Half an hour later, Solomon drifted out to clear the table. An empty plate in each hand, he suddenly boomed, the thunder of his voice parting the waves of chatter:

"Time for them to go! You try to register for pension—nobody care. You go to hospital—you have to wait all day. People come pushing up in front of you, they take them first."

It was Tri who broke the silence, shaking a finger at the group.

"Whatever you do, do it quick," he said, "because better must come."

"What you mean by 'better'?" the former minister asked. "What you want the next government to do?"

"Give us work," Tri said. "I can't find good work all

these years, and fishing only bring starvation wages. It not going to change with these people."

"Especially when the people at the top are so corrupt," said Lambert. "Remember the trucks?"

"What happen to the trucks?" Shad called out.

"You don't read the paper?" the tall woman said. Shad slurped the last of the Alka-Seltzer water in his glass. Beth hadn't read him anything about trucks.

"Eighty trucks, big water trucks," she said, "ordered from Japan by the Ministry of Transport and Works last year. A reporter from the *Gleaner* found out that the minister got a cut from every one of them. Something like two hundred and fifty thousand US dollars went into his bank account abroad. They say they going to investigate, but that only mean nothing going to be done."

Solomon emerged again with one arm lifted and the other holding his order book.

"They is *wicked* people—Sodom and Gomorrah!" he pronounced as he sailed toward the table. "And God will smite them, wait and see."

He stopped beside Jennifer with a grimacing smile. "Dessert, ma'am?"

CHAPTER THIRTY-SEVEN

The flaming glass vase was cool against her legs, her hands resting lightly on both ends. The orange and red lid was taped securely to the jar with cellophane that twinkled in the lamplight.

She wound the purple cloth around the vase and placed it on the mattress. On hands and knees she crawled to the entrance, pushing the lamp ahead of her. Broken tiles scratched her knees and her bandaged right ankle felt swollen and heavy. She shoved the lamp the last two feet toward the doorway and returned to the mattress. Picking up the vase, still wrapped in its swaddling cloth, she settled it in the nook of her left arm.

"It's time, C," she said, the voice deep in her throat, not wanting to come out. She pushed up to a standing position.

"It's been time."

She reached for her fishing pole, reborn as a walking stick, which had been resting against the wall between an empty bottle of water and three books. Leaning on the stick and jumping, the vase cradled hard to her breast, she reached the room's entrance and paused while Cammy ran ahead.

A mild evening breeze tugged at her hair as she bent to tuck in the end of her improvised bandage, strips of a T-shirt wrapped in a neat figure-of-eight. Like the nurse at Bronx-Lebanon Hospital had taught her when Celeste twisted her ankle. She'd left the twelve-year-old doing homework while she went to evening classes at NYU, hadn't expected her to get scared of lightning and fall running down to a neighbor. Four days later, she'd been in the middle of bandaging Celeste's ankle on the living room sofa when a woman from the Administration for Children's Services had knocked on the door. Impressed with Simone's skill at wrapping the bandage, the woman had complimented her, and Simone had never heard from the ACS again.

The ankle was still painful—she had no aspirin—but it had been useful. It had stopped her thinking of Jack. Since Cameron's visit, she'd thought about Jack again, had fallen asleep remembering the taste of the man. She'd felt him kissing her crooked across her mouth, imprinted on cells that couldn't forget. On one occasion, the memory of his acrid late-afternoon smell had been enough to make her juices flow, make her want him for the first time. For the first time since Arlene.

Yes, there is Arlene. He'd said it as if he were making note of a competitor for a new account, the crazy son of a bitch said it as if he were trying to keep her in rational, strategic planning mode.

She'd relived, step by step, the first time she and Jack had had sex. It was on a trip to Paris for a presentation. They'd celebrated the new account with champagne in the little hotel bar. She'd remembered how his sweat had dripped on her as she lay under him for the first time, and how it felt to be a traitor, ashamed and in love, when Celeste and Jeff called the next morning and Jack was still in her bed.

She began her journey down the path, stick, hop, stick, hop, rest. Overhead, stars big and small spangled the sky and a half-moon almost outshone the lamplight on the path.

By the time she reached the tree, breathless from hopping, sweat was sticking the T-shirt to her back. She lowered herself with a groan to the rock where she usually ate. Pieces of charcoal were scattered around like giant raisins, the burlap bag lying on its side with the top open.

A yearning for rice and peas the evening before had caused the accident. It had meant bringing the charcoal closer to the fire. Red beans took time and fuel to cook. But with arms locked around the large, scratchy bag, her foot had hit the dog's smooth side and she'd fallen. At first she'd lain back and screamed with pain, but the loneliness had surrounded her and muted her screams.

Cammy had been watchful since the accident, as if she knew she'd caused it. Now she sat close, requesting a pat. It had been a painful and hungry twenty-four hours. In her stale, sweaty clothes, the foot elevated, the woman had crawled out of her cave only a couple of times to pee in a bush. The rest of the time had been spent lying on her back in the dark, planning her next project.

Beginning the journey again with a kitchen knife clasped to the stick, she headed north toward the long building with the mural. Her breasts bobbled against the vase as she jumped, offering suckle to the bundle. Unseen stones made her stumble more than once. It was dark, but she knew this place, had practiced this walk in her mind many times before.

Rounding the building's back wall, she hopped toward a cliff twenty feet beyond and eased down to the ground. For a few minutes, she waited, resting, allowing her eyes to get used to the darkness, the rocks lighter than the darkness of the sea beyond. Watched by Cammy, who stood guard over the walking stick, she dragged herself—still gripping the vase and knife—to a lower mound of rocks at the edge of the cliff.

Waves were sapping at the rocks below, and for a few minutes she sat with closed eyes and rasping breath, listening for it again. Just before every wave hit, there was a tiny silence. The silence when it strengthened and prepared itself, a split second of quiet she'd started hearing a few days before in her meditation.

She had to be very still to hear it, had to become the water, moving with it, had to suspend herself with the wave in silent intensity before it struck the rock. When she first noticed it, she'd leaned back and listened until the sun went down.

In the crook of her arm, the vase rose and fell with her breath, clinging to the damp T-shirt. Her ankle ached, rebelling from the effort, and she reached out to stroke it—just as a splash out at sea, not far, brought her head up to stare into the blankness of the nighttime ocean she'd come to fear. The fishermen would understand that. Jamaican cowboys who rode into it every night, knowing it could be their last.

Celeste hadn't been around water often enough to grow afraid. They'd gone to Jones Beach a few times, picking their way among the cigarette butts and plump bodies. After she'd left for college, she'd driven down to Key West with new friends, and rented goggles and flippers to swim in an ocean pen with two dolphins. Afterward she'd called home with wonder in her voice.

"The dolphins, Mom, you should have seen them. They seemed to know me, I'm telling you." She'd giggled like she had as a child.

Her mother had said—and meant it—that it sounded like a wonderful experience.

"But can you really afford it?" A parent's caveat. Celeste's voice had deepened in adult defense and lost its wonder.

She lowered the vase to the ground. The place where the vase had lain felt hollow, the pain rushing in, brackish. She groped around in her shorts pocket for a few seconds and brought out a candle, a lighter, and a small bottle, knowing but not seeing the last few drops.

CHAPTER THIRTY-EIGHT

Ashanti's arm curled around her father's neck. She was sucking three fingers of the other hand and shaking with dying sobs about being taken from her older sisters, who were selling vegetables in the market with their mother.

"Want an icicle?" Shad whispered in her ear.

The little girl nodded and her father bought a pink icicle from the box on Aaron's motorbike. With Ashanti licking the icicle in his arms, he leaned on a lignum vitae tree, watching the cricket match in front of them. Two teams of boys were batting and bowling. Elijah was fielding barefoot in his wrinkly uniform.

A ball sailed over their heads.

"Four!" the small captain of the batting team called. The batter ran to the other end of the pitch and Elijah and the other fielders chased the ball. A tall boy picked up the ball and threw it straight at the stumps (four sawed-off broomsticks) behind the batter.

"Out!" he yelled.

A cheer went up from the bowling team, and the next batsman came forward swinging his bat.

Shad smelled her first, sweet and musty, like rumpled sheets. The perfume was called Forbidden Fruit, she'd once told him.

"How's the new baby?" LaSharee said. She was eating an ice cream cone, rum and raisin it looked like, starting to drip on one side.

"Fine," Shad said.

"Where the baby mother, changing diapers?" She brushed her hair away from the cone.

"She's selling in the market," Shad said, and straightened. He juggled Ashanti to the other arm, the child's eyes fixed on the ice cream while she sucked her icicle.

"Selling in the market. Sounds domestic-like, a happy family," she said, and rolled her eyes.

"True. We happy."

"Glad to hear it."

Her toenails were bright red in the silver sandals.

On the field, a shout went up from the boys, followed by scattered applause from the onlookers, men who'd wandered over from the bar.

"Some of us lucky," she said. She sighed and licked the cone, which was dripping faster than she could lick.

"Luck is just opportunity, man," Shad answered. "Some of us use it and others don't."

"Well, I don't know what happen to my opportunity, then." Another lick of the cone, this time swirling it around.

"You having bad luck?" Shad said. Ashanti's icicle dripped onto his arm.

"Every day, it seems."

"What happen?"

Shad set Ashanti down and held her hand. She clung to his leg and stared up at the woman.

"You lost your job?" Shad asked. He'd seen her working behind the counter at a men's store in Port Antonio.

"Which job? I have a new one now, you know. I working in Port Antonio at Titchfield Hotel—receptionist," she said, the wig's locks swinging with pride.

"Glad for you. What wrong, then? You and Tiger?"

She sucked her teeth. "What, Tiger?"

"I thought you and he were—"

"He have other friends now," she said.

"He left town?"

"Seems so. He came in Thursday night and told me he had a work with a 'big man.' He said he didn't need a village girl. That's what he called me—*a village girl*." She frowned at the cone, still grasping the idea.

"Where he gone now?"

"He say Kingston, with all the dance-hall girls."

"You give him my message, about learning bartending?"

"He just laugh and say he don't need that, he making big money now."

"Big money doing what?" Shad said.

"He never say."

"How come you didn't follow him to Kingston?"

"He say he don't want no baggage," she answered, and crunched into the cone, hard.

Shad picked up Ashanti's fallen icicle stick. "You know who the big man is he working for?"

Straightening the shoulder strap of her handbag, she

licked her lips and looked off at the mountain rising behind the village. After a minute, she turned to Shad and
shifted to the other leg.

"Man-O-War," she said. "He call him Man-O-War."

"Man-O-War?"

"Yes," LaSharee said, and handed him the remains of
her cone and napkin. "Throw this away for me."

"Sound like a drug don." The napkin was soggy in
his hand.

"Must be something like that," she said. "Tiger don't
have no skills, you know that. He don't even answer the
phone good. He always get catch up in some stupidness."

Shad bit into his cheek. "This have something to do
with Sharpie, you think?"

"Could be."

"What you mean 'could be'?"

"Sharpie come to pick him up in a car."

Shad wiped Ashanti's mouth with the napkin. Sharpie,
driving a car?

"Let me know if he come back, you hear?" he said,
running out of time. Beth was expecting him to pick up
the baby from Miss Isabel's.

Watching LaSharee saunter away, one arm swinging
in time with her hips, Shad lifted Ashanti, who plopped
her head down on his shoulder.

"Ice cream," she whispered into his ear.

It was only later that night, the first Saturday night he'd
had off in months, that the penny dropped. The chil-

dren in bed, he and Beth were slow dancing to a Temptations song on the radio. He nuzzled her neck, smelling of onions and breast milk, and suddenly remembered La-Sharee's perfume.

"What's the matter?" Beth asked when he missed a step.

"Nothing."

"Like your mind on something."

"Just tired," he said.

Beth didn't need to know, just like she didn't need to know that Dollar had sat on her good-good living room chair, that he'd offered Shad money to tell on his customers.

Oh, God, oh, God, oh, God. He hated secrets.

CHAPTER THIRTY-NINE

A headache was coming on. The forks in the road, the choices made, the guessing game.

Maybe if she'd had another child.

Maybe if she hadn't started with Jack.

Maybe if she'd stayed with Jeff.

Maybe if she'd paid for Jeff to go to college.

Maybe if she hadn't done her master's, spent those nights away from home.

Maybe if she'd accepted the job at Darling and Stone.

Maybe if she'd stayed in New York.

Maybe if she'd kept Celeste at St. Bernadette's.

Maybe if she'd stopped her from hanging out with Ashley and Miara.

Maybe if there'd been a girls' soccer team at West Atlanta Middle School.

Maybe if she hadn't taken those business trips and left Celeste with Do.

Maybe if she'd stayed closer to her family, to Cameron.

Maybe if she'd bought her a new car.

She rubbed her wrist over her eyelids. Let it go, let it go. Stay present. It's not too late.

CHAPTER FORTY

A line of tourists struggled past, their hands clutching those of spouses and strangers behind and in front, helping each other clamber up the waterfall's slippery, round rocks. Another day at Dunn's River Falls and the guide's face was expressionless as he yelled instructions over the roar of the water, telling them where to place their feet. Two teenage boys broke away from the line and dove into a pool that adults were teetering around.

"Jason," a woman called, "get back in the line!"

Shad shouted to Cameron. "The falls go three hundred feet up, you know."

They were resting on a rock under massive cedar trees that spread from one side of the river to the other.

"We're only halfway up, but we can go all the way if you like."

"That's okay," Cameron gulped. "I'm good."

"You did well, man."

"Just trying not to fall in the water. I'm not the best swimmer in the world."

Shad nodded, relieved he wouldn't have to snag his

new bathing trunks any more than he had. It was his first visit to the tourist mecca, thanks to Cameron's purchase of his entrance fee, and he was trying to embed all the details, had had Cameron take a photograph of him next to the falls to show the children. The first thing he'd tell them was that there were lots of tourists, bus after bus parked in the lot. He'd never known there were this many tourists on the island, much less in one place. And the falls were stunning, just like they said, the big, cream-colored rocks sometimes tricky and sometimes easy to climb. The children would laugh to hear how he'd lost his footing and fallen into a pool of water, and how the water was cold-cold and clear.

The two men waited for another line of climbers to pass and then balanced across the rocks to the stairs beside the falls that descended from the parking lot to the beach. Cameron led the way down to the little bar.

"Damn," he said, clinking his beer bottle against Shad's. "That was tougher than I thought. You did pretty well there, buddy!"

"You're in better shape than me, though," Shad said.

"Yeah, but Manhattan doesn't have any waterfalls." Cameron laughed.

"Good experience for you, then."

"Another one," Cameron said, and took a swig.

"People who rich like you and live in America, they have bad experiences?"

"You'd be surprised."

"Name one," Shad said, "and I bet I can give you worse."

"Let's see," Cameron said, poking his finger at the table. "I've been fired twice."

"Try fired four times, twice in the first day." Shad laughed.

"Okay, the big stuff," Cameron said. "I've spent time in jail. Manhattan County Jail, for drunk driving. How about that?"

A few feet away, a large woman was climbing down the last step to the beach, exhaustion on her face.

Shad turned to Cameron. "Kingston Penitentiary, how about that?"

The American's eyebrows shot up. "That's heavy. What were you in for?"

"Foolishness—stealing a woman's purse," Shad said, and turned away.

He burped and placed the bottle in the middle of the coaster. "I was just going to give her back the purse when the policeman held me. She'd given me this sad look when I took it, you know, like she was disappointed in me, and I felt bad."

"How much time did you get?"

Shad drained his bottle. "One year. A year of living hell, but I deserved it."

The trip back to Largo crossed other streams and rivers. Sitting on damp towels in the Mitsubishi, their bathing suits already dry, the men munched on beef patties.

"My mother still doesn't know I was in jail," Cameron said. "I made my sisters promise not to tell."

"She knew you went to court?" Shad asked, brushing crumbs from his mouth.

"I told her it was a driving ticket."

"No one in Largo know I was in prison," Shad said. "Only Beth and Job."

Shad looked up at Cameron and made a face. "Don't tell nobody, you hear?" He might have said too much already.

"Of course not," Cameron said.

He shot Shad a sideways glance. "I guess Eric doesn't know."

"No. I'll tell him one day, but he kind of funny. I don't want to shock him too much."

Shad put a hand on the dashboard. "Watch out for that taxi."

Cameron swerved hard around the braking taxi.

"Damn drivers," he said. "I bet they never went to driving school."

Shad laughed. "They have schools for driving in America?"

"Yes, of course. America is big on schools. Schools for dancing, schools for cooking, schools for wine making, schools for housewives . . ."

"How many schools you went to?"

"After high school? I went to New York University, NYU, we call it. I'm in the school of life now, though."

They laughed, two half-naked men on wet towels eating patties.

"Sometimes the school of life catch up with you," Shad said, and turned serious.

With Cameron weaving around the slowing vehicles in Port Maria, Shad began telling him about Dollar. He told him how one day, when he was doing pull-ups on the bars of his cell window, partly to see the water sparkling in Kingston Harbour, Sergeant Lucas had come into his cell and hauled him onto the mattress. And how, just when the guard, a bulky man who'd made suggestive remarks to Shad more than once, had thrown himself onto Shad's back, Doughnut-Boy had come into the open cell and dragged the man off and knocked him out cold.

"That's the kind of friend you need in prison," Cameron said.

"It wasn't the only favor he did me, either."

"Why'd he protect you?"

"He say I remind him of his little brother. His brother got killed by some guys from another gang, not Doughnut-Boy's gang, I mean, Dollar's—that's what they call him now. I don't think the brother was in a gang. Like he was trying to stay straight or something, and the other gang kill him to get at Dollar."

"Where's Dollar now?" Cameron asked. "Still in prison?"

"Supposed to be—he was in for life, for murder. He killed a man and a woman, some drug business, I think. They almost hang him, but he had a good lawyer and got life without parole." Shad pursed his lips. "And he's out now."

A minibus blasting Buju Banton's latest song roared past, the conductor's head sticking out the open door.

"Somebody must have got him out," Shad said.

"Somebody with connections," Cameron added.

By the time the pair arrived in Largo, Shad's stomach

upset from the twists and turns, the story of Dollar's recent visits had been told. Sitting in the parked car outside his house, Shad recounted the connection between Sharpie and Tiger, and Sharpie and Dollar-Bill.

Cameron rubbed his unshaven chin. "So Dollar works for an American businessman named Manheim, you think. That means he's either gone straight or Manheim is crooked."

"And Man-O-War," Shad said. "Sounds like a drug don, right? I've never heard of him in my life. All of a sudden he's paying big money to Tiger and probably Sharpie, two good-for-nothing guys. To do what? That's what I want to know."

Cameron beat a hand on the steering wheel. "And what I want to know is—why did they visit my sister?"

Four eyebrows shot up at the same time.

CHAPTER FORTY-ONE

L ow, dark skies and dampness everywhere—the rainy season had arrived. The cooking pots would be re-filled by afternoon.

Once alarmed by the heavy showers, she'd gotten used to the lunchtime downpour, always followed by clear skies, and made the necessary adjustments to her schedule. Between the rains and her sprained ankle, she'd created a new lifestyle, the perfect one, she told herself.

It was midmorning already when she sat up today, knowing there'd be no swimming. The skies were too gloomy, and it wasn't worth the pain. She limped out-side to find something to eat—a can of sardines with two crackers for Cammy, dry cereal with raisins straight from the box for her.

After breakfast and in full view of the ocean, she started her bath, her *ablutions,* her father used to call it. Standing on her left leg, her right leg resting on its heel, she poured water over herself with a cup, scooping it from the pot she always kept on the porch now. Cammy, well out of the way of splashes, watched as she rubbed down with a soapy rag and finished off with more water, pouring the whole pot over her head, whooping when it tickled her armpits.

When she'd toweled off, she sat on the bed and sectioned her hair with her fingers, the morning fight with the comb ended. Without a mirror, she'd started creating elaborate hairstyles, a new one every day. This morning she braided small sections in the front and back and twisted the sides into thin, swirly locks, using olive oil to soften them.

She was naked again. Sometimes she forgot to put on clothes even when she meant to. The nudity had started after the sprained ankle because it was easier to spend the day naked than to dress, since almost every movement hurt. By the time the pain had subsided, she'd discovered that she liked being naked. It was cooler without clothes and she felt more honest.

The gun had been abandoned, there being no place to carry it, and she'd held a ceremony where she flung it far out to sea. For days before she'd sensed a sheath of protection around her and she'd had a compulsion to get rid of the gun. Part of it was an acceptance of her fate. Death was inevitable, she reasoned, and if it was to be sooner rather than later, so be it. Whether she lived or died, Celeste would be with her.

The new coiffure complete, she wiped her oily hands on her arms and took up her journal, her back to the wall. She'd found joy in writing after the first clumsy weeks, and most of the time now the words flowed out of her pen without effort, had started sounding even poetic to her ears.

Before the sprained ankle she'd written of Jack and about who other than Cameron knew about the affair, and she'd come to the conclusion that they probably all did, the years of secrecy wasted. She described herself and Jack both crying in a bar in Copacabana, drunk on cachaça, and buying asters together in Covent Garden and leaving them in the hotel to fly home on separate flights.

She described his tennis-trim stomach and thinning hair, remembered how his brown eyes softened the last time she'd seen him.

"Take as much time as you need," he said, and smiled. He'd been peeling an apple, winding the skin around and around, trying not to break the skin. "You've been through a rough time. You need a rest, I can see it. Your salary will be paid as usual, don't worry."

"Thanks," she'd said, her eyes fixed on the peel. Confrontations and nastiness weren't allowed for vice presidents.

His drawing away had started soon after they'd, no, *she'd* signed Arlene. And his avoiding her eyes when she'd asked him if he wanted her to work late (their code), his gradual distancing, had been like a slow poison entering her body one day at a time, and she'd refused to think about it, had been in denial because he was busy, really busy with the new account—until she'd seen them, his hand on her thigh.

And when she'd asked, had stared at herself in the restroom mirror before asking, all he'd said was, *Yes, there is Arlene.*

And it was to a meeting with Arlene and her staff that

she was rushing when she'd last seen Celeste, her voice bitter with Jack, in the kitchen chastising Celeste, and it was Arlene's fault that she hadn't kissed her daughter, hadn't held her for the last time. No, not Arlene's fault; Jack's fault for entwining her, this woman, like a serpent, into their lives and the business they'd built.

One evening, with the air suddenly still and mosquitoes darting around, it had dawned on her that every image of Jack in the office was of him surrounded by hovering women—Jacqueline, his assistant; Deborah, the CFO; Annalisa, the head of PR; even Marybelle, the office maid, who made sure his coffee cup was never empty. And she began to see him as a collector of sorts, a collector of women, and she'd cringed to think she'd been one of those who'd hovered.

After she twisted her ankle, the stories about Jack had shriveled up. When she tried to pick up where she'd left off, the vignettes had become nothing more than dots and dashes without connection. His name even began to look like gibberish on the page, strange and unnecessary.

It was then that she'd started reading poetry from a book Dorella had handed her on the way to the airport. It had come after Do had made the mistake of saying:

"Do you want me to clean out her room for you, sweetie?"

When Simone had said nothing, Do had reached under the seat to cover the awkwardness and handed her the book. The introduction said the poet was an ancient Persian.

One day she'd limped to her reading bench with

Cammy and read aloud about love and the Beloved, which she guessed was God or his woman. After reading a few pages, she'd had an urge to write poetry, to see the short lines under her pen and feel them feeding into one another with a hidden meaning. Not knowing how, she'd copied a poem from the book instead.

Dance until you shatter yourself,
Dance, when you're broken open.

She'd seen an egg cracking, the yellow pouring out of the jagged shell.

Dance, as if you've torn the bandage off.
Dance in the middle of the fighting. Dance in your blood.

An image of a woman lying wounded in a pool of blood beside a lonely road. Trying to be rid of the thought, she'd stood and danced a little, reading and dancing in time with the waves hitting the rocks, trying to stay off her ankle.

After that day, Celeste was the only thing left to write about, and the only thoughts that came were about the last day they'd spent together. She had no interest in describing the reality, her ugly words, her regrets. Instead, she focused on different scenarios for how things could have gone that day, changing the ending each time, editing or altering her own words and actions to come out the way they should have. One day she'd written that Celeste had gotten up from the breakfast table and they'd embraced and she'd hugged her tight, counting her skinny ribs like they did when she was little.

Uncapping the pen, she opened to a new page.

Day 43 on The Island
Today Celeste woke up and came into the kitchen.
I kissed her and told her I was calling her father
To say she would not be returning to school.
She'll be transferring to Spelman College, I'd say,
Or Georgia State, or Agnes Scott, as she prefers.
She'll be living at home or in a dorm at the school,
But she won't be returning to Florida, not ever.

The expanding pain in her chest made her stop. She squirmed, knowing that it waxed and waned with her thoughts and was only her daughter remembered. It was a souvenir Celeste had left her, and if need be, she'd live with it for the rest of her life.

The rain was starting and she tucked herself into bed for a nap, the kind she'd known in childhood, the kind she used to have on a Sunday afternoon after church and a big lunch. The sheet had been folded around the mattress like a vertical envelope so she could slide in and leave a flap for air. Her head covered, only her nose sticking out, she listened to the spatters on the tarpaulin, the drops gradually drowning out the waves and wind.

Later she'd go to Celeste, but this she needed to do right now, sink deeply into her mattress chrysalis while the rain did its work cleaning the earth and sea.

CHAPTER FORTY-TWO

E ric sopped seawater on the back of his neck. He would have done this faster if he'd done it alone.

"Want me to row?"

"No, thanks, I need the practice," Cameron said. One oar missed the water again. "I'm getting better, right?"

"Let's just say we're still afloat," Eric said. The water was choppy, anticipating the coming downpour.

Twenty-four hours earlier, Cameron had approached Eric, who was clipping the parking lot hedge, a bandanna tied around his forehead.

"Can you come with me tomorrow?" Cameron had said. "I want to row out to the island."

"She's not ready to get off," Eric answered, and continued clipping, anxious to finish before the rain came.

"I'm nervous about her. She might need something."

"She's fine. Sam took groceries out."

"That was last week," Cameron said. "I just need to make sure she's okay, but I'm not ready to row out on my own." And Eric had agreed.

Halfway out to the island, Cameron was already pouring sweat.

"Get a better grip," Eric said, "and dig in deep."

"At least we're pointed in the right direction," Cameron said.

Eric grunted and looked up at the darkening clouds as the first drops fell. There wasn't any reason for Cameron to keep hanging around. She'd probably told him to stay away. If Cameron would leave it to him, everything would be fine. He'd thought it through already. He'd keep visiting her every couple of weeks, and one day she'd say she was ready to leave the island and he'd bring her back. She could stay in Largo with Miss Mac, just as a transition, and Miss Mac would fatten her up.

A steady rain was falling by the time they pulled onto the beach. Sheltering their heads with their arms, the men splashed through the puddles on the path, Cameron calling Simone's name. They found her asleep in her room—under what looked like an intricate crisscross of sheets—and snoring loudly. The dog eyed them for a minute before laying its head back down, and they left. On the return, gusty winds from the departing shower made the canoe zigzag toward shore.

"Are you satisfied?" Eric said.

"We know she's alive, and that's a good thing."

"She'll get through this."

"From your lips to God's ears," her brother said, skimming the water again and cursing.

After they put the canoe on its logs and were walking back to the bar, Eric patted Cameron on the shoulder.

"She's made a decision, and you know how women are."

"There's got to be a better way to take care of her," Cameron said. He crossed his arms and held tight to the elbows. "We can't lose her too."

"Everybody knows she has a gun." Eric cleared his throat. "We can get her some more protection if you like."

Two days later, Eric and a frowning Cameron were standing at the door to the obeah man's office.

"Mr. Keller, an honor," the Doctor said, shaking Eric's hand with a too-firm grip. "Last time I saw you was when my daughter got married."

"I wouldn't normally—," Eric said, feeling his face redden. "This gentleman—he's the brother of the woman staying on the island—he's a bit worried, you know."

"Come in, come in," the Doctor said, his gold tooth leading the way into the office. Cameron lagged behind and closed the door slowly.

The potion dispensed was in a larger bottle this time, one labeled *Oil of Never-Fear*, and it came with some modern advice.

"Why don't you get her a small dinghy, or at least some flares?" Zachariah said to Eric at the door, while Cameron rummaged in his wallet.

Cameron's head popped up.

"I offered," Eric said with a tight smile, "but she said she didn't want any form of escape."

"And you agreed?" the Doctor said.

Cameron wanted to drive to Ocho Rios then and

there, and Eric, as if told to say ten Hail Marys in penance, offered to drive him.

"You wouldn't know where to go," he said, and they left in the Jeep with enough rope to tie the boat down.

In Ocho Rios they parked next to the local market with its hundreds of rickety, improvised stands. Vendors were displaying clothes, bags, sunglasses—all from China—and yelling at passersby. A strip mall near the market boasted a few shops.

"Do they sell flares?" Cameron said above the racket. He was pointing to a dry-goods store with colorful rolls of fabric leaning against the outside wall.

"No, we're going to the chandlery."

"What's that?"

"Boat supply place," Eric answered.

They threaded their way through the mix of tourists and locals, Eric walking briskly ahead to leave his negligence behind.

At the chandlery, and over Eric's protests, Cameron selected a red fiberglass dinghy, the most expensive in its size. After they'd strapped it down in the Jeep and thrown in a box of flares and a large air horn, Eric turned the Jeep around to head home. Cameron slapped the dashboard.

"You'd done me a lot of favors, I know," he said, "but I have one more. Do you know where the Free Zone is?"

They circled the town to the industrial outskirts on a road that went south through the mountains. Eric pulled over opposite a chain-link fence that surrounded a large compound. The fence, some twelve feet high and topped with twisted barbed wire, ran for a quarter of a mile on either side of a guard house. Three long warehouse buildings were visible within the compound. All were connected by well-paved roads and separated by neat patches of grass. The closest building had a parking lot where several tractor trailers, some with cabs attached and others without, stood before warehouse doors. Two of the doors were open and men on forklifts were filling the backs of the trailers with large crates.

"Pull up to the guard house," Cameron said, and motioned Eric forward.

"Why?"

"I'm doing research."

Eric pulled forward and a uniformed guard came out of the booth.

"I'm looking for Mr. Manheim," Cameron called out.

"He's not here now," the guard said, eyeing the red boat in the rear.

"These are his factories, right?"

"Yes, this is Kentone Industries." The guard started to make a note on his clipboard. "You have an appointment with Mr. Manheim?"

"No, I'll make one. Thanks," Cameron said, and gestured for Eric to back up.

"I thought you didn't know anyone on the island!" Eric said, the Jeep jerking backward onto the road.

"I'll explain later. Let's look around for the nearest bar."

Sharkey's Hideaway was half a mile away. Two men were drinking white rum at a table on the sidewalk, their faces intent on the game between them. From the bar, Cameron brought back a beer for himself and tonic water for Eric, who continued to sit in the truck.

"Ever play dominoes?" Cameron said, opening the car door.

"No," said Eric, "and I don't feel like starting now. We have to get back."

"Fifteen years in Jamaica and you don't play dominoes? It's about time you learned."

Cameron pulled up a chair to watch the men. Eric found a stool and nodded to the barmaid, a woman with breasts like watermelons who smiled at him from inside the bar. The domino players—Jethro and Peter, they said—pointed out their strategy, besting each other at giving the visitors tips.

"Never, never show anything in you face except victory," Peter said.

Jethro placed his last domino flat on his forehead and grinned, the black spaces between his teeth outnumbering the teeth.

"Especially when you got the winning card!" he said, and smacked the domino down on the table to loud laughter.

Cameron glanced at Eric and back at the men. "Deal me in next time."

Eric took a sip. It was going to be a long, dark trip home.

"You better play good." Jethro smiled.

"Don't worry about that," Cameron said. "My daddy taught me well."

After the dominoes were dealt, he cupped them in his palm.

"You guys work in the Free Zone?" he said.

"Used to," Jethro said. He let out a crowing laugh and slammed down the opening domino.

CHAPTER FORTY-THREE

A seagull sat on the verandah wall, throwing back its head in the rising wind, trying to keep its balance. Coaxing Cammy off the bed, she bent down to smooth the sheets, her breasts swinging with her movements. She pleated the corners and tucked them in like Grandma Adina had done, saw the large rear end in the long skirt, the cracked heels in front of her, heard the song her grandmother always sang around the lace-curtained house.

For His eye is on the sparrow,
And I know He watches me.

the granddaughter hummed and then sang.

Under the tree she spooned out cornmeal cooked the day before and fed it to Cammy—Jamaican dog food, according to Sam. Returning to her room, she sat on the bed and replaited her hair, waiting for the rain. Cammy stretched out on the tiles and rested her muzzle on the woman's ankle, a new habit.

Grandma Adina had had a watchdog with a high-pitched bark, a dog that stayed chained to an iron post.

Brutus, hush up you barking, her grandmother would

call. Lucille made up stories about what Brutus would do if you got close. He was going to tear you to pieces and feed them to his mongrel friends at night, she said. No one touched him.

A gust of wind pulled at the tarpaulin above, making the plastic flap against the wires. Gray clouds became grayer and rain spattered the verandah. Too early to nap, so she reached for her journal.

Five pages of scribbles later, the day's work emerged.

Open without fear,
One with sea
One with sky
One with storm—
As God decides.
Surrender and survive,
No more need
No more want
Nothing sought—
As God provides.

A *Third World banana republic,* Cameron called Jamaica, and Shad puzzled over what that meant, at least as it applied to Miss Daphne at the Parish Council, who looked like she'd never walked in a banana field in her whole life.

"What fucking country would let a woman live by herself on an island?" Cameron had shouted. "That's what I want to know!"

Cameron's face had started turning purple. "First, she goes all weird and turns against the family. And now she's gone crazy! I saw her from the boat, walking around stark naked, her hair sticking up on her head!"

Earlier that morning, Cameron had rowed over in Minion's boat, towing the red dinghy behind him. Shad, on his way to work, had seen him weaving toward the island. Half an hour later, Cameron had returned, rowing at a speed, with the dinghy still trailing behind him. He'd run up from the beach to the bar, shouting for Shad, calling Eric a bastard for letting his sister live on the island.

He'd insisted that Shad come with him to Port Antonio, and he'd told Shad to take him to whomever he needed to see about getting help for Simone. At the wheel of the rented car, Cameron had flown down the road (Shad clinging to the door), hurtling around corners, overtaking taxis, leaning into the wheel and the horn.

Their first stop was the Parish Council, where Cameron ran up the old gray steps by twos, and it had taken a panting Shad a minute to catch up with him. Simone was now legally insane, Cameron had declared to Miss Daphne—Shad leaning in for the details—and he needed to take her back home to the States. He needed help getting her off the island.

"It sounds like a police matter to me," Miss Daphne had said, dry as a bone as usual.

"So what do I do?" Cameron's eyes had been huge. "I want to get her into a hospital or something."

"That's for you and the police to work out," the secretary had said, and smoothed back her hair like the case was closed.

Descending the steps of the old building, Cameron had called Jamaica all manner of names, a God-forsaken hellhole, a primitive Third World island, and a banana republic.

Eric came in for a pounding, because he'd allowed Simone to live on the island in the first place. He should have known better, Cameron protested to Shad, who nodded, amazed that Americans could get as vexed at each other as Jamaicans. He let Cameron's words flow in one ear and out the other, because Cameron didn't really know Eric.

And Shad had kept nodding, because Cameron was a man of action who'd thought things through and found a solution, who'd recovered from his confusion and rage when he first came back from the island, when he'd shouted the boss's name for all to hear. Even if the boss had only made things worse by trying to defend himself, protesting that it made sense that the woman walk around naked since she had no reason to dress.

Things only got worse when they went to the police station. The first bad sign was that they had to go around through the Guard Room because of the leaks in the lobby ceiling and flooding from yesterday's downpour. The place was empty, only a junior constable on duty who had no idea where the sergeant was. He'd said he'd be back later in the afternoon. Cameron wrote down the young man's name and badge number.

"It's *urgent*," Cameron insisted, staring down the recruit. "What do you do in emergencies?"

"We haven't come to that in training yet, sir," the recruit said with a shaky smile.

Shad asked for directions to the sergeant's house in Port Antonio. Out in the parking lot, Cameron turned to Shad.

"Do you know how to drive?"

Shad nodded.

"Drive fast, just drive fast," Cameron said, and handed him the keys.

At the wheel of the Mitsubishi, reminding himself it was an automatic and he didn't have to change gears, Shad drove up the narrow mountain road overlooking the port. It twisted and turned, alternating between steep valleys and inclines. At a corner shop, Shad asked a woman leaning against the door where the sergeant lived, and Cameron wrote down the directions.

When they arrived at the bungalow, a dog greeted them, yapping behind an iron gate. Shad knocked on the metal house number with a stone and a maid came out and shouted at the dog to stop.

"Yes, what you want?" she said, her half-Chinese eyes narrow.

"Is the sergeant here? I have an American gentleman who want to see him. It's *urgent,*" Shad said.

"Hold on." The woman went back inside.

Ten minutes later, the dog barking every few seconds, a man emerged from the side of the small verandah. He was wearing a blue chenille bathrobe, his large belly peering out of an undershirt.

"Can this wait?" he said in a deep voice.

"A tourist man need to see you, sir," Shad said, embarrassed for the man in his woman's bathrobe. If he knew Cameron was a foreigner, he might go inside and change.

"We have an emergency situation here," Cameron said, and stepped out of the car. "We need you to take some action. Please."

"What is it?" the man said. A hand reached out of the verandah's shadows and passed the man a banana, which he took and peeled slowly.

"My sister, she's been living on an island by herself, an island off Largo Bay, and she's mentally ill. She was fine when she left America, but now she's not herself. She's walking around naked."

The sergeant looked at Shad, his thick eyebrows twitching.

"She refuses to leave," Cameron tried again, his voice louder and firmer, "but I need to take her back to the States for treatment. I need the police to help me remove her, get her to the hospital and then the airport."

Still at the gate, Shad nodded at the end of Cameron's sentences, affirming the logic of the man's statements. The sergeant munched the banana and looked from Cameron to Shad and back again.

"The Coast Guard," he said at last. "You need the Coast Guard. We don't have any jurisdiction at sea. Go down to the wharf office and ask for Lieutenant"—he pronounced it *left-tenant*—"Archibald. Tell him I sent you."

With that, the man and his banana vanished inside, and the dog started yapping again.

At the Coast Guard, they were ushered into the lieutenant's office, a cubbyhole with a window looking out at the wharf area, no boats in sight. The desk was cluttered with papers, some of them with the letters *US DEA* stamped across them.

"Yes?" Lieutenant Archibald said, his white captain's hat on top of the lampshade making a statement. Cameron, knees jammed against the desk, explained again, slower this time.

His lips squeezed together like he'd just eaten a sour plum, the man listened to every word before answering.

"The first step is to get a medical officer to come with

us," he said. He sounded like the governor-general, slow and serious, with good English. They must have gone to the same school, one of those private boys' schools in Kingston.

"Go to the Port Antonio Hospital. Get a doctor to come on board the boat. If he sees her and declares her incompetent, we can then return with the police and remove her."

"If I get a doctor to come with us, when can we go across?" Cameron asked.

"The earliest is next week. One boat is on dry dock, and the other is at sea on drug patrol duty."

Shad leaned forward. "If I can get a boat, can we go earlier?"

"No, we have to do it in our boat. Otherwise, it could be construed as kidnapping."

Shad thanked the lieutenant and led Cameron out by the elbow. He knew where the hospital was. If Job hadn't come home already, he could have visited him at the same time.

CHAPTER FORTY-FIVE

His head was down, the blade of the knife cutting at the solid mass of ice in time with the music, a sweet dance-hall piece by Shaggy, his favorite singer.

He had to prep the bar early, before going with Cameron to the hospital again to find a doctor. When they went yesterday, there'd been only two medical residents in the whole place. Neither knew what to do, and a matron had told them they needed a fully qualified doctor to certify Simone as crazy.

Forbidden Fruit drifted between Shad and the ice, and he spun around.

"LaSharee, you frighten me!" Shad said, and put down the knife. "What bring you here?"

"Just passing by." She dropped her pocketbook onto the counter, the gold vinyl like a pot of gold in the sunlight.

"It's hot, eh?" she said under the new brown wig.

Shad opened a Red Stripe and placed it in front of her. "First time you come since you get back. I never see you in here before."

LaSharee took a sip and put the bottle back on the coaster.

"I know you don't come just because you hot," Shad said.

She picked up the napkin he'd placed beside the beer and fanned herself a couple of times. "I didn't want to go to your house, disturb your wife and everything."

Shad started chipping at the ice again, half turned away from her. "Good idea, she not easy."

"I wouldn't want her to know how you leave me in Largo, don't write me a word, and show up four years later with her and a pickney."

"You right, she don't need to know." He turned around, his stomach signaling early distress. "That's fourteen, fifteen years ago, anyway. Plenty water under bridge."

"At least you could say you sorry," she said, and puckered her lips for another sip.

"You right. I owe you an apology. You want to know what happen? I was an ignorant young boy, went to Port Antonio, and got into trouble, because I wanted money quick. Four stupid, bad years. The only good thing was that Beth was there for me." His gaze drifted to her purse, the strap unraveled on one end.

"You right to be vex, I treated you bad. But you disappear right after we came anyway, so I couldn't explain. I'm sorry."

"I didn't come for that, but I glad for the apology." She drained the bottle. "I have a favor to ask you."

"Talk to me."

"Tiger back in town. I see him late last night."

Shad ran his hand over his head and squinted. "The two of you made up?"

227

"No, he just come to pick up the rest of his things."

"What he doing back?"

"He have *business* to do here," she said.

"What kind of business?"

She shrugged. "He say he get paid every week."

"Get paid to do what?"

"I dunno. Probably some funny business."

"He still around?"

"He gone by his mother's. Say he have to do something tonight."

"Like what?"

"Something big, he say." She drained the bottle. "I want him back, you hear? Get him out of whatever—that's the favor—but I want him clean and straight, ready to settle down, have a family. It's the least you can do." She slung the bag over her shoulder and walked out, her pink sneakers making not a sound.

Cameron was leaning on the Mitsubishi outside of Miss Mac's when Shad approached.

"You're late. We have to catch the first doctor we find."

"I had a customer."

On the road to Port Antonio, Shad turned off the air conditioner and opened the window.

"I got some news. Tiger is back in town."

"The guy who tried to rape Simone?" Cameron glared at Shad.

"Watch out!" Shad called. Cameron swung around a small girl walking on the side of the road.

Shad leaned back and exhaled. "We don't know if they were going to rape her."

"Can we get him arrested?"

Shad raised his arm above the window and let air into his shirt sleeve. "No proof," he said. "Your sister couldn't identify the men, and he and Sharpie would deny everything."

"Why is he back? Is he still working for Manheim?"

"Yes. Doing what, I don't know."

"Maybe it's drugs," Cameron said.

"Whatever it is, he going to do something important tonight, though."

"Like what, I wonder?" Cameron frowned at the canoes bobbing in Manchioneal Bay.

"Something for this Man-O-War guy, probably," Shad said.

Cameron slapped his knee. "Oh, my God, I forgot to tell you, with everything going on. Peter, this man in Ocho Rios that I met, used to work for Manheim. He said that Manheim has connections with the government. He said that Manheim is a big shot with the 'right-side party' in America—I guess he meant the Republicans. When Obama won and the party lost, he and some partners bought Kentone Industries. That makes sense, since the government here is conservative. They must have made it easy for Manheim to set up shop in the Free Zone."

"He probably bribed somebody, you mean."

Cameron's eyes grew bigger. "Maybe, but guess what the workers call him?"

"Man-O-War," said Shad.

"You got it."

Shad hit the doorframe. "So he doing the government a favor in Portland and Largo Bay, making sure they win. And if Dollar is involved, is dirty business he doing."

"That's how it's sounding." Cameron made a noise as if he was trying to suck his teeth. "But why Largo? That's what I want to know."

"People in Largo not going to vote for the party next time, and Portland is the prime minister's seat. The People's National Movement can't afford to lose any part of the parish, even little Largo—but it not looking good for them. Too much neglect, too many complaints about corruption. The Jamaica Workers Party moving in and is going to be a fight."

"I don't understand how Tiger comes into this, though. Why would they need him?"

"Could be some connection between Manheim and drugs," said Shad.

"But what would a small-timer like Tiger do for him?"

"Maybe move ganja to the factory, to ship out in the clothes containers. That would make a good cover."

Shad narrowed his eyes at the pickup in front, loaded with worn tires. "But something don't feel right with that. Tiger chats too much to trust him with something like that."

"What would he do, then?" Cameron slowed down behind the smoking pickup.

"I think it have something to do with the party, dirty party work."

"Damn!" Cameron said, and rolled up his window

against the pickup's fumes. "I'd heard about the corruption."

"Is how they work things here, sad but true," Shad said.

"But what would Tiger be doing tonight? He couldn't even . . . do anything to Simone."

"And people in Largo still laughing at him."

Shad pictured Tiger and Sharpie over a ganja spliff, cooking up another stupid scheme. He rolled up the window and turned on the air.

"Before people take him seriously—," Shad said.

"You thinking what I'm thinking?" Cameron said. He gripped the steering wheel and leaned forward.

"The hospital can wait," Shad said.

CHAPTER FORTY-SIX

The moon so close I can touch it, but won't,
Not needing to tarnish perfection.
Who dreams and creates a perfect moon?
Makes tiny hands and feet in sets of perfect tens?
There's power in knowing, power I should have owned,
But never thought to experience,
Choosing only what I touched and owned,
Wanting what I couldn't have, not seeing what I had.
The only power that matters now is opening to truth,
Finding perfection in imperfection,
Seeing the gifts behind the veil, finding She
Who makes me wise and whole, the God who forgives.

She closed the journal and blew out the lamp beside her bed. Cammy jumped up and wagged her tail. The ocean before them reflected the moonlight broken to small pieces of glitter on its surface. There was no breeze tonight.

Soon it would be over. She could feel it in her bones, as Grandma Adina used to say.

CHAPTER FORTY-SEVEN

The beach under the full moon looked like a Broadway scene where two lovers were to meet in secret, the sea a silvery prop in the background. Standing beside the boat at the water's edge, Eric looked around at the outlines of coconut trees behind him. The fishermen had gone out already, all except Minion, asleep in his bed after renting him the boat for the price of a good catch.

"She's gone crazy!" Cameron had yelled two mornings before. The normally cool eyes of the man had opened wide, exposing the whites, making him look mad himself. And Eric, unwilling to see her ruined and weak, had waited, thinking that maybe Cameron was right, and he'd . . . enabled her, whatever the word was, wanted to make love to her while she was going through a mental breakdown, and probably wanted her even more because of it.

Shad and Cameron came hurrying toward him, talking in low voices.

"What's this all about?" Eric asked, relief dropping his shoulders.

"Long story," Cameron said, and turned over the red dinghy, lavender in the moonlight. He threw a coil of rope into the dinghy and started dragging the little boat toward the water's edge.

"Something going down with Tiger tonight," Shad said. "We thought we should—"

It was at that moment that Eric Keller saw something he'd never forget. A barefoot man walked out of the shadows carrying a burlap bag and a long, striped staff. His cape and turban shimmered white in the moonlight against his silver-black skin, and under his protruding eyebrows, his eyes had disappeared into deep shadows. Two white stripes were painted on each cheek, one across his forehead, and dots of white ran down his nose.

"Holy Mother!" Eric muttered.

"A little insurance," Shad said at Eric's elbow.

Without greeting the men, the obeah man tossed the sack into Minion's boat and placed the stick on the bottom. He tied the ends of his cape in a knot at his waist and, familiar with boats and fishing in the dark, started pushing off the canoe. Eric joined him, pushing the boat out to knee-high water. They climbed in from opposite sides, balancing for each other.

Behind them, Shad and Cameron climbed into the red dinghy and Shad took the oars.

Minutes later, his heart pounding, Eric ran the canoe onto the eastern beach of the island. Zachariah stood up with his bag and stick. He swung overboard, the snake ring glittering platinum for a second. Shad and Cameron pulled up next to Eric and climbed out of the dinghy, Cameron holding the coil of rope.

At the top of the cliff, the Doctor untied the knotted cape from his waist and looked at Eric, who pointed toward the almond tree. With light enough to see every stone and rain puddle in their path, the men walked in single file. The daytime sounds—the breeze, the almond leaves, the barking of the dog—were gone, replaced by the sea-silence of water at low tide. In the blackness under the tree, they paused for a minute. Zachariah pointed to the old dining room. A dark form behind the wall was moving, lowering onto the ground.

The men approached the roofless building and crouched inside the window. Beside them, Jennifer's mural was barely visible under the love-bush vine and its heart-shaped shadows. From the village came the howl of a dog calling to the moon.

Fifty feet in front of the men, moonlight painted the woman's back like a sculpture in a museum garden, spine curved and head bowed. Her thin arms were wrapped around her knees like a dream. She was sitting on a folded cloth, a towel perhaps, on rocks above the water's edge. Behind her sat the dog, ears erect, staring at them in silence.

"What do we do now?" Eric whispered to Shad.

"You and the doc stay here. We going to keep watch."

"And then what?"

"Don't leave her," Cameron hissed.

Zachariah, intent on the woman, said nothing, and Cameron and Shad crept away.

Simone turned and knelt sideways to them. Moonlight bathed her erect torso, her face, her legs, her breasts. Eric flicked his hair back and lowered his eyes, raising them in time to see her reaching inside a small mound of rocks. Weak yellow candlelight fluttered over her hands as she withdrew a vase—the one she kept beside her bed. She placed it on the ground and touched the lid.

They could hear her talking, too softly at first to make out the words, but loud enough to hear half-whining syllables and chuckles. The sounds of a woman gone mad, cracked, like Aunt Betsy, his father's sister, who'd walked around their house singing and turning pictures to face the wall.

Words drifted in, phrases clear, not clear, soft laughter creating commas in between.

"—as though he'd seen a ghost, C—stood up in the boat—almost turned it over . . ."

The Doctor opened the bag. A goat-skin drum appeared on the floor, then a statue about two feet tall, a man's head on one end, the torso covered with beads and bones.

"—never leave you—," she was saying.

The Doctor stood and untied his cape, which he draped over Eric's shoulders. Then he unwound the turban with his long fingers, slowly revealing a round, bald skull. His only garments now were a pair of black briefs and a dozen necklaces, some with large pouches, others strung with teeth and seeds.

Moving a few inches away, Eric held on to the window ledge and breathed into his clamped lungs, willing himself to stay calm. In front of his white knuckles was an insane naked woman, beside him a witch doctor. He suppressed a laugh, thinking of Father Bradley, the collar always too tight at his neck, the Shaker Heights exorcist.

Picking up the drum and the statue, the striped stick already under his arm, Brother Zachariah rounded the wall and stepped into the open. He started speaking in a low voice, strange, guttural words. Cammy stared, paying homage behind her mistress's back.

Simone stood up and raised her arms to the side, her feet and ankles gold in the candlelight, her body silver. She spoke louder and stronger, and even with her back to them, every word was clear.

"God of the Ocean, the Earth, and the Skies," she called, "I come to you with all humility, asking you to protect my daughter, Celeste."

Zachariah shoved the flat end of the sculpture into the soft earth in front of the window. He started tapping one finger on the drum, like rain dripping from a roof.

"Mother God, Father God, I celebrate the love of my child and her love for me," Simone continued, "and I ask you to bless her and keep her safe forever."

Zachariah kept tapping, now shuffling forward. Moonlight radiated off the man's skull in a halo of white.

"Lord, have mercy," Eric whispered, making the sign of the cross—the altar boy's response. The drumming got louder, two fingers, larger raindrops.

Simone's entreaty stopped. She stood motionless, her head tipped to one side, listening. She turned in slow motion, arms extended, a crucifix against the glittering ocean.

Shuffling in time with the pulsing drum, the obeah man approached the woman, Cammy quivering between them.

CHAPTER FORTY-EIGHT

Drumming, in my head, then behind me.
When I turned, he was there,
Naked like me,
A snake under his arm, and the drum.
It was time, the drum said,
Speaking to my heart,
Beating, beating.
He had come for her.
Go, I said, releasing her, it's time to go,
And she escaped among the splinters,
Plunging down
Into the sea, into a new home,
Among clumps of ash.
A cloud of dust lingered
Near my hands,
And left with the wind.

CHAPTER FORTY-NINE

Cameron walked toward the bed in the dark corner, made darker by the bright slash of moonlight on the verandah. Shad stayed at the doorway, his gaze rotating between the lobby and the exterior, the bushes frozen in blue light. He adjusted the cloth-wrapped knife in the waistband of his shorts.

"They're not here," he said. "Let we check the beach again."

They should stay together in twos, he'd told Cameron earlier, because Tiger was too lame to come alone. They'd need as many men as they could muster, men who could keep their mouths shut. Eric and Zachariah were the only candidates.

"Do we have to take the obeah man?" Cameron had asked.

"Of course," Shad had said, and that was that.

They'd sent Elijah to run up the hill. Shad had pictured the boy, his little chest heaving like his used to, standing in the obeah man's office, hopping from one foot to the other, asking him to meet the men at midnight on the beach.

While Shad worked behind the bar, Cameron had cruised the two bars close to the square. He'd ordered a beer at both, played dominoes at one, but got no further information about Tiger or his activities. At eleven o'clock on the dot, Shad had closed the bar and sent Janet and Tri home early. Then he'd woken Eric and told him to get dressed.

"Meet me and Cameron on the beach with Minion's boat," Shad had said. "I made the arrangements already. He's waiting for you."

"What's wrong?"

"Just need you to come," Shad had answered. And he'd come. That was the boss, a man you could rely on most of the time.

On the eastern side of the island, Shad and Cameron stood on the cliff looking down. The two boats they'd just rowed over sat parallel in the sand. The long canoe looked old and primitive next to the new plastic dinghy from America.

A breeze had sprung up from the south, a land breeze, rippling the top of the water. Cameron sat on the coil of rope, and Shad looked south toward the village.

"I hear a noise!" he said.

"Where?" Cameron said, and jumped to his feet.

"There." Shad pointed in the direction of a hum, the murmur of a boat engine.

"Could be a fisherman," he said.

"Is it coming from the village?"

"Sounds so."

"Over there," Cameron said.

A boat was bobbing toward them. In the bright moonlight they could make out its zigzag course, probably steered by Tiger pointing the tiller at the island, forgetting the current's pull. He'd never gone fishing, Tiger, had never had an uncle to teach him how to steer a boat or set a lobster basket. So he'd sat under the big cotton tree talking foolishness, selling cigarettes and weed, an easy target for the likes of Sharpie.

The boat drifted south of the island, heading for the western beach—near Simone's room.

Running, stumbling in unseen ruts, Shad and Cameron dashed across the island and skirted the old guest rooms. Above the beach, they squatted down behind a bush on a palm leaf. The sound of the engine got louder.

"What's that?" Cameron whispered.

"What?"

"That smell."

Shad sniffed. "Oh, God, we found her shit hole." He laughed, a quick *hee-hee* behind his hand.

Below them the boat engine cut off and the boat slid onto the sand. Someone jumped over the side of the boat, followed by another splash and wading sounds.

"Where you put the gun?" a rough voice said.

"In my pocket. What you expect?" It was Tiger's voice, high and defensive.

Cameron grabbed Shad's arm and handed him the end of the rope. Shad scooted across the path on all fours. He crouched behind a bush, the rope slack between them.

Voices grumbled upward. "Only because I don't have a pocket, I letting you carry it, you know," the other man said, irritated already. "Not like last time with the bone, you hear?"

"Stop talking about that. We big-time now."

"I going in front. I don't trust you."

Grunts and groans followed. The top of a man's head emerged, followed by a hand grasping the cliff edge. A fat man pulled up and sat on the edge, his breath rasping, and put out his hand for the other, leaner and quicker than the first. Tiger's basketball shirt gleamed in the moonlight.

"Where you think she keep the money?" Sharpie said, brushing sand from his feet.

"Must be wherever she sleeping. She pay big rent every month to the American man, I tell you. She have plenty money, man."

"Come, let we do it, then."

His palms sweating on the rope, Shad stopped breathing as the intruders started forward.

When they'd made a few steps, Cameron shouted, "Pull!"

What happened, Shad told Beth the next day, was in black and white, like an old-time movie at the Rialto. Sharpie and then Tiger went tumbling forward over the rope, arms flailing. Sharpie made a loud thud when he fell to the ground.

"What the *blood claat*!" he yelled.

Sharpie lay still for the second it took Cameron and Shad to wrap the rope around his legs. Tiger jumped up looking dazed. Shad grabbed Sharpie's sweat suit by the arms so Cameron could sit on his back. They tied the fat wrists together while Sharpie cursed nonstop.

243

"Leave him! Let him go!" Tiger skipped backward and fumbled in his right shorts pocket.

Shad jumped at Tiger.

"Me and you, man!" Shad said, his voice coarse and unfamiliar. He held on to Tiger's hand and dragged him to his knees.

"Get the fuck away from me! What you want with me?" Tiger said, trying to shake off his attacker. "Shad?! What you want with me?"

Shad hung on to Tiger's hand and shoulders. "I know what you come to do, you worthless good-for-nothing."

Tiger reached into his pocket and Shad wrestled him to the ground.

"Who these idiots?" a kicking Sharpie called to Tiger.

"The woman's brother, that's who!" Cameron sang out, riding Sharpie's back like a bucking bronco.

Shad and Tiger rolled on the ground. Tiger wrapped his legs around Shad and faced him.

"Get the gun, Tiger! Get the *rass claat* gun!" Sharpie shouted.

"You're going to have to shoot me on top of him, because I'm not coming off!" Cameron yelled.

"I know what you trying to do," Shad said. He got one arm around Tiger and yanked him back to the ground.

"You don't know nothing," Tiger said. He rolled over and pulled the gun out of his pocket, his left arm across Shad's throat.

"You not going to find her," Shad growled. The knife was pushing into his groin. "She have protection."

"What you mean 'protection'?" Tiger pushed himself up, pointing the gun at Shad's head.

"Just shoot him!" Sharpie shouted.

"What kind of protection?" Tiger said, his eyes bugging out.

"You'll see." Shad turned his head toward the almond tree and away from the black gun, shaking in Tiger's hand.

Still staring at Shad, Tiger shouted to Cameron. "Untie him!"

"You wasting your time," Cameron shouted back. "I'm not getting off him—even if you shoot Shad!"

"The Lord is my shepherd—," Shad said to the tree.

"Shoot him, you idiot!" Sharpie yelled. Shad closed his eyes. If anything happened, Beth would give him a good funeral. White lilies, she knew already, like at his grandmother's funeral.

Tiger yanked on Shad's arm. "Get up, get up!"

On his knees, Shad brushed the dirt from his shorts.

Tiger waved him to his feet with the gun. "Take me to the woman." He sucked his teeth loud and long. "You going to be my protection tonight, star."

Shad glanced toward the old dining room and started walking.

"You leaving me here?" Sharpie called behind them.

They walked along the cracked old road the buses used to drive up loaded with tourists. Rounding the guest rooms, Shad stepped onto the pavement, the gun a tumor growing out of his back, the knife a dead weight in his side.

CHAPTER FIFTY

Brother put the drum back in the bag. He was as cool as a cucumber, cleaning off the spade end of the statue with the burlap, plopping it into the bag. As if nothing had happened. He handed a plastic bowl to Eric, gestured with his thumb to Simone, and started toward the boat, the stick under his arm. The dog trotted after him, wagging her tail. When the man stopped and frowned, the dog returned to the woman and sat watching her.

Retching once, twice, three times, Simone sat slumped over, her face buried in her knees, the hair a fluff ball on top. Eric rounded the wall, skirting what looked now like eggshells the Doctor had scattered, and stepped down onto the shelf where she sat.

He held out the white cape, blocking his view of her nakedness. He placed the robe over her, front to back, trying not to touch her too much. Easing down to the ground beside her, clumsy with pain in his knees, he put an arm around her shoulders. She recoiled with huge eyes, then surrendered and leaned into him with a howl, her hair surprisingly soft against his chin.

She cried with a vengeance, like damned-up water rushing through a sluice, his mother would have said. Nothing held back. And as she cried, he holding her close but not too close, a cut somewhere under the cape seeping blood and the candle dying in the grotto, Eric felt the tickle of tears behind his eyes.

His own crying surprised him. But if there was ever a time to cry, this was it, and after a few minutes he gave himself permission to let it rip. So the two friends sat in what was left of the moonlight. Her tears were violent, her body vibrating with loud wails, water pouring from her eyes, her nose, her mouth, and his soft, running down the gullies between his nose and cheeks, dripping off his chin.

Later, when he tried to remember the last time he'd cried, he couldn't remember, but he must have needed a good cry because it had felt like a purge. He'd probably started crying for Simone, thinking of the Christmases ahead of her without photographs. Or maybe the tears were for his wretched parenting—as pathetic as his father's—and his own living children far away.

And under it all he was crying for his dead hotel, the child he had birthed, for the Orchid Bar, where he hung the orchids he'd found in the Blue Mountains, for the kitchen, with its industrial stoves and copper pots hanging from the ceiling, for the staff's jokes and the New Year's Eve parties, and for the garden, with its circular driveway and the fountain with koi fish.

The moon had already started its descent when the woman's wails were reduced to sobs, and then to whimpers. Making sure the cape covered everything he was not supposed to see, Eric fed her the rum-smelling drink in the plastic bowl, using the lid to catch the drips. She made a face at each sip. Afterward she laid her head back with her eyes closed, little spasms quivering through her every few minutes. Her weight on his arm felt good, her small boniness and his roundness needing each other.

Drained and content, cheeks tight with salt, Eric looked up. Almost above him were the Hunter Orion and his Belt—his father's favorite constellation. Then he heard the gunshot.

CHAPTER FIFTY-ONE

The island looked like a cemetery, a dead place with jagged tombstone bushes. The barrel of the gun was still warm from Tiger's pocket.

The Lord is my shepherd, I shall not want—

Yea, the valley of the shadow of death . . .

The Lord is my shepherd—

The words tumbled around in Shad's head, moved his lips.

"Where de woman?" Tiger said behind him. "Where she sleep?"

Shad pointed to the lobby and Tiger signaled him to go in.

Stepping into the darkness inside the lobby, Tiger skipped to one side.

"Wake her up!" he said. Shad walked over to the bed. Tiger came alongside and sucked his teeth.

"*Rawtid.* She gone! Why you didn't tell me?" He hit Shad's arm with his free hand. "Take me to her, man!"

Back outside, Shad pointed toward the walls of the dining room.

"Why you didn't tell me in the first place? Just wasting a man's fucking time."

They resumed their patrol, this time toward the shadowy tree. Shad stepped over something. Behind him, Tiger tripped and grabbed Shad's shoulder, and they both looked down. A brown sculpture lay face up, scowling at them.

"What the *bumba claat*?" Tiger said.

When they straightened, a dark, naked figure stepped out from behind the tree. Shad would have said it was the devil if he hadn't known better. The white paint on the man's face jumped out at them as he came forward.

"Jesus Christ!" Tiger grabbed Shad's shoulder and ducked behind him. "What that?"

Zachariah raised both arms, his stick in one hand.

"De obeah man!" Tiger screeched. "And he have a snake in he hand!"

Tiger threw an arm around Shad's neck and started shuffling backward, Shad stumbling, opening and closing his mouth. Zachariah kept walking toward them. He reached into his necklaces, muttering and throwing small objects, animal teeth they looked like. He was saying words Shad had never heard before, rough words that sounded like wildness.

The staff high in the air, the Doctor stopped and called:

"Oludamare, Father of all divinity, heal this man."

Tiger froze, his fingernails digging into the shoulder of Shad's shirt.

"Is the obeah man?" he whispered. Without waiting

for Shad to answer, he released him and turned to run, looking back over his shoulder.

It was like he'd seen it before, Shad told Beth, like something you think you know already, Tiger tripping over the ugly sculpture. Even the gun flying out of Tiger's hand he'd seen before.

Zachariah, his dotted nostrils flaring, walked past Shad, leaving a musty trail behind him. He stood over Tiger, who was curled up like a baby, his eyes shut tight. Shad swore to Beth that the Doc had light coming out of his whole body, even coming out of the staff, and that he sounded like Pastor McClelen when he was receiving sinners at the altar, when he threw his head back and shouted:

"Olofi, hold this man's heart in your hands.

"Make him see the evil he brings to this town.

"Cleanse him of his iniquitous ways."

Across Tiger's chest and down his body, Zachariah scattered something flaky, ashes it looked like.

"Fly away, Evil One, fly away from the Myal." He circled the scrunched-up Tiger, shuffling his feet, grunting more strange words.

When the obeah man was gone, Tiger lay whimpering on the ground. Shad edged over to the gun and picked it up.

"Stay there! Don't get up!" he said. The gun fit perfectly in the hollow of his hand.

Tiger raised his hands, palms up, his eyes still squeezed shut.

"Why you come over here?" Shad snarled at Tiger.

Tiger was silent and Shad repeated the question, louder this time.

Tiger opened one eye. "I looking for the woman."

"What you want with her?"

"I not telling you nothing." The skinny man pushed up and stretched out one hand to Shad. "Give me back me gun. Sharpie give it to me."

"You really a fool." Shad sucked his teeth. "You don't see I holding the gun and you on the ground?"

"You not going to shoot, I know you. You too soft!"

"Oh, no?" Shad said. He pointed the gun at Tiger's chest and released the safety catch.

Tiger jumped to his feet. "Don't shoot! Don't shoot! It loaded!"

"Tell me, then! Why you come—with a loaded gun?"

"Sharpie say if we going to work for Man-O-War, we must prove weself first to the village. People still laughing at us since the first time, when she chase us off the island."

"So you were working for Man-O-War the first time you come out here too?"

"No, no. That was just fun we was looking, little action, you know? We working for him now, though. He looking strong man who can run things, like me and Sharpie."

"You a real clown!" Shad said. "You going to rape a woman to prove you a man?"

"Not going to rape her, just give her little company, give her little sex."

"That called rape, fool."

"Sharpie say if we can handle the woman—we wasn't going to hurt her, you know—we would show people that we in charge."

"In charge of what? What you doing for Manheim?" Shad said.

"I don't know 'bout no Manheim," Tiger said.

"Man-O-War, whatever."

"Sharpie working for him about a year now, he say. Man-O-War even pay his rent. But he don't tell me yet what Man-O-War want me to do. He was to tell me after we done with the woman. But he pay good, Shad, real good!"

"Pay good, eh? You tell your mother about your fancy job that pay so good? You don't think she will shame when she find out you try to rape the woman out here, not once, but twice? The poor woman already ashamed of you. She have to hide you and the new engine in her house."

"Just lemme go." Tiger turned and called over his shoulder. "You can keep the gun."

"Stop, I going shoot," Shad shouted. "So help me, God!" Tiger started running.

Shad pulled the trigger, aiming above the man's head into the darkness. The gun jerked against his palm, the roar filling his ears.

Tiger dropped to his knees, his back to Shad. "Don't kill me, don't kill me!"

A dark brown spot spread across the seat of the shiny basketball shorts.

Shad frowned behind Tiger. "What dat on the back of your pants, boy? You shit yourself?"

Tiger half turned, forehead puckered, and Shad laughed. "You a true coward, you know that?"

He walked up close behind Tiger, his voice hard, his palm itching. "You think you a man now? You hear a gun fire and you shit your pants?"

Shad circled Tiger and faced him. The gun was steady in his hand.

"You know what they say on TV? Don't do the crime if you can't pay the time. Suppose you went to prison, boy? You don't even know what it like in prison. You know what it feel like? It feel like sitting in shit for a whole day, a whole night. Just how you feel now, that how it feel every day of every year you in there. And like how you so skinny and coward, they bound to rape you, grab you crotch and haul you down to the ground, you hear me? And stick you from behind! Slam you up against a wall when you turn a corner, and pull down your pants. Open your asshole and jam you! You know the shame you carry around with you after that, big man?"

A whimper escaped from Tiger. "You not going to send me to prison, right, Shad?"

"Why not? You a criminal!"

"No, Shad, no. Please." Tiger was crying now, the tears squeezing out the corners of his eyes.

Shad smiled and rubbed the nozzle of the gun in Tiger's little beard. "On one condition."

Tiger sniffed. "What dat? What you want me to do?"

"Two things. I want you to go back to LaSharee."

"I can do dat."

"And you have to turn bartender."

"Bartender?"

"You deaf or what? That what I said. Didn't you tell me you want to learn to be a bartender?"

Tiger got to his feet, wiping the tears from his cheeks. "That don't pay big money, Shad."

"You decide. Kingston Pen and living in shit—or bartender. Which you want?"

"Who going to teach me?"

"I, same one. I will teach you. And if you learn, you can work at a big hotel in Port Antonio. Good tips."

"It hard? Bartending?"

"A nice job. You keep your hands clean and you meet a lot of people."

Tiger shrugged. His shirt slipped from his shoulder. Shad pulled up the fallen sleeve and patted it, sticking the gun between Tiger's ribs.

"And, by the way, I have a cousin who a sergeant in Port Antonio. If you even dream of changing you mind, you gone straight to the Pen, you hear me?"

CHAPTER FIFTY-TWO

The moon gone, Zachariah was a bundle of darkness sleeping in the stern, the stick reptilian beside him. Eric pushed off and started rowing, and the Doctor lifted himself onto a seat.

"Where Shad and Tiger? And the other man, the brother?" His voice was smooth and soft, not that of a man who'd just woken up.

"They're on the beach. I'm going back for them."

"Want me to row?"

"I got it. Stay where you are."

There was time, between the dipping and the pulling, the bottom of the canoe smelling of old rope, to tell him as much as Shad had time to tell him after he'd tiptoed out of Simone's room. Cameron had argued for taking her back to Largo.

"She needs more time," Eric had countered.

"But we—she could—suppose she hurts herself?"

"Leave her alone. She's going to be fine." Eric had stood with firm legs, his back to her doorway.

When he'd held her after the gunshot, calmed her and

himself with soft words, he'd felt closer to her than he'd ever felt to a human being, had felt the opening—and knew it was shared with her—to whatever life brought, had known it was possible to cut the albatross of grief from the string around your neck and wait for the new to appear. If she needed to be alone to do that, like she'd whispered before she fell asleep, she'd earned it.

They left the red dinghy pulled up high on the rocks with the oars in the bottom, to be discovered tomorrow or the next day. The Oil of Never-Fear she'd see next to her bed in the morning.

Eric pulled on the oars and looked at the silhouette that was Zachariah, the dots already fading from his face. "I want to ask you something, though."

"Speak your mind."

"Why didn't the dog bark?"

"A dog don't bite the hand that feed it." The little mutt, an obeah dog.

"What happened to her in the first place?"

"Grief—it awaken her. She never knew who she was before. The shock bring her back to her true animal spirit."

Zachariah pointed to his solar plexus, the middle of his darkness. "She had to go down to the bottom to find her true-true spirit."

The man's voice had a smile in it. "And she did it alone. You hardly ever see that. She a strong woman, hard to protect."

"Then why did you come? Why did you smash the

urn?" Eric said, his voice turning sharp. "You saw how she snatched it up, tried to protect it from you. It was all she had left!" She would want to know one day.

"She was holding on to the child's spirit. The child was trapped, and she need to move on."

Eric pulled harder.

"What's that sculpture thing you brought, that wooden statue?"

"A *boccio,* for protection. It come from Nigeria, but I got it in New York."

Zachariah striding down 125th in a sharp white suit. He'd probably worn alligator shoes and sunglasses.

"I learn the art from my grandfather in Trelawny," Zachariah said. "He practice me and then send me to school in America."

"You went to college?" said Eric, who'd never even thought of going to college.

The man rested his head on his fist, the ring now muted in the darkness. "What so strange about that?"

"Nothing. What did you study?"

"Psychology," Zachariah said, and smiled, his tooth winking.

"And you don't owe me nothing," he answered into Eric's silence. "The village needed it, so I do it for all of we, for myself too."

In the predawn darkness, a glimmer of light on the horizon, the man leaned over the edge of the canoe, making it tip a little.

"That's my job, you know," Zachariah said. "Your job

is to bring people together. My job is to keep them in balance."

He took a handful of salt water and rinsed his mouth. When he spat, it sounded like a dart hitting a bull's-eye.

"Everybody need a little balancing now and again," he said as the canoe straightened.

CHAPTER FIFTY-THREE

A four-day hangover drooped over her, dimming the midmorning brightness. On her lap was Cammy, motionless, pretending to sleep.

With one hand she brushed the dog's side and with the other she turned to the poem she'd written the day before. She read aloud in a flat voice.

Naked on a slab in the morgue,
Slender face cracked like an egg,
Black hair matted with dried blood.
She had found the fruitless path,
Following in her mother's footsteps,
Looking for love in all the wrong places.
Standing there, I knew I had killed her
The frozen words a knife still in her heart.
No visible wounds, no open casket to remind
Of guilt so heavy I threw it to my mother,
A woman whose path was steep and rough,
Who did whatever it took to make ours smooth.
So now I have to claim this millstone,

Knowing it was I who never said I love you.
I who never danced in the rain with her daughter.

Without warning, without sound, one dolphin, then two, leaped out of the water a couple hundred yards in front of her. She narrowed her eyes and waited, the patting hand in midair, and yes, here they came again, arching up into the air and sliding down into the water. They were playing, jumping for the joy of it.

She stood slowly, fearing that sudden movement would stop the show. She waited to see which one would break first out of the water. The one farther away it was, followed by the other. They glistened, their silver backs streaked with blue and gold. Stunning in thoughtless beauty, loving the ocean, celebrating life, making her heart leap. Joy, sheer joy, nothing more.

If Celeste had been here, she'd have laughed and said, *I told you so.* She'd have said again, *I'm coming back as a dolphin, Mom.*

Far out to sea the dolphins disappeared and she fell to her knees.

CHAPTER FIFTY-FOUR

"And before you pour the beer, tilt the glass, so. You see what I mean? You pour the beer halfway, easy like, and then straighten the glass up and put a head on it." Shad took another bottle from the fridge and placed it on the counter.

"What kind of head?" Tiger said, touching his neck and the absent gold chain.

"The foam on the beer, that's what they call it. You want about two inches on top the beer. Try now."

"Like this?" Tiger snapped the top off the bottle. He brought the glass up to eye level and shrugged his shoulders. When he finished, he had a half-inch head.

"Pshaw, man. I never thought it so hard," he said, twisting his mouth.

"Next time, don't worry. It get better with practice."

Shad looked at his watch. "You can take your break now. Carry this into the kitchen and share it with Solomon. And when you done, I need you to count the beer bottles and soft drinks in the closet behind the kitchen. Ask Solomon to show you where. I come to check you in ten minutes."

Tiger strolled off with his hip-hop walk. On the bar counter Shad assembled the ingredients he needed: vodka, tonic, lime. And bitters, don't forget the Angostura bitters. He reached up to the shelf for the small brown bottle and glanced at his watch again. Three minutes to eleven. They were expected in Port Antonio at half past.

It had been harder than he'd imagined, setting the whole thing up. There'd been Cameron to be talked into making phone calls from Miss Mac's bedside phone, and Tri standing next to the pink tufted bedspread giving instructions about what to say, and disappointment all around when they couldn't make contact and there was no return call for a while.

"Somebody named Myers here?" a voice said. The man had appeared like a thief.

"Donovan Bailey." The handshake across the counter was strong, the politician's hand bony.

"Shadrack Myers. Call me Shad."

"I remember you from when we came last time." Behind him, a dusty Toyota SUV waited in the parking lot, a driver in front.

"The message Tri left said it was 'urgent'?"

Shad grinned. "Gin—sorry, vodka and tonic, with bitters. Right?"

"You remembered." The man's Adam's apple rose and fell as he slid onto a stool.

While he cut the lime into eighth-inch slices, measured the vodka and then the tonic over three cubes of ice, and added the bitters, Shad recounted the recent events with Sharpie and Tiger on the island.

"What does that have to do with me?" the politician said.

"Plenty, sir." Shad placed the glass on a coaster in front of the man. "It turn out that they working for a man name Man-O-War. Ever heard of him?"

Bailey took a sip. "Who's that? Sounds like a ghetto don."

"You ever hear of Milton Manheim?"

"Of course. The American with the big factories in the Free Zone."

"What else you know about him?"

"He doesn't pay a scrap of taxes for ten years, and the contract that the government signed allows him to get an extension on that deal when the time comes. All he has to do is hire cheap Jamaican labor." Bailey scratched his chin. "My gut tells me someone got paid off along the way."

"But you didn't know they call him Man-O-War?"

"Man-O-War?" The minister frowned and pulled in his chin. "That's the kind of name you only get when you play with criminals."

"Some of the people who work for him give him the name."

Bailey's frown went deeper into his forehead. "What kind of people? Is he dealing drugs?"

"We not sure what going on, but it smell like a fish and it look like a fish, so it must be fishy." A little smile escaped as Shad settled on his stool. "Okay. First thing is that his chauffeur is an ex-criminal, a man who always up to something shady. I know the man a long time now, and I never know him to go straight. And he don't do any small-time business either. He used to work for Barry Segal, the man who ran the horseracing racket they shut down eighteen years ago, remember?"

Shad leaned over the bar and lowered his voice. "Anyway, this guy used to twist a man's arm, and worse, when he wouldn't pay Segal his money. Now he's working for Manheim, hanging around Largo, asking people to tell him how the town going to vote. He paid a couple of guys, one of them a real tough man, and gave them a gun."

Bailey put down his drink and rubbed his neck. The Adam's apple bobbed up and down.

"There's only one thing other than drugs they would be doing for Manheim." The man was talking to himself now. "Makes sense. He's a conservative, everybody knows that, lockstep with this government, and he's afraid that if we get in, we'd make him pay up, or find out about a bribe."

He looked hard at Shad. "How you know they working for Manheim?"

"One of the men told me. He called him Man-O-War, but is one and the same."

"The government must be providing the guns." Bailey stroked his cheek, digging his fingers in deep. "Can you prove it?"

"Sure, I can prove it." Shad looked toward Miss Mac's. "I have a partner coming soon. He'll give you the full score."

It was after a second vodka-tonic that Shad, Cameron,

and the former minister arrived, driven by Bailey's chauffeur, at the old police station in Port Antonio. Sergeant Neville Myers was waiting for them. Minutes later the group circled the building single file. In front of a large wooden door, they wiped their feet on the grating. The lock on the door was a new computer dial pad, looking American.

"We just holding him until you tell us what to charge, you know," the hefty sergeant said, and looked hard at Shad, the once-errant cousin. "We can't keep him here forever. Two weeks maximum before the judge have to see him."

Bailey spoke up while the policeman coded in a number, his broad back blocking their view. "By the end of this visit, Sarge, you'll have your answer, don't worry."

The stench of urine and sweat hit them as soon as the door swung open. Cameron took a handkerchief out of his pocket and covered his nose.

"Breathe deep and quick," Shad said at his shoulder. "You get used to the smell after that."

A corporal with one stripe on his epaulet sat behind a grill in the lobby, his feet on the desk. From a radio on the desk came the voice of a woman talk-show host.

"The country don't need any more teachers," the woman was saying. "We full of teachers. What we need is better teachers."

The young man jumped up to open the gate leading to four cells. A pair of hands hung from a crossbar of the last cell.

"You have visitors, Sharpie," the sergeant called, stopping at the first cell. "Big man from Kingston."

The corporal leaned into the cell's lock and turned the key with a grating sound. At the end of the corridor, a gruff voice called out:

"My turn now! Come open me up, nuh?"

In Sharpie's cell, a barred window high on the opposite wall cut through the gloom. There was space for only two men, Myers and Bailey, to stand beside the mattress where Sharpie lay. Outside, Cameron glanced down at the open gutter that ran alongside and Shad held on to the bars and peered down at Sharpie, the steel cold on his cheeks. The feel of the bars too familiar, he rubbed his arms with a sudden chill.

"You look like you disappointed, Sharpie," Neville said. "Who was you expecting, boy?" His thick black belt extending well in front of him, Neville laughed with a deep *ho-ho*, a kind of Santa Claus laugh. He spread his legs, the toes of his shiny black boots hitting the mattress. He was born to be a police, Granny used to say, even though Aunt Jasmine wanted him to be a preacher. He'd even changed his name from Ezekiel to Neville because it sounded more like a police.

"Sharpie? That your name?" the former minister said. Sharpie pushed up on one arm. The deep folds under his eyes seemed deeper since Shad had last seen him. His prison uniform was stained and stinking already, the man whose sweat suits were always dry-cleaned.

"I hear you working for Manheim," Bailey said. His Adam's apple jerked up and slowly descended.

"I dunno what you talking about. You have the wrong man." Sharpie tried and failed to grasp his ankles. He left his arms loose in his lap and stared at the mattress.

"Man-O-War? You never heard of him?" Bailey said.

Sour silence from Sharpie.

The talk-show host on the radio pierced the silence. "Where are the best of our teachers? Gone to America, that's where!"

"I also hear you attempted to rape a woman," the politician said, and crossed his arms, "not once but twice. We have witnesses who ready to speak up now. Serious business that."

Cameron sneezed into his handkerchief, and everyone's head swung toward him, including Sharpie's, who narrowed his eyes. Shad stifled a smile.

The politician cleared his throat. "Armed assault the second time, I hear. With an unlicensed firearm."

Shad held on to the bars again. "I see you and Dollar-Bill together, and he working for Manheim, and we know you and Dollar working for Manheim." He had to ask. "Where you know Dollar from?"

Sharpie kept staring at the mattress, his lips crooking into a small smile. "Same place you know him—Kingston Pen."

All eyes turned to Shad, who shrank back, the bars suddenly hot.

Bailey jumped in. "How many years we looking at this time, Sarge?"

"With his record? Ten to fifteen years, Penitentiary again."

"—the authors of our own destruction," the radio woman was saying.

"You want to get out, boy?" Neville said. "This your chance."

His jaw clenched, an angry beggar on a sidewalk, Sharpie looked up and blinked in the dim light.

CHAPTER FIFTY-FIVE

Two heads bobbed above the water, the dog's small head bobbing twice as fast as the woman's. She raised one arm and waved, shouted something, but the groaning and splashing of the oars drowned her out. He pulled harder to reach her, then glided up leaning on his oars. Hugging the dog, she reached up for the side of the canoe and hung on, and he wanted to touch her fingernails, short and wet.

"I have a bone to pick with you," she said, frowning. Her lips quivered but she held the corners down. The swimsuit bubbled around her like a giant jellyfish, and drops of water sparkled in her locks.

"Come pick all you want," Eric said. She released the dog and started stroking toward the shore alongside the canoe.

He climbed the cliff ahead of her, saving her embarrassment about the baggy suit.

"Wait here," she said when they got to the tree, and she went to her room holding the suit up with both hands.

Eric sat down beside the coal pot. His legs wouldn't

cross, so he hugged them, the knees high in the air. Whether she liked it or not, he was staying, he would last her out. Five days he'd waited for some sign that she needed him, and nothing had come. He'd be doing his accounts at the table and look up, hoping to see her standing on the point waving. And every afternoon he'd walked down to the beach to check if the red dinghy was still on the eastern beach, and it was. Last night on his verandah, scrutinizing the shadows in front of him, he'd decided to come across with no excuse.

Emerging from her room she tripped on the edge of the step and caught herself, the dog glancing up at her. She was wearing an orange and blue sarong tied above her breasts, the fabric billowing in the wind. On her head she'd tied a towel into a turban. He stayed where he was and hugged his legs harder.

"I feel like a total idiot, you know that, don't you?" she said when she got closer. Her eyes looked hard, almost like that first day.

The words came spitting out. "You brought that man out here—I was naked as a damn baby! I was—in the middle of—something very private."

She paced around in the shade of the tree, holding the sarong down with one arm and throwing out the other. "How do you think I felt, Eric? You saw me naked, and the—this total stranger saw me naked."

"I need to—," he started. There'd be no mention of seeing her naked before.

She held up her hand. "Let me finish."

Stopping abruptly, she turned, eyes flashing. "You

should have told me you were coming out. You invaded my privacy. This is my—you had no right to bring him here."

Rocking to give himself momentum, Eric uncurled and brushed off the back of his shorts. "Let me—"

She shook her finger at him. "And you were peeping from behind the wall, watching, like . . . a fucking voyeur! Don't think I didn't see you!"

The breeze whipped hair over his face. "We were trying—"

"Trying to do what? I know I said I wanted to meet him, but not like that. Bringing him at midnight, dancing and drumming away like a crazy man? He scared me shitless." She hugged her arms. "And he broke the urn, Eric. He broke her urn. I was going to do it myself."

Her voice dropped almost to a whisper, and she sat down on the rock under the tree. "It was time for her to go, I know, but it happened so suddenly. I hadn't expected it."

"I'm sorry, I didn't know what to expect either."

"Why did you bring him anyway?" she said, her eyes filling with tears.

"We heard that Tiger and Sharpie, the same two men who'd come before, might be coming back. This time they were coming to prove a point. We wanted to protect you."

"That was a strange way to protect me. The men didn't even come, and this crazy man almost frightens me to death, that snake under his arm and everything."

"It was just a stick."

"It looked like a snake from where I was." She patted the dog's side. "Cammy didn't bark, like we were both hypnotized."

"And the two men did try to get at you again."

"They did?" she said, her head snapping up, the hand to the throat.

"I'm telling you." He took a step toward her. "They came up on the beach behind your room. Cameron and Shad took care of them."

"Cameron and Shad were here too?" She raised her eyebrows under the loosening turban.

"They weren't with us, so they didn't see anything, don't worry. But the men have been taken care of—one is in prison and the other is in a training program. They won't bother you again."

"Thank God," she said. "Or maybe I should thank you."

Standing, she unwound the turban, unleashing the hair beneath it. "I'm glad you stayed with me afterward."

"I wouldn't have left you."

She made a sharp sound, something between a laugh and a choke, and looked away. "I don't know if I've ever heard that from a man, from anyone, before."

"I don't know if I've ever said that to anyone before," he said.

His feet were rooted to the fine pebbles under them, his arms folded, fingers gripping elbows. Maybe it had been too many years to take one more chance. Too many years to face another disappointed woman and say, *This isn't working.*

She came closer and put one hand on his shoulder, the other holding the towel. The remnants of tears sat on her eyelashes.

"Thank you," she said. She tiptoed and kissed him on the cheek.

He held her arm and kissed her back. Her cheek felt soft and he was glad he'd shaved.

"You're welcome."

She stood close to him, the towel between them.

"Would you like something to drink?"

"Like water?"

"No, like a real drink." She threw the towel onto the rock and delved into a box. "I have some rum somewhere."

The wind wrapped her sarong around her legs, and he wanted to pull it loose. The last time he'd touched her, he'd been holding her hand beside the bed and her hold had slackened. He'd felt her slipping into sleep, and he'd wanted to crawl into the bed and kiss her awake, but he'd let her go away to wherever she had to. He'd listened to the sleeping breath coming from her and the dog, and, his back aching, he'd pushed up with only a soft groan and took one look before leaving.

She held out the drink, no ice. "Would you like to drink it in my room?"

"Why not?" He was blushing—the blush spreading up his cheeks.

"So—how have you been?" he asked after they stepped into the lobby.

"In a vacuum, I think." She folded the sarong around her. "I don't seem able to do much of anything. I sleep a lot, but I'm not really tired, and I have these dreams, dreams about animals."

She sat down and patted the mattress. The dog jumped up and Simone sent her to the foot of the bed, where she turned in a circle before lying down and staring out to sea.

"You probably need some downtime, whatever that means." He eased down to the spot she'd patted and stretched his legs out. His knees looked old and scaly.

"You want to know if I'm staying, don't you?" she said.

"No, I don't. When you're ready to leave—"

"I'm waiting for a sign, but no one's told me what to look for."

"Take your time." He made a slurping noise with his rum and wished he hadn't.

"Time is all I have left, I suppose," she said with a short laugh.

He glanced at her and looked away, at the view he loved. "I'll miss you when you go." At the end of the verandah the water was choppy and dark blue.

"Hurricane season coming," he said, placing his empty glass on the floor.

"I know."

"Just wanted to remind you, in case—"

"I'm a big girl, Eric." She put down her glass and leaned into him. Her eyes moved up to his eyebrows and down to his mouth.

He reached up and pulled her toward him, the hair springy in the palm of his hand. Her warm rum breath came to him first, followed by quick, strong kisses.

"I have—wanted you—so—so—much," he said.

The liquor warm in his belly, he pulled her down to the mattress.

She smoothed back his hair and kissed him. The knot of the sarong stabbed his chest.

"I know," she said.

"I didn't want to—I was afraid of you."

He untied the sarong clumsily, and she had to help. When he finished she lay beside him, a bronze stamen in the middle of the fabric's bright petals. He pulled her toward him and ran his hands down her back, remembering moonlight on a curved spine.

"I'm sorry he broke the urn," he whispered, and kissed her shoulder.

"It was time."

He waited for her tears and then her breathing to calm, stroking her back. Then he kissed her again and she arched up to him. He ran his fingers down her arm and down her hip and kissed her other shoulder.

"And I have to get on with my life," she said. She hooked her fingers around the waist of his shorts and pulled down.

When she took his penis in her hand, he caught his breath and let out a moan that covered the years since a woman had stroked him like that. He nuzzled down to her breast and sucked the nipple hard, then gently, while she laid her head back on the pillow. Slipping his hand down, he ran his fingers back and forth through the curls of the pubic hair he'd stroked in his mind for weeks. He kissed her neck and pushed his fingers down farther to touch her wet folds.

When he touched her, opened and pressed, slid his fingers in and out, she groaned, her eyes closed. She threw one leg over his. Their space was filled with musty vagina smell.

Thanking God, he eased down into the petals of orange and blue.

CHAPTER FIFTY-SIX

B eth slipped her hand through his, the way he liked when they were in church.

"Prepare the way of the Lord," Pastor McClelen sang out, his wiry little body jerking with each syllable.

"Hallelujah!" shouted Sister Arida.

"Make his paths straight. And every valley shall be filled, and every mountain and hill shall be made low."

Miss Louise jumped up and raised one arm high. "And the crooked shall be made straight. Amen, amen, brother."

"The rough ways will be made smooth." Pastor ran a hand over his pomaded head. "You hear that? The *rough* ways will be made smooth."

Pastor paused, the way he always did before he got to the point. "And all flesh, yes, brothers and sistahs, *all* flesh, yours and mine, shall see the salvation of God." The handkerchief would be coming out next.

At Shad's elbow, Elijah wriggled his shoulders in the new suit. Next to him sat Cameron, sweating despite the overhead fan, starting at the outbursts from the congregation.

Pastor lowered his voice. "Prepare for your salvation, brothers and sistahs." Out came the handkerchief.

"Or for your damnation." He wiped his sinewy face, wiped it again.

Shad glanced out the open window at the gathering clouds. Sharpie had been in the Pen with Dollar, and with him. He remembered him now, one of Dollar's lackeys, another one that Dollar had protected, because nobody liked Sharpie, and there were a couple of guys who would have stabbed him for five dollars. He'd kept to himself and had this sour look on his face all the time, like he'd been beaten so much as a child that he hated the world. He'd worked in the laundry, not speaking to anybody, making sure Dollar had clean uniforms every day. But he was thinner then and didn't wear a gold chain.

Pastor's voice called out to the beams in the ceiling, willing them to rise up and float out of the room. "Are you ready? Are you ready, brothers and sistahs, for *eternal life*?"

Yes, thought Shad. But not right now.

"Are you ready? Are you *ready*?"

"Yes, yes," Louise shouted. Pastor sat down and the choir started a low moan, the segue into the hymn they always sang after the sermon and before the collection.

"My God and I, we've been through hills and valleys,
"My God and I, we've seen the battle won."

Shad squeezed Beth's hand. By this time next year they'd be married, the first married people in either of their families as long as anyone could remember. It would only be right in God's eyes, Pastor had said. When they'd watched a woman on *The Young and the Restless* walk down the aisle, Beth's eyes had lit up. She was going to make a new dress like that for her wedding, she'd said, a white one with no straps.

The reception would have to be in the bar, because the whole village would be there. The older half knew him from baby days, when they used to take care of him if his grandmother had the ague. The younger half he knew from school days. Then there was Beth's aunt and uncle and cousins coming from Port Antonio. They couldn't invite the Doctor, though, since Pastor would be performing the ceremony. Pastor had said once in a sermon that there were "agents of the devil" living right here in town, and he'd rolled his eyes up to the hills where Zachariah lived. Everybody had nodded, knowing that Pastor's wife had gone to the Doctor when she lost her last baby.

As soon as he stepped out of the church door, Cameron opened his shirt another button.

"Sorry I was late, man," Cameron said, and looked down at Elijah. "Miss Mac had to take up his suit. I enjoyed it, though, more energy than I've ever seen in a church. Leaves you feeling high."

"It's good for the boy," Shad said. He patted the sleeping baby's back.

"It is. He needs more of that." Elijah pulled free of Cameron's hand and dashed after Rickia, who'd walked ahead with the other children. Cameron looked down at his empty hand. "I'm going to miss him."

"I'll look out for him when you go," Beth said. "We'll take him on Sundays, now that he have a suit and shoes."

"Thanks," Cameron said. "I need to get going soon, just waiting to hear from Simone. Has Eric said anything? I saw him rowing out there a couple times."

"He hasn't been around much."

"Damn." Cameron rubbed his head. "I have to talk to him."

"What happen with Sharpie? You hear anything?" Shad said.

"Bailey called this morning to say he's holding a press conference tomorrow."

"Press conference?" Shad said. Words with wings, sounding like Kingston and power.

"It's a meeting where you invite the press, the newspapers and TV, like that. The people who call the meeting make a big announcement and the media publicize it."

"He must be going to announce about Manheim."

"Manheim's in trouble, man, big trouble." Cameron shook his head. "Sharpie as good as sealed his fate."

"There is a God," Shad called up to the skies, opening his mouth wide. Joshua woke from his nap and started crying. Shad handed him to Beth.

"But Sharpie in trouble with the PNM, not true?" Beth said, hushing the baby.

"He going to be running for a while," Shad said. "Teach him a lesson." At least he'd go to another town, wear a new sweat suit.

Beth clucked her tongue. "A man like Sharpie never learn."

"He going have a tough life, then," said Shad. He turned to Cameron.

"I come over to Miss Mac's tomorrow night, so we can watch the seven o'clock news." He'd put Solomon behind the bar, and Maisie to watch Solomon.

"How is Tiger doing?"

"Terrible. I was bad at first too, couldn't remember vodka from gin," Shad said, and laughed with a whinny at the end.

"You're doing all right now, though," Cameron said. "Life has turned out good for you."

"Thank God, and I turn teacher now," Shad said. "I love it."

"And tour guide, don't forget. We still taking that drive into the mountains tomorrow, visit one of the Blue Mountain coffee estates?" Cameron said.

"Yes, man, the earlier the better. They say it's going to rain in the afternoon, and I have to go to work at three." Beth called to the children and they turned down the lane to their house.

"I'll come for you at eight," Cameron said. Elijah ran after Rickia and gave her a slap on the arm.

"Last lick." The boy laughed and ran back to Cameron.

"See you in the morning." Shad waved. "Eight o'clock."

CHAPTER FIFTY-SEVEN

In my dream I'm dead. I've just died and my old friends can't see me, but I can see them.

I am in a new body that bruises easily and I'm learning how to take care of it. I'm learning to stay away from sharp objects and rough walls.

I want to buy a gift for a man who is still alive in a human body, so I go to a store where people like me, dead people, buy or get gifts for living people. The store has many rooms but it's entirely natural, with streams and plants and fish, like an indoor jungle. It's enclosed like a store but is a magical place, full of running water and trees. I love it here.

I choose a bright green, neon-green, frog and hold it flat between my hands.

In a room at the end there's a place where they package the gifts. I give my frog to a man behind the counter. He takes it and nods. He knows what to do with it.

CHAPTER FIFTY-EIGHT

Holding the necklace he'd picked out, still uncertain if she'd like the colors, Eric approached the cashier. The woman was talking to a customer, her voice high and excited.

"—and they said it was expected to hit us at six—"

"What's going to hit?" Eric said.

"The storm. It was going to skirt the South Coast, but it turned north all of a sudden. It's heading for us and getting stronger. I'm going to lock up."

Throwing down the cash without waiting for change, Eric ran to the Jeep. He roared out of Ocho Rios east along the coast. His car radio was dead. The sea was getting rough and the sky was darkening. Simone wouldn't be able to get to shore.

Rain accompanied by a clap of thunder started at Annotto Bay, just as he was crossing the stone bridge. People were dashing to and from grocery stores, preparing for days without water or lights. A woman screamed from the sidewalk a second after lightning lit up the sky.

With heavier rain in Buff Bay, the Jeep's wipers started scraping and sticking. Eric rolled down his side window and stuck his head out. Water stung his face and neck. He slowed down only for corners, or when he thought there were corners.

"Hang on, I'm coming," he shouted into the rain.

By the time he pulled into Largo two hours later, the storm had hit. Lightning flashed every few minutes. Houses and shops were shut tight, a few with plywood boards nailed at odd angles across windows. Banana plants and sugar cane in backyards were bending to the point of breaking, and small tree branches lay across the road.

The bar was empty, chairs and tables on their sides, some swept against the wall of his apartment. Rain blew in from the open sides, but the new roof was holding. Eric glanced toward his apartment. His louver windows were open as usual and his bed would be soaked.

Outside the concrete house of Tiger's mother, Eric leaned on the horn. After a few minutes and two more honks, Miss Armstrong opened her door a crack. Eric turned off the Jeep and jumped out. If Shad was right, this was the answer.

"I want to rent your boat," he shouted above the wind, "and the new engine. I have to go over to the island—the woman."

Miss Armstrong nodded slowly, shook her head at the money he held out. She pointed to the hen house on the side.

The new engine sat ready in the shed, covered with clear plastic. Eric lifted it off the wooden stand, hoisted it onto his shoulder—stooping low with the weight—and headed for the boat. Down on the beach, the rain slashed horizontally in the driving wind. The surf was crashing higher than usual, almost reaching the few canoes that the fishermen hadn't dragged home. He put the engine on the sand and turned over the green plexiglass boat. Just as he lifted the engine onto the stern, a wave surged around him and started pulling the light boat as it retreated.

"God, help me," Eric cried out. The engine slid down the stern into the water. He held on tight to the engine, hooked his arm inside the stern of the boat, and looked around for help. The water was winning, pulling him and the boat out. Trying to plant his feet in the sand against the pull, he looked up again. A man was running toward him, blurry in the deluge, holding a jacket over his head.

"Here," Cameron shouted when he got closer. He grabbed the engine while Eric held on to the boat.

Five minutes later, they were under way. The water was kicking up, surprised by the storm, anxious to be part of the action. Cameron bailed water with a plastic bottle tied to the side. Eric, at the tiller, measured the height of the waves. Four feet up, four feet down. Five feet up, five feet down.

"If we turn over, just hang on to the boat," he yelled. Cameron held on tight to the side, his eyes like saucers.

The powerful motor kept driving them forward, undaunted by the air it sucked in on the peaks, biting again in the troughs. A shock of thunder in their ears, then lightning, a couple of miles out to sea. The current was pushing them sideways and he had to keep correcting. For a half hour that felt like hours, Eric held fast to the tiller, his grip never released. His eyes stayed glued to the island, misty in the rain.

When they arrived on the eastern side of the island, the beach had disappeared. Waves smashed against the bottom of the cliff. Eric steered north, keeping his hair out of his face with one arm, staying parallel to the shore.

On the northern side, he pulled up to a lower shelf with a small mound of rocks. Kneeling in the bottom of the boat, the engine on neutral, he made a loop with a line and threw it over the rocks. It missed. Cameron threw it again and it caught. He leaped out and secured the boat with a second line, and Eric shut off the engine and clambered out and onto the shelf where she'd stood like a crucifix, the mound of rocks once the altar with her daughter's ashes.

Pressing into the gale, the men rounded the dining room wall. The almond tree had lost half its leaves already, the big branches swirling and bending overhead while they splashed through the water beneath.

Inside Simone's room, everything above—the tarp, the ropes and wires—had vanished and rain poured in unhindered. A jumble of furniture had been blown into the corner where she slept. Her mattress stood upright, flattened against the wall by the wind.

Water was gushing from the lobby into the dark corridor like a ghetto gully. Cameron started wading down the hallway, holding on to the walls for balance, Eric in tow.

"Simone, Simone," they both shouted. Wind whistled

through the doorways, and rain blew in from the open-sided rooms on the windward side.

They found her in a room halfway down the corridor, sitting on top of a shelf with the shivering dog under her arm. A wavy smile across her face, she held out the other hand.

"I'm ready," she called. "Let's go."

CHAPTER FIFTY-NINE

Only a week on solid ground and the hermit, the gypsy, the
     nomad,
is at rest, surrounded by the settled, the curious, the others.
My little Cammy is gone. She disappeared after the storm,
     somewhere between the boat and the boardinghouse, and
     I miss her.
Now an old goat with a beard stares at me (a Capricorn, to
     boot) when I sit on the porch writing.
He wonders where I came from, and I wonder where he's
     going.
I once read that goats have unusual eyes with rectangular
     pupils, not round,
and the circumference of what they see is twice more than
     humans.
We have something in common, with our narrowed eyes and
     square pupils.
I too see the world differently, see the superficial now for what
     it is.
The watershed was the storm and its horror. I was terrified
     when it hit and ran with Cammy to a room usually filled
     with bats. The bats were gone.

I remembered my passport and journal, and went back to get
them, holding on to the damp walls to keep from being
blown over.

I got to my mattress, dug in my suitcase, and found the
documents, my wallet, my keys, wrapped them in the
white cloth Eric had covered me with.

Above me, the tarp was singing, but it was holding, and in
front of me, the rain was catapulting down, spray blowing
in, wind pinning me to my seat.

In the midst of the chaos, I knew I would be safe, knew what
to expect. Nothing would happen to me and I could stay,
should stay.

There was no fear, just gray beauty in front of me, the power
of the water and the wind. Inside, where once I had pain, I
felt nothing but peace.

My body began to blur with everything around me. There were
no boundaries. I became part of the storm: I was the rain,
I was the wind.

We were all moving energy, one energy, the wind and rain
faster, swirling around a slower, tranquil center, all in
perfect harmony.

Throughout the frenzy I felt awe and wholeness in the face of
power so vast

I could never recapture it. And I knew it was her last time.

It was her farewell gift to me—the gift of inner peace I never
had and she

was born with. I thanked her, blessed her, and said my good-
bye.

Cammy brought me back, barking, warning me that rain was
pouring in.

The tarp had pulled away from the walls, the floor was
    underwater.
I crawled to the corridor, up to my elbows in water, Cammy
    leaping ahead.
Behind me, an uproar, the zinging of wires slashing the walls!
When I heard Cameron's voice and saw him standing drenched
    at the door,
my heart almost stood still with love and gratitude.
The sea was rough and green on the trip back, the men a bit
    green themselves. Cammy was soaking wet, her heart
    beating fast against my chest.
Now I sleep in a real bed, and am fed June plum juice and
    chicken soup with dumplings by Cameron's landlady, now
    my landlady, I suppose.
She says the braying sound comes from doves, mourning doves
    she calls them, and that they mourn the dead and comfort
    those who mourn.
I remember now lying enfolded by soft sheets, early coolness
    seeping through
open windows, listening to soft coos signaling daylight and
    school.
So many childhood memories refreshed, made flesh at last, the
    wholeness
settling me—sounds, smells, tastes, people, feeling like
    home.
Eric bridges America (all that I have been) with the present,
    represents
things left behind, and of being neither one thing nor another.
He fidgets when he visits, afraid to let anyone know we've
    been lovers,

asks about my health and diet, invites me to his birthday party.

He presented me with a necklace with strange purple-green-
blue colors

that remind me of the little fish I threw back into the water.

I have no expectations of Eric, a distant man who lives on the
culture's edge,

Who approaches love as a dilettante would, with fear of
complication.

And I, a Capricorn, will take a long time to heal, to walk the
paths of love,

And I, finally healing, discover that love is nothing if not
complicated,

And love him only with gratitude, a blossoming love without
tendrils.

Cameron has been babying me. He makes sure I eat well and
take a tonic.

I love him deeply and tell him often, but not enough to
embarrass him.

A little boy named Elijah peeps in on me but says not a word.
Cameron is adopting him. His uncle is a drunkard and
happy to get rid of him.

As the Sufi poet said, If destiny comes to help you, love will
come to meet you. Cameron's destiny is this boy's life.
Mine was my daughter's death.

Through her death I have found my own life, her gift to me,
and am reborn.

She has made me proud, a girl who knew how to love and
loved me.

She has shown me the way, through her red door, the door
that I will enter

to learn what I need to teach others how to love, before it's too
late.

And now I find myself filled with purpose for the first in a long,
long time.

No more adapting to the dreams of others, no more the
chameleon.

Another chance at life and, like my little fish, alive and
iridescent.

CHAPTER SIXTY

The party was under way. Elijah had been dispatched to invite half the village—some repairing roofs and others clearing branches—to tell them to come tomorrow, because it was Mistah Eric's birthday, even if the power wasn't back yet. It had taken a while for the boy to return to collect his dollar, walking around the mud puddles in the car park, his blue and white sneakers still spotless.

The bar had been mopped clean, the parking lot swept, and Maisie's cake tested for freshness. Shad stuck his head in the kitchen door. Solomon was placing garlands of red and green pepper slices around the sandwiches, his little finger extended.

"Nearly ready with the food?" Shad shouted above the generator. "The guests coming in."

Casey, Jennifer's daughter, holding her little brother Wayne, appeared under Shad. "You don't need balloons to make a good party, right?" Wayne wiggled to the floor.

"This is a grown-up party, no balloons this time," Shad said.

When you got to be sixty-five, you didn't want balloons. And the guests weren't coming to see the boss anyway. They were coming to see the woman. It had been the best way to get the village to come out for Eric's birthday, telling a few strategic people that she was coming. Everyone wanted to see what she looked like, what a woman who was brazen enough to live on the island alone would look like. Was she big and masculine? Were her eyes wild? Her mind would definitely have changed, they'd been saying. Two months alone and she wouldn't be the same. A man might make it, but not a woman.

Shad set the glasses on the bar counter, bringing them down from the shelf in twos because they were the good glasses with the stems. The chairs, borrowed from Holy Sepulcher Baptist Church, had already been arranged, the old bar stools and chairs a pile of sticks behind the building.

A dozen children had already arrived, Shad's four and Elijah among them. The boys wore clean white shirts and shorts. The girls wore pink and blue dresses with lacy collars and hems. They sat around a table holding their drinks in paper cups, giggling and shoving each other. More children were running toward the bar. Elijah had invited every child in the village, it looked like, impressing them with his new status.

Fishermen stood in groups around the tables, downing their Red Stripes and talking about the storm's damage to their houses and boats. At the big round table near the bar, Jennifer and Lambert sat chatting with Beth, who was bouncing Josh on one knee. The orange dress Beth had been sewing for the last two nights reflected off her shoulder blades and matched her new earrings. It had been a long time since she'd worn lipstick, and her lips were shining—straight into Shad's groin.

Cameron walked in, shorts and shirt stiffly starched, Miss Mac's laundry style. He was carrying a newspaper under his arm.

"Is she coming?" Shad called to him.

"She's coming." Cameron said.

"How's she doing?" Jennifer asked, little Wayne tugging at her arm.

"Her appetite is back. The doctor said she just needs rest."

Eric appeared, bathed and shaved. Every silver strand had been pulled back tight in a ponytail and he was wearing a new peach shirt still creased from the package.

"You didn't invite Tiger, right?" he said, settling on Shad's stool.

"No, boss."

Cameron walked over to the bar and held out his hand to Eric. "Happy birthday, man."

He threw the newspaper down on the counter. "Did you see this, Shad?"

Shad leaned over the paper, making out a few words in the headline.

"'American mill—,'" he started. The word looked long and oppressive.

"'—millionaire controls election,'" Eric finished. There was a picture of Manheim leaving his home, caught by surprise by the photographer. He wore a suit, a handsome man, thin and tall with gray hair slicked back, looking like he'd never apologized for anything he'd ever done.

"Oh, sweet Jesus," Shad said, hitting his forehead. "I forgot about the—"

"—press conference!" Cameron clapped his hands and they all laughed.

Eric picked up the paper and, retrieving his glasses from the top of the fridge, started reading the article about Bailey's announcement. The former minister had stated at the press conference that he had evidence, based on a confession to police, that Milton Manheim of Kentone Industries and "some of his employees" were hiring men to influence the voting in North Coast parishes, including Portland. Shad winced inside thinking of Dollar—the man who had saved him, the man he'd betrayed—and what vengeance he would be planning. He wasn't a man to forgive and forget.

"According to new information from a reliable source," Eric continued under raised eyebrows, "the governor-general will be convening an independent panel to investigate the relationship between Manheim and the government, any contracts signed between them, and the PNM's possible corruption of the electoral process."

Eric looked up at the two men and took off his glasses. "Looks like you turned things around, guys."

Shad and Cameron high-fived, grins all around.

"I tell you, though," said Cameron, shaking his head, "I was worried that Sharpie wouldn't cough up the information. He had that tough-guy face on, like you'd have to burn him at the stake to get him to say anything. But once he heard about going back to the Pen—boy, that was the trick!" Cameron threw his arm up high, the fraternity brand peeping out, and his voice rang out like a preacher's. "He started singing like a bird, and I knew we were home free. And when he admitted that Dollar had recruited him last year to *persuade* Portland—"

"I like how he call himself a *persuader.*" Shad laughed. "I must try that one at home!"

"I guess that's the new name for a political thug," said Eric. He smoothed back his hair and looked around, probably checking on Simone's arrival, not wanting to ask.

"The PNM has a lot of explaining to do," said Cameron. "It might just be the tipping point to sink them in the election."

"And Manheim's in big trouble," added Shad. "He bound to leave the island."

"Damn straight." Cameron grinned. "It's time for a celebration, right?"

"One beer coming up," Shad said. He might even have a drink himself later, his stomach felt so good.

"It's been a crazy week, man," Cameron said. "And, oh, my God, that boat ride . . ." He gave a mock shiver. "In a ninety-mile-an-hour wind!"

"Reminded me of—," Eric said, and broke off. "That's the last time I go out in a storm, I promise you."

"Sorry I couldn't go with you," Shad said. He pushed the newspaper aside and placed the beer on the counter. "I had to help Beth board up the windows." He'd show her the article later and they could read it together.

In front of them, Joella was spinning a little girl in circles, the child's hair clattering with multicolored clips. Three others vied to be next.

Cameron took a sip of his beer. There was a small cut on the back of his hand. "We would have come back earlier, but—"

"Shad told me," Eric said. "A landslide."

His eyes boyish, growing larger, Cameron repeated the tale.

"You should have seen us, man. I'm driving down the mountain and we see these clouds coming. Then the rain starts, like it's slamming into the side of the car. I'm skidding and slipping all over the place. I don't know how we didn't go over the cliff. When we're almost at the bottom"—he paused, his hands in the air—"we turn this corner and, oh, my God, we see this landslide, must have just happened. Then we have to turn back and find another road down, about three miles back."

"Shad's version was in Technicolor," Eric said, laughing and glancing at Shad.

The radio sprang to life in the middle of a news report.

"Electricity's back!" Shad said, and tuned the radio to a Cuban music station.

"Turn off the generator, please," he called to the kitchen.

The bar was getting crowded. Job walked in leaning on his wife, and three people rushed to get him a chair. Elijah approached the bar and stopped a few feet away from the men.

"Come here, kid," Cameron said, and reached out.

The boy moved forward, his tongue sticking out the side of his mouth, until Cameron's hand rested on top of his head.

"Eric," Cameron said, "I have a birthday present for you. A potential birthday present, anyway. I was speaking to one of my clients today, Daniel Caines, a businessman in the Bronx. He's looking at investing outside of the States."

Balancing a tray of lemonade on one hand, Shad paused and opened the fridge door, waiting for Eric to respond. The boss was standing still, only his eyes blinking. After a few seconds, Shad closed the fridge.

"What about a little hotel?" Shad said, adding a little laugh as if it were a joke. "Maybe a little island?"

"Could be, could be," Cameron said. "He's thinking about it, anyway." Elijah slid his hand into Cameron's.

"You're not serious." Eric shook his head, his eyes big, almost unbelieving. "How would he—there's no—"

Shit! (Shad asked God to forgive him.) The boss was going to let it slip through his fingers.

"I've been talking to him about investing in Largo," Cameron said.

He spun Elijah around like a dance partner and the boy laughed. "Investing in Jamaica—I never thought I'd be saying that. I told him your equity would be the island and the cliff land with the bar. Interested?"

Eric was looking like a child who wanted something so bad he couldn't speak. Shad put the tray down.

"Yeah, man. He interested—he can live there and manage it. I'll help him, don't worry."

Elijah ran off to a table with children, and Cameron rushed on, salesman-style. "You'd need more land for a hotel, of course. We could speak to Miss Mac."

"She'll sell for the right price," Shad said, nodding, nodding. "She's ready."

A murmur went through the crowd, a few hands clapping. Simone was walking in, arm in arm with Miss Mac. She'd cut her hair close to her head. The obeah man's white cape was tied at one shoulder, cinched with a gold belt. Around her neck was a purplish necklace and on her feet a pair of sandals, the kind Miss Olive sold in the market.

She'd gotten thin, her arm tiny enough to put your fingers around, and she wore no makeup, but her eyes were bright. A smile started small and shaky, as if she didn't know what people would think of her, and then it grew until it stretched from one ear to the other as she looked around.

Waving to the three men and nodding to everyone else, the two women headed for a table in the center of the room. They were pretending not to see everyone gawking at her, the woman who looked like a pretty Kingston lady, who'd survived the island, who'd gotten the better of Sharpie and Tiger, a woman who didn't look crazy.

Cold coconut water would be her drink, Shad decided. He reached into the fridge for the bottle.

"Boss, why don't you take this drink to the lady?" Shad said. Woken from a dream, Eric looked at him, then turned to Cameron.

"Listen, man," he said. "The only way I'm going into

this is if Shad has shares in the company." His voice was different, louder, like it used to sound when he was ordering a round of drinks at the hotel bar. "If it hadn't been for him—you know—"

He glanced at Shad for a second. "This time around I'll need a local partner, a younger man on the scene."

"That seems fair," Cameron said. "I think we can organize some sweat equity or something." He winked at the bartender and strolled away to join his sister.

Not feeling the ground beneath him, Shad moved into the crowd, handing Simone her coconut water, doling out lemonade to the children, telling the adults there was beer if they wanted. His head was light. Even his stomach was light.

An "Ooooh" from the crowd. Maisie had placed the birthday cake, square and yellow, on the food table. Elijah and the other children stood around the table staring at the cake and taking sandwiches from trays. Behind the group stood Beth, the orange dress a magnet for his eyes. She handed the baby to Rickia and took the candles from Maisie. She leaned forward, poking them into the cake, showing more cleavage than usual, a dark pathway down the middle.

Shad circled the bar and poured two glasses of Johnnie Walker Red. He handed one to Eric.

"What's this for?" Eric said.

"The future," Shad said.

"It might never happen, you know that, right?"

"My God is a patient God," Shad said, and grinned.

He clinked his glass against Eric's. "To us, boss, to us."

"I thought you didn't drink."

"'Drink your wine with a joyful heart'—Ecclesiastes." Shad took a sip and grimaced.

He wiped his mouth with the back of his hand.

"And look like you need a little courage to walk over to Madam Goat."

They sipped at the same time. Then they burst out laughing, blessing each other with spluttered scotch.

ACKNOWLEDGMENTS

The emergence of a first novel needs the encouragement, recommendations, and deep breathing called for by any first birth. Dozens of supporters and advisors appear, too many to name, all essential and appreciated.

My lifelong urge to write was first nurtured by the late Tess Thomas, my English teacher in high school, followed by a host of journalism instructors and editors. After the book started taking form, writing teacher Carol Lee Lorenzo took me gently through the roughest patches. My readers, LuAnne Dowling, Baji Daniels, and Farah Ebrahimi, told me the truth, however hard to hear.

I owe a great debt to the Algonkian Writer Conference where I got invaluable advice from the attending editors, advice that made my work publishable. Expert assistance came from Beverly Langford and Anne Schewe, both of whom lost their daughters and survived the pain.

My deepest appreciation goes to my editor, Malaika Adero, who has a way of making her writers feel honored while giving of her wisdom. My publisher, Judith Curr of Atria Books, has made this book possible, something I will never forget.

ACKNOWLEDGMENTS

Thank you, friends and family—my daughter Lauren, my entire family, the Girls Night Out crew, the St. Croix posse—for believing in me throughout. And a Jamaican *big-up* to the University of the Virgin Islands for bringing me back to my beloved Caribbean.

To all of you: One love, one heart.